Shifting Meta

by Rye Fields

Adult Readers Only

SHIFTING META

Published by Bewere Books
Flagstaff, Arizona
https://www.bewere.us

ISBN 978-1-62475-172-1
Printed in the United States, United Kingdom, or Australia
First trade paperback edition: July 2023

Cover art by BadShade
Edited by David M. Sula

To the friends and family who have supported me on my long journey to becoming an author.

Chapter 1 (Zach)

I've gone up and down the stairs leading to our apartment too many times to count. I've soared down them on my way to work after sleeping through my alarm, shoes banging on wood so loud you'd think the whole staircase was collapsing. I've trudged up them after escaping downpours, thankful to be under their protective cover despite my clothes and fur already being soaked. I've slid down them, tripped over them, cracked one of them. I've picked at the flaking paint while waiting for a ride and filled them with the sounds of my rapid giggling.

Now I'm going down them one step at a time, maybe with too much caution, because the only thing that could make this day worse would be tumbling end-over-end and breaking my glasses like the time I was a bit too tipsy coming home from a bar. I don't know if I'll ever use these stairs again, or see the apartment, or even this city block. I never thought it'd be my home forever, but you get used to a place after four years.

The plastic milk crate in my paws feels too light. I think about how when someone in the movies or on TV is leaving a place for good, they'll have a box overflowing with their belongings: a framed photo, a little plant, all the tacky decorations that'd littered their desk. All I've got in this final load are a few odds and ends. There's nothing of meaning in it, nothing symbolic that'll rekindle the relationship that just ended or give me hope for a brighter future. It's junk. There are a few utensils we think are mine, a pride keychain that had sat in a drawer for years because I was too afraid to use it publicly, a broken set of headphones, and a pair of too-short-to-be-useful ethernet cables. I don't think the crate is mine, but if Jay put the last of my things in it then he probably doesn't want it back. Everything of value was moved out earlier in the day.

I reach the landing halfway down the stairs, where they turn to head down in the opposite direction. My fluffy gray and white tail is limp, and my ears are drooped. I haven't heard the door close yet, so I know Jay's still standing in the doorway. Is he waiting for me to drop the crate and bolt up the stairs, tears wetting my fur as I tell him we shouldn't give up, that what's going on is just a bump in the road we'll laugh about later? Am I waiting for him to come after me and do the same? I hold my breath, as if the world needs complete silence before I hear him shout, "Zach!" or, "Fox!" or even just, "Wait!"

All I hear is a car driving past and the TV in a nearby unit. The world continues without me. There is no cosmic need for us to make it work and be a happily-ever-after pair, no audience cheering as we share a passionate kiss before the credits roll. Life goes on, and so must I.

So I resist the urge to look up and catch a glimpse of Jay, to see the lizard's scaly, sea green tail flicking about. If I see him again I'll start crying, and I don't want that to be his last image of me.

Jay and I were together for six years. My snout quivers thinking about it, and I feel my eyes watering. It feels like it was longer, and that only makes it worse. We'd met during freshman year, part of the same quad in Moore Hall. Fourth floor, west wing. The gay wing. The university was trying to find ways to celebrate the legalization of same-sex marriage in Washington State the year before, and settled on creating an LGBT-friendly section in their newest dorm.

My best friend Noah was the one who'd found out about the program and convinced me to join it. I hadn't had a choice, really;

we'd always talked about being roommates in college, and I wasn't about to back down from that just because being out of the closet made me nervous. My parents knew by then, and some of the extended family, but it was still very much a semi-private thing for me. Getting gay marriage didn't change the fact the east side of the state was predominantly rural and conservative where the majority voted against the referendum. But Noah's always had a way of forcing me to focus on the positives.

There were three dozen others like me in that wing, all dealing with their own dramas and dreams. I should've gotten to know them all—for better or worse—but instead I found Jay. Jay, the tall lizard who greeted me on the first day in the dorm with the enthusiasm of someone reuniting with a long-lost friend. His personality was—and still is—bubbly. Not in the fake way of a retail worker trying to get through their shift or a stranger desperately craving conversation while waiting in line. Genuine joy, the kind that's contagious and gives you hope.

I learned later it'd been a coping mechanism for him, to get him through a childhood where his father believed every slight could be fixed with a beating, and slurs were spoken at family gatherings as often as blessings. But in Moore Hall, he was away from all that, and he could be himself.

It wasn't love at first sight. Originally I was simply jealous of Jay's confidence. Then I idolized it. I looked up to him during our freshman year and tried to imitate him. When he got a nose piercing, I got a small teal stud earring on my right ear and kept it even after he decided to ditch his. I joined any event he took part in and hung out with him more than anyone else. I realize now that was when I started shaping my life to revolve around Jay at the expense of other friends or acquaintances who could've *become* friends. Maybe that was my first mistake.

Jay, Noah, and I moved out of Moore Hall after freshman year and into a student apartment a bit north of it, where we spent the last three years of college. My memories of that time have always been wonderful, but as I walk away from the life I began there, I see how my oblivious, self-imposed isolation only intensified once we were on our own.

On Halloween, Jay got us invited to a party on Greek Row. I don't remember which frat it was at, or even what my costume was. I only remember that Jay dressed as a devil. He wore a pair of cheap plastic devil horns from Hillmart, a cape borrowed from a friend in the theater department, and a red shirt with a faded Cane-Cola logo. He hadn't been able to find a toy pitchfork to complete the costume, but sometimes it finds its way into my memories anyway, as if to make the moment perfect.

The contrast between his kindness and the costume amused me probably more than it should've—even more so once I'd had a few drinks. I clung to him that night more than I had any night before. We danced to cheesy remixes and watched beer pong games between members of rival frats, who'd hoot and roar in victory before drunkenly slapping their opponents hard on the back. We ended up out back, alone, and talked about life. We were drunk enough for everything to sound meaningful. Then Jay kissed me.

It wasn't my first kiss, but in my memories, it might as well have been. I'd never kissed outside of a locked room before. It'd felt bold and daring, despite the fact it was nearly midnight and there was no one in sight. Neither of us forgot the morning after, and we were dating by New Year's.

From that point on, Jay was my whole life. I started thinking of my future entirely in terms of being with him. My own ambitions were nudged aside, not that I had many at that point. I majored in Creative Writing, since writing had been my only skill, but I had no clue what career I'd get out of it. I didn't think I'd make a good teacher and didn't have any interest in technical or journalistic writing. I became an editor for the school's literary journal after being recommended to the position by a professor during sophomore year, but the world of publishing sounded daunting. I really just wanted to write my own stuff.

So I put off the issue year after year, in part because I believed it wouldn't matter what I did as long as I was with Jay. His degree was in Viticulture, and he stayed on top of scholarships and internships and had seemingly figured everything out by his sophomore year. When I envisioned my future—*our* future—I saw us sitting on the porch of a small house further south, him sipping on the wine he'd cultivated while I wrote the next great fantasy series. I put no thought into how we'd reach that idealized point.

Jay never pressed me about what my plans were after college. I appreciated that then, what with all the questions my parents and family asked regarding it. Maybe some concern would've been better. But no, I can't blame Jay for my mistakes.

We had to move out of the student apartments after graduation, and Jay and I decided to get a new place just to ourselves. We chose the third apartment we looked at, a cozy one-bedroom unit on the second floor of a complex south of campus and Old Downtown, with easy access to I-90 for Jay's commute to the winery he was interning for.

The apartment was on the very edge of the city, where homes abruptly end and fields begin. It can't expand any further in this direction, so the area has remained relatively unchanged these last four years. From our little corner balcony, we can watch the sun rise above the low hills while the stars fade as the sky turns from black to orange to blue. When we first moved in, we swore we'd watch it together almost every day. The reality of our sleep and work schedules made the events rare. It's already May and I don't think we've seen it together once this year. I can't remember when the last time was. Maybe it's better that way.

The first year in our new apartment was great. We were done with classes for good—no more tests to study for or papers to finish at the last minute. I got a job at a small antique shop in Old Downtown to pay my half of rent and have something to do while Jay was at work. Just a temporary thing, to hold me over until I got something published. But I didn't publish anything that first year. Or the year after. I still haven't. My computer is filled with the starts of a dozen abandoned stories, a digital reminder of my lack of confidence. It's been almost two years since I even thought of starting something.

Again, Jay never pressed me on my writing, or the lack thereof. It never came up. We paid little attention to each other's ambitions.

Jay didn't know what I wanted to write; he just thought me writing was "cool." In turn, I never learned exactly what he was doing at the winery. I knew when his coworkers annoyed him and when his bosses were stressed out, but beyond that, his career—his *passion*—was a void to me. I should've asked. How can you be with someone for six years and not know even the simplest thing about their job?

Hindsight is 20/20, but now that I'm seeing all the warning signs, our relationship was fragile. I feel like I spent the last six years blind.

So much of our socialization had been at parties and hangouts, as part of a group, not just a couple. When college ended, people moved back home; people got jobs. Parties became a rare treat. We had so much less in common than we'd originally believed, and neither of us wanted to accept that. Time to ourselves defaulted to watching TV, our attention more on the programs than each other. The sex continued to be good, and I wonder if that's all that kept us together these last few years as our relationship slowly deteriorated.

Things finally started falling apart this year. I can't remember a single serious argument between us until January when Jay abruptly asked me if I was going to look into getting a better job. It was an innocent question, but I'd heard it from my parents, my sisters, and pretty much everyone else in the extended family while visiting for Christmas, and I became defensive. I tried to shrug it off, but he pushed. I snapped at him, he snapped right back, as much to his surprise as mine. He dropped the issue, we apologized, and that night we had our first ever makeup sex. The relief it brought was temporary.

The question came up again a week later and never went away. Then a conversation about rearranging the furniture in the living room turned into a full-blown argument, with him wanting to move everything and me just wanting to tweak things here and there. We'd never so vehemently disagreed over something so petty before. Even the makeup sex after felt desperate, like we were convincing each other everything was alright. But the floodgates had been opened.

Every little issue we'd kept bottled up poured out. If he pointed out something I'd done that bothered him, I'd bitterly counter with something he'd done, whether it was related or not. He did the same.

We spent less time together and saw each other in bed more than anywhere else. His birthday was a quiet formality, lacking in the care of previous years.

One night we finally sat down and forced ourselves to confront the weeks of discord. We tried to list out reasons for staying together, but all we found were faults and doubts. It'd left us both in tears. It was still a few more days before we decided to separate.

I know it's the right choice, that the passion and care we had six years ago just isn't there anymore, and that dragging things out will only make it worse and ruin any hope we have of becoming friends again. But—standing at the bottom of the stairs, paws shaking—I want to hear Jay pounding down the steps to convince me we can fix things. Why can't I have a miracle, just this once?

I hear the door close above, and with it, a chapter of my life I was certain would last forever, ends.

I walk across the dark lawn and put the crate on the passenger seat of my car. The second I'm in, my muzzle is quivering, and tears are running down my cheeks. My claws dig into the steering wheel, and I sit there for a few minutes, not making a sound, feeling like I'm about to cave in on myself. I only start driving when I realize Jay could be watching me from the apartment.

It's all my fault. I had six years to connect with Jay and get to know his interests better. I could've asked more questions; I could've listened better; I could've opened up more. What if I'd looked into a new job with actual opportunities for advancement or found a way to write?

The exhausted remnants of my self-esteem are trying to tell me Jay and I were both at fault, but I'm not listening. Pretty little shallow words can't fool me. I screwed up and may have ruined both our lives in the process.

My drive north isn't even ten minutes but I've got my GPS on, just in case. Noah's place is just down the street from the old student apartments. It's close enough that I could've walked over, but I've only seen it once before today. He's still in school, since he's aiming to be a professor. I'd love to pretend that's why we've barely spoken these last four years, only chatting at holiday parties and sending sparse texts. The truth is, I neglected him in favor of Jay, for all the good that did me.

Noah was the only one I could think to talk to once I realized my relationship with Jay was falling apart, and he comforted me as if we'd never stopped hanging out. He offered me a room before I had even begun to address the difficulties of moving out on my own. I obviously couldn't stay in my old apartment.

I head up Chestnut, past the hospital and block after block of small houses. At University Way I take a left, then right on Cowboy Way, skirting the edge of campus. Every time I pass it these days, it looks small and lonely without peers I recognize milling about.

Central Washington University is far from being the largest college in the state. It's hovering in the top ten, always shifting spots with Eastern and Western, well below the University of Washington and Washington State University. No one outside the state knows it exists, but the rest of the country tends to reduce us to a single city and an abundance of rain and coffee regardless, so that's not surprising.

I chose Central over everything else because it was close and cheap, and Noah had made up his mind to go there before he'd even figured out what he wanted to do in life. It's a family tradition, and he gets along well enough with his family to actually care about that sort of thing.

Rows of trees hide the red brick buildings of the college, but they can't block my memories. I see the clustered dorms and halls with paths crisscrossing between them. I see the irrigation canal that cuts campus in half, which I soon find myself driving parallel to. And I see Jay and me walking to the library to study, blind to how fleeting our love will turn out to be.

I fear all my good memories of college will be forever tied to Jay and our failed relationship, preventing me from looking back on any part of those four years fondly. I have to believe I'll get over it eventually, because otherwise I'll be forced to pretend four years of my life simply didn't happen.

I'm worrying so much I almost miss my turn. The modest CWU football stadium and various sporting grounds are to my right, while nothing but apartments are to my left. Noah's complex is eight buildings looped around a parking lot just ahead. I park and spend a few minutes in the dark collecting myself so I won't be in tears when I get inside, leaving only when I'm sure the light gray fur around my eyes doesn't look matted.

The milk crate hasn't gotten any heavier or more meaningful since I dropped it in the car. I don't know why I bothered bringing it back with me. It's all stuff I'd forgotten and done without for years now. I should've just told Jay to keep it. Would that have come off as petty? "Thanks, but no thanks; it's your junk now"? What if it'd come across as a pitiful attempt to leave reminders of myself behind, either out of spite or a last-ditch ploy to make him love me again? I feel like my brain's working overtime to worsen the situation. I wish it could've put in this much effort of thinking things through *during* the relationship.

Noah has a second-floor apartment in the building closest to the street. Every building in the complex looks slightly overdue for a fresh coat of paint, the wood siding fading unevenly. Their elevated walkways are exposed to the elements and remind me of a cheap motel. The stairs leading up to Noah's apartment are louder than the ones of my old home. My feet *c'thunk* and *creak* on each ancient wooden step. I don't have a key yet so I have to knock on the door. I hear a muffled shout from within that I assume is something along the lines of "I'm coming!" and shortly afterward the deadbolt is undone, and the door swings open.

Noah greets me with a warm smile. The king cheetah's ditched his shirt for a tank top since I've been gone, one he seems on the verge of outgrowing. He's always been on the plump side, and he's obviously filled out more since graduation. I hadn't noticed until we met up to discuss me moving in, and I'm still getting used to the change. He carries the weight well, though.

"That's the last of it, right?" he asks as I walk in, the door closing behind us.

"Yeah." I hear my voice break a little. I need a few seconds to recover so I hurry off to drop the crate in my room.

The apartment feels smaller than my last one, despite having a second bedroom. The living room is split in half by an angled couch aimed at a tv in the far-right corner. There's a deck past it though the blinds are currently shut. The other half has a table and a bookshelf. A corridor kitchen is to the immediate right of the entry. It looks cramped, but at least it has all the essentials. On the left is the bathroom and master bedroom, which is Noah's. I think his little feral cat Mr. Wiggles is still hiding in there. My new bedroom is just past the kitchen. I slide the crate into my room and wipe my eyes again.

"I ordered the pizza while you were gone. Should be here in about twenty."

"How much do I owe ya?"

Noah shakes his head. "Nothing. It's on me."

"I broke up, but I'm not broke." I thought the joke might lighten the mood, but I sigh rather than smile.

"Look, we'll trade off paying for takeout, just like old times. So unless you're planning on cramming money into my waistband like you're at a strip club then don't worry about it." Noah chirps and wiggles his hips at me before disappearing into the kitchen.

I let out a single laugh, as much as my depressed brain will allow in my current mood. "Do you take credit?"

"Zach, buddy, if you stick a card in there you aren't getting it back," Noah's voice echoes from around the corner, and I spend a moment too long visualizing that. I hear the fridge open. "You want a beer?"

Anything to take my mind off everything. "Sure."

"I've got plain Cascade and some Konig Light Lime."

"Cascade's fine."

"Ah, showing loyalty by sticking to local?"

"They're not even local anymore; one of the national brands bought them out decades ago."

Noah walks back into the living room, a beer in each paw. "When did you become a beer expert?"

"I didn't. I just... know people who are." Jay's almost as fond of beer as he is wine, and gets chatty about it when drunk. Noah doesn't press me. He probably guesses I'm talking about Jay, or someone who reminds me of Jay. Hopefully this knee-jerk way of associating alcohol with Jay will pass. When college memories make you sad, you can drink, but if drinking makes you sad, you have to start going to meetings.

He hands me my beer, and we settle down on the couch. It's ashy gray, light enough that my winter fur probably won't stand out as much when it starts shedding. I wonder if Noah remembers the hardships of living with a platinum fox. "Why couldn't you have sensible scaly skin?" Jay would always tease every time he had to empty the clouds of fur out of the vacuum. Noah has the three slots on the back of the couch punched out so our tails don't get painfully bunched up while sitting. I think I've only seen a couch not set up like that by default once while at a rabbit's house.

I wince at my first sip of beer. Cascade isn't exactly known for its taste, but I'm only drinking it for the buzz, so I don't care. I prefer ciders, anyway. Something fruity like me. Again I fail to make myself smile, and I take another drink.

"Noah, thanks again for taking me in. I'm not... I'm not quite sure what I'd be doing right now otherwise." Preparing to sleep on the couch again? Staring at listings for bad apartments I could barely afford? Another round of muffled crying in the bathroom?

"Dude, it's nothing." Noah pats me on the back. "It'll be nice having a roommate again."

I wish his enthusiasm was contagious. "Yeah, like the good old days." But even then I still had Jay, in one way or another. I can't believe it's over. My stuff's all moved out, and Jay has my key, but I frantically try to imagine I'm only visiting Noah to catch up. My heart begins to pound. "Did I do the right thing?"

Noah's smile wavers momentarily. "I obviously don't know what all you've been through recently, but I'm sure the decision you and Jay made was for the best."

"Six years." That's all it takes to make my eyes water. "I didn't do enough. I should've been able to make this work. Why didn't I?" My muzzle quivers, and I give up trying to hold the tears back. My glasses slide forwards. "All I did was tell myself things would get better over and over and over again and didn't do jack shit to make that happen! He deserved someone so much better than me."

I'm hunched over, ears flat, my shaking paws wrapped tightly around the neck of my beer bottle. I've never cried this hard in front of someone else before, but I've almost forgotten Noah's even there as I lose myself to a torrent of regret and self-loathing.

Noah quickly slides over on the couch and wraps an arm around me. "Hey, hey, hey, you weren't the only one in that relationship. Figuring shit out goes both ways, so don't put the blame solely on yourself. Sometimes things just don't work out, and sometimes it takes a while to realize that. It hurts, but you can move on. You've done it before. Remember us?"

I'd started realizing I was gay my freshman year of high school. The reason was Clyde Barrows, an alligator in my gym class. I was entranced seeing Clyde rush around the court in volleyball and then shirtless in the locker room after. I found myself wanting to see more of him. After a week of nervous ogling, it dawned on me I was into guys.

Naturally, I panicked. If my classmates found out, I'd be called a fag, beaten up, and maybe even suspended. That'd happened to two girls caught kissing at school the year before I got there. Both were suspended, and I'd heard one was sent to a Catholic girls' school by her parents to purge the sin from her or something. Since my parents weren't all that religious, I assumed they'd skip the penance part and just kick me out. I was ultimately wrong about that, thankfully, but it still took me four more years to come out to them.

Noah was my closest friend and the only one I felt I could trust, so I came out to him the next time he slept over. I'd imagined him reacting with disgust, begrudging acceptance, or even apathy. I hadn't expected him to come out to me as well. Apparently he'd figured out the year before, after becoming enamored with the Seattle Star's new forward, a young zebra who dyed his mohawk neon colors. That was also when Noah had started dying the tuft of fur on his head. Twiddling with my ear stud, I realize now that we both seemed to have a penchant for taking on the traits of our obsessions when we were younger.

Our new connection brought us closer together than ever. A month later we secretly started dating, first to confirm we were what we thought we were, and then because we didn't know anyone else who was gay. Mostly we just held paws in private and flustered each other with kisses. We couldn't do much else in the conservative city of Wenatchee. Sometimes we talked about moving to Seattle after high school, where no one cared you were gay. It was youthful naivete on our part. Things were better in the big city, but it wasn't the utopia free of hate crimes we desperately wanted it to be.

Eventually, we grew bold and lost our virginity to each other. It was an embarrassing but sweet night of experimentation, our voices quieted and our ears constantly on alert for noise, as if Noah's parents were poised to break down the door and catch us in the act. We got better at sneaking around, but the fear of getting caught never went away.

Our relationship only lasted a year, slowly petering out as we realized we didn't mesh well as a couple. There was no heartache or mourning, just shrugs and the promise we'd still be friends. Jay and I have made the same promise, but I can't help but feel the situations differ too greatly for me to remain hopeful. I worry that I'll be as good of friends with Jay as the with that alligator I'd crushed on all those years ago, which is to say, not at all.

"Our relationship was different," I point out.

"Well yeah, I'm a cat, and he's a lizard." Noah's trying to cheer me up, and I want to laugh, but instead my ears droop.

"Six years, Noah." I feel nothing else sums up my despair over what I lost than repeating that mournful number.

I slump back on the couch. Everyone I'd been hanging out with recently are Jay's friends, first and foremost. They're people he took classes with, people he's worked with, people he met through mutual acquaintances. I was always Jay's boyfriend, and they were always my boyfriend's friends. I'm starting to feel like I've just woken from a six-year sleep and everyone else has moved on. But that's not true. Noah's still here, with his arm wrapped around me. I can smell the lingering scent of his citrusy shampoo and the light orange dye in his fur.

"I'm not saying it's gonna be easy, Zach. You might be left with a lot of bittersweet memories and a lot more crying, but you're gonna get through this. You'll find the right guy someday."

I thought I had with Jay, I want to say, but my muzzle's back to quivering, and I'm sure I'll be sobbing before I get halfway through it so I only whimper.

We sit there, him offering a flood of genuine condolences as I stare at my reflection in the blank TV, a fox with no future.

A knock at the door jolts me free of my gloom. Is it Jay? I imagine him sitting on the floor by the door after watching me leave, reduced to tears in the same way I've been, until struck by an epiphany, he flies out of our apartment, down the stairs, and into his car, racing past campus to take me back.

"Pizza's here," Noah says, unaware he's just crushed my silent delusion.

The hope leaves me as Noah gets up and heads to the door. Of course it's not Jay. He doesn't even know where Noah lives. There'll be no eye-opening flashbacks or conveniently-discovered declarations of love. We won't run into each other seeking shelter from the rain and reconcile, embracing while a romantic song swells around us. No mutual friend will magically solve our problems and nod from a distance as we kiss again, our relationship stronger than ever.

Sometimes a relationship simply ends; the connection you swore was indestructible crumbles to ash and blows away, reduced to scattered memories and nothing more.

The door opens and closes, and something is slid onto the table. "Zach, come grab some pizza, and we'll find something dumb to watch?"

I lack the energy to do much right now, but I force myself up. I don't want to spend my first night here in a daze. Noah passes me a paper plate once I walk over. The pizza box on the table has a cartoonish otter in a toga happily eating a pizza slice. I can smell the cheese and pepperoni.

"Hope you don't mind Little Nerva's. Their stuffed crust is really good," Noah says, opening the box. He takes two slices of pizza for himself. I grab one, hesitate, then grab a second. All I've eaten today is cereal, so maybe greasy food will make me happy.

Noah gets out a pair of TV trays so we can sit on the couch while we eat. He turns the TV on and flips through a row of streaming services, settling on one filled with shows from all of the home and garden networks. We used to watch those a lot back in the student apartments. He scrolls through the lists and starts up *Home Finders*. The episode starts with quick shots of streetcars, hills, and the bright yellow Golden Gate Bridge so we immediately know it's taking place in San Francisco. It's just like how any show set in Seattle sets the scene with a view of the Needle and Mt. Rainier.

The budget for the couple is absurd, of course. "God damn, I wish I could casually claim to have a million and a half to spend on anything," Noah laughs. "What did they say they do again?"

"She does photography and he does something in technology," I say, having already mostly forgotten.

"Wanna bet they have one or more loaded parents?"

"That's like betting if they'll find a house or not."

"Or if they'll complain about the pool not being large enough."

"Or the place not having stunning views of downtown, the mountains, *and* the water." I let out a laugh, and it's the first genuine one I've had all day. I've got a love-hate relationship with these shows, where I'm jealous that I can't afford a home even a fraction of the size as the ones depicted, while also enjoying guessing which home they'll be willing to "make sacrifices" for.

Within five minutes the couple is complaining about a potential house not having a large enough home theater while I dig into cheap pizza. Little Nerva's gets a bad rap, but I'm hungry and struggling to hold back a flood of depression so it tastes like the best pizza I've ever had. The beer helps, too, letting me dwell upon things other than my failed relationship.

In between mocking the show and eating, Noah and I talk about our hometown, Wenatchee, which is about an hour and a half north of here. It's a little smaller and a little greener, and while our memories of growing up there aren't traumatic, neither of us have any intention of ever moving back there for good. For Noah, it's because he wouldn't have any job opportunities. For me, it's because the only connection I've got left is my family, and I'm fine having a modest distance between me and them. I'm not on bad terms with them or anything, but lately it just feels like we all put up with each other at best.

By the time we've gone through three episodes of *Home Finders* and a couple of beers, I'm no longer constantly on the verge of tears, and I'm only thinking about Jay a lot rather than non-stop. I've gotta piss so I slide off the couch, grunting as I do. Having a third slice of pizza may have been a mistake. I'm not a heavy eater so this is enough to leave me feeling stuffed, but that's probably better than feeling empty. I need all the distractions I can get, even a food coma.

When I return, my gaze falls upon a nearby bookshelf. The lower shelves are a mix of textbooks, cookbooks, and the occasional dieting guide, which I suspect were gifts from his parents. Above are board games, along with card binders and some deck boxes. I pick up one of the deck boxes and smile. Engraved on the front is a circle in between two crossed rings in the shape of an "x", like a partial atomic symbol. I haven't played in years, but I'd never forget the logo for Adamant: The Godless Age. It's a collectible card game, one of the oldest and most popular still around.

I started playing Adamant in middle school, after seeing a bunch of other kids huddled around a game in the cafeteria. I hoped to make friends by playing and begged my parents to buy me a deck. They hadn't been fond of the name, but eventually caved after a week of pouting and whining. I'm pretty sure the real reason they gave in was because I'd just gotten glasses and they wanted me to feel better.

It was how Noah and I first met, and our earlier bonds were over him teaching me how to play. We, and a few other kids, played Adamant all the time growing up: at home, in school, and in small weekly tournaments at a local card store. I stopped playing when we got to college because I couldn't afford new cards anymore, and my interests had drifted elsewhere—to Jay, mainly.

How many hobbies have I been neglecting because of Jay? He was never against any of them. It's just that we always did whatever I thought *he* wanted to do. Maybe if I'd bothered asking, he would've tried the game. The thought doesn't help me shake away my solidifying belief that I was the problem with our relationship.

"I haven't played Adamant in forever," I say, looking over the deck box in my paw.

Noah looks over his shoulder and his face lights up. He bolts up with far more grace than I did and is with me in an instant. "I took a pretty long break myself. Roy got me back into it like two years ago." Another acquaintance I haven't chatted with in years. "We've been going to the Friday Night Adamant events again, too."

FNA are weekly tournaments held at game stores. Noah and I attended one or two a month back in high school. Only family obligations and the costs kept us from going every week.

"I've barely paid attention to Adamant since I quit. I see packs at Hillmart and that's about it." I never felt tempted to give them more than a cursory glance. They were just a childhood fad squeezed between the Gardemon stuff and sports cards.

"The game's changed a whole bunch, but it's still basically the same as when we were both playing." I raise my brow at the ridiculousness of what he's just said. "Dude, you know what I mean. There are a few more card types, some rule adjustments, and a new core cast, but I'm sure you'd be able to stumble right back into it no problem."

I hadn't actually considered playing it again. But Adamant is something from before I met Jay, something guaranteed not to remind me of him. Maybe that's the kind of distraction I need right now. "I guess it could be fun to play again."

"Want to right now? I've got more than one deck." Noah's looking at me expectantly, like I'm on the verge of giving him an early Christmas present. I've never been able to say no to that soft smile of his.

"Sure."

Noah chirps in joy before his face twists in embarrassment. I chuckle at the display. He grabs the rest of the decks from the shelf and brings them to the table, shoving the leftover pizza to one side so we've got room to play. I add the deck I'd been holding to the collection.

"Zach, you liked red aggro decks, right," Noah asks me.

Cards in Adamant are split between five colors, one of which is red. Aggro is just a shorthand for "aggressive" and describes how the deck plays. "Yep."

We both look at the deck boxes. They look color-coded to me, and none of them are red. "I don't have any Red Aggro decks at the moment, unfortunately. I've got a White Ghosts deck you might like, though."

If my memory's correct, the deck Noah's suggesting should have a similar playstyle to what I like. I'm sure I'd be fine with anything, though.

I lift the lid off the white box and take the deck out. The cards are all in glossy protective sleeves that have a zebra print on the back. I wave the deck at him with a smile on my face.

"What?" he asks, with a note of defensiveness.

"Nothing, just admiring the stripes."

"They were on sale, and they match the deck's color!"

"Uh-huh."

"Look, my green deck has anaconda sleeves. It's a theme!"

"So you've finally realized how good reptiles are, too?"

Noah's jaw opens and his ears lower. "It's. A. Theme." He furiously shuffles his deck.

I leave things at that. His excuses are sound, but we both know he's attracted to zebras. Your first crush tends to stick with you, and Noah wasn't always the best at hiding his porn in college. I've teased him before that we broke up because I didn't have stripes.

"So, mister fluffy smartass, do you remember how to play?"

"Pretty sure I do, splotches. I'll have to ask you about new keywords, though. And don't get mad if I do anything that's now against the rules." Adamant's been around for nearly thirty years, and the game's made so many changes in that time you can usually guess when someone started playing the game just by the basic terms they use.

"Fair."

I shuffle my deck and place it on the table in front of me. At its core, Adamant is all about reducing your opponent's life points from twenty to zero using various cards. Accomplishing that is the tricky part.

Both our decks have the standard sixty cards. You can have more, but that makes it harder to get the cards you want. We each draw seven to begin with—the starting hand.

Four of my cards are locations, which produce a resource called *aether* needed to play other cards. White's locations are all called *sanctuaries*, and the art on them depicts training grounds and temples. Aside from the locations, I've got two creatures and a spell.

White's overall theme is order, and it's filled with cards based around war, religion, and the afterlife. My two creature cards are both ghosts, like Noah said, so the deck will be leaning more into the afterlife theme than the others.

I win the dice roll and, thus, go first. I can only play one location per turn, so I drop one of the sanctuaries. The deck I'm borrowing is all about getting low-cost cards out fast. I turn my sanctuary card sideways—referred to as *tapping* it—to produce a single aether. I then use that single white aether to play a creature card. It's a spectral soldier with glowing blue eyes on a devastated battlefield. The art makes them look fierce, but the card is pretty weak and won't hold up against any threat. They've only got one strength and one defense, which means they can deal one point of damage to players and other creatures, and they can only take one point of damage before they're destroyed. Its true power is as part of a swarm. I've gotta get more than one out for that to happen, though.

After playing my location and creature, there isn't anything else I can do. My sanctuary is used up, and most creatures can't do anything the first turn they come into play anyway. "Done," I announce.

Noah draws a card at the beginning of his turn. He quickly drops a location—his deck is green so his are called *groves*—and ends his turn.

"Ramp?" I ask, untapping my resource and drawing a card. It's another creature.

"Maybe," Noah replies with a smile.

Ramp is a deck type that focuses on producing extra resources so you can ramp up to expensive cards fast. Our game will be a race between my fast hoard and his slow heavy hitters. As this is my first time seeing either deck in action, I've got no clue who's more likely to win. Noah has the edge simply because he's been playing more recently than I have, and he built the decks. There's always a chance I'll get lucky.

I play a second location and then tap both to play the spell card I started with. It shows a cleric with their staff raised high before a mausoleum, from which two ghosts are rising. Yet again it's a case of the art being more dramatic than the card. It creates two weak ghost tokens, which are just generic creatures. I use a pair of dice to represent them.

My army is growing. I tap my original ghost and attack Noah with it. Noah has nothing to stop the attack, so he takes the measly one damage, taking him down to nineteen life. For all I know, this single attack will prove decisive in the end and be the reason I win. Right now, though, it's utterly unimpressive.

It's Noah's turn. He draws a card, plays a location, and then plays a creature that can produce a green aether if tapped. He ends his turn.

I draw another location, which isn't what I need right now. Of course, with a third location down I can play a stronger ghost now; at least I think it's stronger. It's got an ability I've never heard of before, and no explanation as to what it does. That usually only happens when the ability appears in every—or almost every—set. I play the creature anyway.

"So what does 'Report 1' do?" I ask.

"When the creature comes into play, you can look at the top card of your deck, and either put it back or discard it. It's a variant of Peer."

Another keyword I've never heard before. I don't need to know about it now, though, so I just nod and look at the top card of my deck. It's a location, which I've got plenty of already. Since I need literally anything else, I choose to discard the card. That's essentially getting rid of it. It'll sit in my discard pile for the rest of the game unless I use another card to retrieve it, but a retrieval card for locations would be unlikely in this deck. True to the ghost theme, white retrieval cards tend to prioritize interacting with discarded creatures, so I'll just consider the location gone for good.

I look across at Noah's cards and attack with my three active creatures. His creature *could* block one of mine, but they'd both destroy each other in the process, and his aether maker is far too valuable to lose. He takes three more damage.

On Noah's next turn, the tide of the game starts to turn against me. He finally gets a second creature out, and his is a giant plant monster that's as strong as all four of my creatures put together. I have no way to beat it—yet—but I can still try to outlast it.

On my turn, I draw an exploit card. Exploits are cards that broadly affect the game while they're in play. Mine shows a grave surrounded by dozens of candles and flowers. It provides an extra strength and defense to every ghost I have in play, suddenly making my fragile swarm more imposing. They're still not a match individually for the one Noah has in play.

I've come to the first real choice in this game. If I attack right now, he'll block and destroy one of my creatures, but I'll damage him some more. If I hold off, he might swing at me with his large creature, which I could gang up on and destroy at the cost of half my forces. Or he could just sit there, playing more and more large creatures until I have no hope of stopping him.

If there were any real stakes on this game, I might take more than a second to think about my plan of action, but this is as casual as it gets. I attack with everything and hope for the best. He destroys one by blocking it, of course, but takes six damage and is down to ten, half his starting life total. I haven't been hit once yet.

It's fun to imagine what our little battle would look like if it actually took place in the Adamant universe, my squad of ghosts versus his lone plant. "How does a plant even kill a ghost?" I ask, musing aloud.

"Maybe it just entangles them?" Noah says, going along.

"And the ghost just poofed into a little white cloud after, like in cartoons?" I laugh.

"Well then maybe it ate them!"

"And they didn't just float out after?"

"Doesn't the setting have monsters that specifically eat ghosts?"

It does, now that I think about it. I'm more into the lore of Adamant than most, so the odd things always stick with me. "Yeah, it's some weird dragon thing involving stealing souls for power. It's why a bunch of dragon cards have bonuses against ghosts."

"Well then that's what my plant did!"

I just laugh.

My little attack doesn't seem to have intimidated Noah. He plays a pair of beefy creatures on his turn and passes. The tide of battle is turning against me. Once Noah starts attacking with his creatures, I'll be forced to block so I don't get crushed, but my creatures aren't strong enough to survive that. I have to find a way to outnumber him, maybe even take out a heavy hitter or two. Without knowing exactly what kind of solutions this deck has against large creatures—if any—all I can do is go on the defensive and hope I draw something I need.

I never do.

Noah starts throwing his creatures at me, and I do my best to delay the inevitable. I lose creature after creature to his plants, which gradually begin to outmatch me. It turns out what I thought was a ramp deck is closer to an aggro deck. On paper, the game seems close, with Noah's life total getting whittled down while mine gets large chunks taken out of it when his plants get through. I know I'm not going to win, though. His deck gets stronger the longer the game is, while mine flatlines around the midgame. The nice thing is, I don't care. I'm remembering how fun Adamant is—the back and forth, trying to figure out strategies on the fly to deal with unexpected threats or bad draws, foiling an opponent's move and buying yourself extra time. When I'm playing Adamant, I feel clever.

A massive attack finishes me off, and my first game of Adamant in close to eight years is over. Both of us are smiling. "Still throwing your weight around with big green decks?" I laugh.

"I never grew tired of them," Noah says, neatly collecting the cards he'd played and adding them back to his deck.

I pick up the rest of my deck and start skimming through it. You can have up to four copies of each card in your deck so I'm already familiar with a lot of them by now. I stop to read every card I never drew, asking Noah for clarification about keywords and unusual formatting. A cluster of powerful cards is towards the bottom, any one of which could've given me a chance of victory. Sometimes bad luck plays just as big a role in a win as strategy does.

"Want to play again?" I ask.

"Hell yeah! You wanna try a different deck?"

"I'll stick with this one." I'm still trying to learn how the deck plays and don't want to start over from square one, which is what I'm basically doing with my real life. Even though this deck isn't what I'm used to, enough familiarity is present, and there's satisfaction in being able to build upon my missteps rather than start over the moment things stop working out.

The second game goes by much faster. My starting hand is bad, and I don't draw anything better, so Noah plows right through me while only taking a couple of points of damage. The loss doesn't deter me; I've gotten lucky before and inflicted the same thing upon others, and I'm not about to get bitter over a casual game. The third game is closer, and Noah has to fight to earn his win.

Everything clicks for me in the fourth. I know what to expect out of my deck and what threats Noah's can create. While poor draws leave him struggling to get out locations, I put together a formidable swarm of ghosts boosted by exploits and spells. I finish him off before he can stage a comeback.

The games and beer had already livened me up, but victory leaves me bouncy. I didn't realize how much I'd missed playing Adamant.

"Maybe I should've made my other decks weaker," Noah says.

"You won three out of four. I think your deck's strong enough!" I glance at the other decks sitting on the table. "You know, I still have my whole collection and my old deck with me."

"Here?"

"Yeah, I brought them down to college and never got around to sending them back home, even when I stopped playing." I didn't think my parents would throw them out—they keep everything—but I was afraid they'd get left in a box in the attic and either be forgotten or ruined by mold. I've carried them in the same storage bin from place to place, always shoving them in the back of a closet until the next move. "Maybe I'll have to finally get it out and start playing again."

Noah's smile finds a way to grow wider, pinching his soft cheeks. It's faint, but I can hear him starting to purr. I want to tease the dork but I hold back. "That'd be so awesome! I'd be able to play more than one day a week."

Seeing Noah excited makes me happy. I feel like I've found a way to give back to him for his generosity and make up for the years away. "I'm gonna guess most of my cards aren't tournament legal anymore. I'll have to buy some new stuff." There's a hint of eagerness in my voice.

Adamant has been around long enough that allowing players to use every card ever printed would lead to chaos and make balancing the game nearly impossible. Because of that, the game is split into formats, each of which limits the sets of cards you have access to. Each has its own unique list of banned cards to maintain a degree of balance. The most popular format is called Standard, which is the mainstay of Friday Night Adamant and the big tournaments. It generally only includes cards from recent sets, creating a constantly shifting environment where different deck types have a chance to shine or falter.

"There's a great place to get cards in Old Downtown called Cascade Games. If you'd like, we can check it out tomorrow, maybe get you a new starter deck to build off of."

Tomorrow's Sunday, and I hadn't had any plans for it. Hadn't had any plans for anything, really. Going to a game store will be better than lingering around the apartment in despair. "That sounds great."

We play one more game, which I lose, before packing up the decks and putting them back on the shelf. We return to the couch to watch bad TV, sticking with *Home Finders*. The buzz from the beer has worn off, but my mood doesn't plummet.

My thoughts aren't free of Jay, not by a longshot. I don't think they ever will be. And maybe that's for the best. If I can find even a few things to cherish about our old relationship then it won't feel like a total waste. I need it to have meaning—another annoying habit from my college degree—even if only as a moral to do better, or try harder, or care more.

A small part of me still fantasizes about figuring out the solution to fixing my broken relationship, and I can't bring myself to brush the thoughts away completely because that feels too much like giving up. If I have a chance to redeem myself and undo my past mistakes then I should take it. But that's a big if.

Drowsiness and the joyful rush from playing Adamant again hold the depression at bay for the rest of the night. I smile and chat as I sit beside Noah, my oldest friend, the one who came to my rescue without hesitation when everything fell apart. It's hard to feel deserving of a friend like him. We gradually get closer, and at some point, my eyelids close and I fall asleep leaning against him, soothed by his soft side and gentle purrs.

Chapter 2 (Zach)

I struggle to wake up the next morning. All I remember from my dreams are muddled feelings of dread, so I'm thankful none of the details stick with me. Few of my dreams lately have been good. Jay has been in most of them, sometimes distant, sometimes hostile. The ones in which he's nice have been the worst, though. I hate being taunted by my memories.

When I finally bother opening my eyes, the room confuses me. The TV is on a different stand, and it's sitting at an angle. The shelf full of games and movies that's always been beside it is missing, too. If Jay had rearranged things in the night I would've woken up; I'm not *that* heavy a sleeper.

Then I remember I'm not in my old apartment; I'm in my new one. The breakup hits me all over again, my eyes watering not even five minutes into the day. One nice night won't be enough for me to get over Jay. I don't want having a breakdown to become part of my morning routine.

I'm still in the clothes I was wearing last night, and a light sheet is covering me. No doubt I've got Noah to thank for it. When I try to move, though, I feel an odd weight on my legs. I look over and see

Mr. Wiggles curled up in a ball in the valley between my legs. He's a white feral cat with big black spots and resembles a tiny, short-haired snow leopard. He opens his eyes and gives me a look of irritation. I'm being judged for waking him up.

Mr. Wiggles is adorable, and I don't want to be mean to Noah's cat, but I'm not about to be held hostage while he sleeps the morning and maybe even the afternoon away.

I try to slide my legs free without disturbing the cat too much, but I don't have much room to work with so Mr. Wiggles is rocked from side to side in the process. He eventually lets out a long, mournful meow and stands up, allowing me to slide into a sitting position. He then lays back down and dozes off again. I begin to suspect the couch is his favorite spot to sleep, and me being there had nothing to do with his decision. My absence certainly doesn't seem missed once I get up.

My back is stiff from sleeping on the couch, and stretching only does so much. I go to my room and look over my sparse belongings. Aside from the crate, there's my computer and desk with a chair that's just beginning to fall apart. I've always bought cheap ones, and they never last. My clothes are crammed into a bin along with my laundry bag. Three small boxes hold mostly books. There's the bin with my collection of Adamant cards, of course. And that's it. All my worldly possessions could fit in the back of a pick-up truck. Or in a dumpster.

Living with Jay, I always felt like I had a lot of stuff, forgetting the majority of it was his. He owned the TV and the GameCom and all the movies and games that went along with them. The furniture was all his and so was every poster and painting on the walls. Some of the kitchen appliances belonged to both of us, but I didn't feel like figuring out how to split such things so I just left them all behind. I don't even know if Noah would have needed any of it.

I imagine the old apartment won't look much different with me gone. A clear spot where my desk was and some extra space in the closet. I'm leaving a pinprick-sized hole in Jay's life that'll be filled in with a few slight adjustments. Suddenly the milk crate of junk seems symbolic of my life with Jay, maybe my life in general.

I feel like I brought more to college than I did here to Noah's place. It's like I'm starting all over from scratch. No relationship, few belongings, same dead-end job. Changing any of that will be daunting. Getting a new bed needs to be my first priority though. Noah's offered me an air mattress, which lays inflated and unused on the floor with pillows and a neatly folded sheet atop it. It's not much of an improvement over the couch, but at least I'll be able to feel like I actually live here. I should have enough in my savings to buy a cheap mattress to start with. I can worry about a bed frame later.

I dig out a towel, shampoo, and soap and head to the bathroom to take a shower in the hope it'll distract me. Distractions are all I'm craving lately. Having showered in the same bathroom for four years, I immediately feel like an intruder in Noah's. *Well, it's mine now, too, I guess.* The tub is as wide and deep as the one in my last place. I've never been one for soaking, so I doubt I'll ever use it for baths. They're more for amphibious and aquatic folk than foxes like me.

The fur dryer is on the wall beside the tub, a long nozzle angled downward. I've heard of older places not having one, so seeing it is a relief. Before they were invented, anyone with fur mainly cleaned with powders rather than water, if at all. I've seen images in text-books of ancient automated fans powered by waterwheels, too. I can't imagine how long drying must have taken using one of them.

I bring my thoughts back to the modern world. I find a spot for my shampoo and soap, shed my clothes, and get the shower running. It turns out the shower only highlights how everything's changed. The nozzle is completely different and I have to adjust it a bit before it feels right. When I'm ready for my shampoo I reach for where it's always been, only to remember I'm in a new shower with my stuff in a different spot; the same is true for my soap. Even after I've rinsed and turned the shower off, my instinct is to turn left to exit, when I'll now be turning right. It's all little stuff, and I know I'll get used to it soon, but I'm not sure I'll have a peaceful shower until I learn to override all this muscle memory.

Wet foxes aren't very majestic. My puffy fur is flat, making me look emaciated, and clings together in clumps that resemble short needles. There's a reason that even in swim suit advertisements you always see fox models posing around and atop the water, but rarely in it. Even computer touch-ups can only help so much.

The rasping howl of the fur dryer makes my ears flatten. I slowly rotate in place, raising my arms as I let the hot air blast me. My longer fur means I'll probably still be damp when I'm done. I expected that though; it's why I have the towel to finish off with. I'm jealous of people without fur. Jay never even needed to use the dryer at our place. He could just wipe down his scales and be done.

After a few minutes under the dryer and a lot of toweling down, I'm as dry as I can be. The remaining dampness will just need time. I leave the bathroom and hear noise from the kitchen. Noah is watching over a pancake sizzling on the stove, shirtless. I stare, then suddenly feel like I'm intruding on a private moment and avert my eyes. A second later I remember it's nothing I haven't seen before and calm down. When summer rolls around and the heat really settles in, I'll be going around shirtless, too.

Fortunately, Noah doesn't see my reaction. "Morning, Zach. You still like pancakes, right?"

I'm more of a waffle guy, but pancakes are nearly as good, so I nod. "You didn't have to make breakfast."

"We can't all sustain ourselves on air," Noah says with a smirk.

"I mean you didn't have to make *me* breakfast."

"And what were you going to have if I didn't?" He has a point. I was so caught up in the move and the breakup that I didn't bring any food over with me. More stuff I need to buy. "All you've got in the fridge is leftover pizza, and that's not a *real* breakfast; that's an 'oh shit I slept through my alarm' breakfast. And I'm not gonna let you fall into bad habits right away and get blamed for you getting fat."

I laugh. "My waistline survived my piss-poor eating habits in college. I'll be fine." I hope. I'm dealing with enough at the moment though and don't want to add "unexpected weight gain" to the mix. Suddenly I feel guilty fretting over a few hypothetical pounds when Noah is right in front of me, probably twice my size through no fault of his own.

Something brushing past my leg offers a welcome break from my thoughts. I look down to see Mr. Wiggles, who has left his couch to rub against Noah.

"Mornin', Wiggles," Noah says, beaming. The cat meows at him, and he chirps back, earning a second meow.

"Shame I don't speak cat," I say.

"We can always head out into the woods and find you a fox to yip at."

"I doubt we'll find any platinums out there." I've never seen my coloration in the wild before, only online. Even the zoos I've been to have only had regular red foxes. Most people don't even know platinum foxes exist, which is why I'm usually mistaken for an arctic fox or a hybrid. Or a Samoyed, though that only happened once, and the dude was drunk so I'm surprised he didn't confuse me for a tiger.

Mr. Wiggles rushes over to me and rubs up against my leg, before returning to Noah to do the same. I think it has to do with scent marking and claiming things. Cat stuff. Even Noah will rub his cheek on yours during greetings if you're a friend. We didn't lose all of our animalistic instincts when we went upright.

"Does he like pancakes?" I ask.

"Nah, he just thinks I'm making bacon, even though his adorable little kitty nose should be telling him otherwise." Noah leans down and gently pokes Mr. Wiggles on the nose. He turns his attention back to me once he's finished toying with the cat. "You still interested in checking out the game store today?"

The uncertainties that have been lingering in the back of my mind since I woke up fade some. "Yeah."

"Awesome. Wasn't sure if you were dealing with a hangover or anything since you passed out hard last night. You didn't even budge when I slid off the couch."

"No hangover. I was just tired." I'm also a bit of a lightweight. Jay likes to have wine with dinner, but I don't drink with him much; at least not for the last couple or so years. Was that another sign I stubbornly ignored? Damn it, I'm gonna be reading too much into every little interaction we ever had now.

"I'm thinking we can go right after breakfast. That way we can get it all handled and have the rest of the day to do whatever." Noah flips the pancake and relocates it to a plate with two others. He pours the last of the batter into the pan.

I don't have anything else going on. I used to just loosely hang out with Jay on weekends, watching TV or finding something to chat with him about. "Works for me."

Breakfast is pleasant. Noah tries to hinder my expectations, but the pancakes are honestly some of the best I've had in a while. They're light and fluffy and soak up the syrup and butter nicely. I wish I had more than two and then wonder if I really will have to keep an eye on my weight. I don't tell Noah, because I know he'll start teasing me about bringing home more junk food and fast food or offer to let me borrow his clothes if mine are feeling too snug. When his weight was mocked back in high school, he responded by rolling with the punches and turning it into a bit of a joke. Kids wanted him to look sullen or embarrassed when they called him fat, not hear him claim he was training to be a pro wrestler named Wrecking Ball.

I take care of the dishes while Noah takes a shower. It gives me time to acquaint myself with the kitchen. I notice Noah doesn't have many plates or cups. I'll need to buy some extras so we don't run out of dishes every other day. There's probably more the apartment needs to comfortably accommodate two people. My mental list of necessary purchases just keeps growing while my savings dwindle. I'm lucky Adamant's the only hobby I've got right now; I doubt I could afford any others.

An overcast rolled in overnight. The weather report says there's a chance of rain late in the afternoon, but the clouds look light and harmless at the moment. I'm glad for the brief reprieve from the sun, though I know it'll be back. Summer comes early on this side of the state, and I'll be missing seventy-degree weather once it hits the nineties and hundreds later.

"How long is the walk?" I ask once we've left the apartment complex.

"About half an hour. It's not too much for you, right?"

"It's the same as my walk to work. Uh, same as it was."

I expect the need to slow my pace so Noah can keep up, but the opposite proves true. I can't even blame breakfast, since we ate the same amount. I guess being overweight isn't enough to stop a cheetah from being a speedster.

We turn at the first corner and enter the northern half of the CWU campus. Tatham Stadium is to our left, the name written in big print on the side and flanked by two banners showing the scowling face of the Cowboys' mascot. By default, they're a dark red feline with a cowboy hat tilted to cover their eyes. The university sells species variations of all their gear to be inclusive—I've got notebooks and hoodies with a scowling red fox, while Jay's all sported generic lizards.

Past the various sports complexes I never paid any attention to, we cross Dean Boulevard and enter the campus proper. I haven't been here in four years—didn't have a reason to after graduation—and it feels at once familiar and foreign to me, like visiting a place I've only dreamed of. I guess I *have* been dealing with a resurgence of bad college dreams lately. Not quite nightmares, but none of them have been fun.

I don't see many students on campus right now. Finals are in two weeks, so most are probably either studying or procrastinating. I tended to do the latter. *And look where that got you*, I grumble. I don't remember ever being so down on my time spent in college. I know the breakup is to blame, but that's not enough to fend off the onslaught of negativity I find myself struggling against.

The irrigation canal that winds through campus is right ahead. Trees line both sides of it, providing shade. As we cross a bridge, I see the stumps of thick branches that had once reached over the canal.

The university made a big deal about cutting them after students kept injuring themselves while "fishing". They weren't actually fishing, of course. Students with a long prehensile tail—usually monkeys or snakes—would hang from a branch by it and try to snatch someone swimming below.

It was fun to watch, but often ended with the "fisher" losing their grip and falling head over heels into the water, sometimes right on top of their target. It took three gorings in a single weekend and a lost eye for the university to crack down on the tradition.

We go over the bridge and past the big student recreation center that looked amazing the two times I actually went. I can still access it as an alumnus—God, it feels weird to refer to myself as that—but I don't think hitting the gym will make me forget about Jay. If anything, just being on campus is reminding me of him too much.

I endure memories of parties and drunk walks home. We always cut through campus on the way back to the apartment from Greek Row. One night Noah stumbled into the canal. On another, we all went to Moore Hall, the freshman building, only remembering we didn't live there anymore after trying all of our keys on an entrance in vain. Then there was the time Jay and I kissed in the dark beneath a cherry blossom tree in the Japanese Garden. I make an effort not to look at it as we pass even though it's one of the prettiest bits of landscaping on campus.

Noah talks about stuff he's seen on campus lately and points out things that have changed in the last four years. I'm too distracted to respond with anything but the bare minimum, and most of what he says is immediately lost to me.

My mood improves once we leave campus and approach Old Downtown. Cascade was founded about a century and a half ago, but Old Downtown is the only place left that still has the feel of that age. Most of the buildings are red brick squares two to three stories tall, filled with small businesses and covered in signs that look like antiques. When you look down a street there, you can see glimpses of an old west town. There aren't any general stores or stables, though. It's all real estate offices and restaurants, along with a few aging major retailers holding out in the shells of storefronts they'd had since the fifties.

Down one of the wide, one-way streets lined with parking spots is the antique store I work at. I look towards it as we pass and check the time. The new walk is only a couple of minutes longer than the old one. At least I won't have to adjust my morning schedule much.

"How's work been?" Noah asks. I must have been staring too long.

"Same as always," I say, not even exaggerating. The only thing that's changed in the past four years is my coworkers. No one stays for more than a year. No one but me.

"Cool," is all Noah has to say to that.

He's not pressing me about my mediocre job, but I know he must be considering it. At this point, I've heard the "you can do better" speech a thousand times over from everyone in my life. I half expect my boss to give it one day. The speeches vary wildly in their sympathy. Family has usually been disappointed, as if a guilt trip will magically inspire me. On the other hand, my friends can be a bit overly bubbly about my potential, claiming I'm capable of anything when I'm clearly not. Jay was like that at first, before it started leading to arguments a few months back. Now I can't help but doubt the sincerity of any friend who's ever tried to inspire me to find something better.

Noah leads us down Oats Street, just a block past work. In the middle of a row of identical red brick buildings is Cascade Cafe and Games. It looks like three whole lots were merged to make it, with separate entrances for the game store and the cafe. I've been down this street often to grab dinner after work, and I don't remember seeing the game store at all.

"How long has this place been here?"

"Zach, it's been here forever. You should really get out more," Noah snickers.

"I get out plenty." But when I think about that for more than a second, I realize it's a lie. I rarely went anywhere without Jay, and he stayed in more often than not once he got his internship and then job. Rather than be adventurous and suggest we check new places out, I simply clung to him and decided things were perfect. Did I bring *anything* good to our relationship? Anything at all?

Once we're inside, my relationship despair falls to the wayside. The store is bright, with polished floors made of an almost golden brown wood. Floor-to-ceiling shelves cover the walls, and aisles full of board games stretch all the way to the back of the store. Signs above the aisles say things like "fantasy" and "science fiction," reminding me of a bookstore. The ones saying "deck builders" and "resource management" swiftly break that illusion.

To my right, there's an opening to another section of the store filled with supplies for miniatures games. Across from it, on my left, is another entrance to the cafe. From a glance, it has the feel of an old west saloon, which doesn't surprise me. Half the bars in this part of Washington are themed like that.

I played lots of board games growing up, but the sheer number in the store leaves me speechless. I don't recognize any of them, though I spot the names of a few familiar video games and movies. Back in Wenatchee, the local card shop only had a single shelf of board games. The rest of it was dedicated solely to cards. They had cases filled with valuable sports cards and even some paraphernalia, like signed photos and balls. Adamant and Gardemon filled out the rest. I don't even see any cards yet. "I didn't realize there were so many games."

Noah pats me on the back and chuckles. "Oh, you don't know the half of it. They've been getting really popular the last few years. I'm sure Roy could tell you all about them."

The chipmunk at the counter gives us a polite nod and a smile as Noah leads me into the section with the miniatures. We pass rows of paints and tables displaying dioramas, and reach the card games.

Finally, I'm in familiar territory. Adamant dominates the large space. Art prints of classic cards hang on the walls in between racks and shelves. One wall is almost entirely boxes, packs, and individual cards. The others have card sleeves, deck boxes, and card binders—everything you need to keep your collection in good condition. Tables crowd the middle of the room, where I assume the Friday Night Adamant tournaments take place. They're pretty beat up, but they're still nicer than the folding tables the card shop back home used.

I walk up to the wall of product. Row upon row of card packs hang on hooks. I don't recognize the names of most of them. Only when I look to the very top do I spot a pack from the last set that came out before I quit Adamant. I shouldn't be surprised; four sets come out a year, and I haven't played for eight years. Even a creative writing major like me can do the math to know how far behind I've fallen.

Booster packs are the product most people associate with card games like Adamant. Packs include fifteen random cards, so you never know what you're going to get. If you're lucky, you'll pull a big-money card that'll more than pay for the whole pack. You're just as likely to end up with a fifty-cent card as your most expensive pull, though. Packs were all I could afford with my allowance and birthday money when I was younger.

Below all the packs is a much smaller collection of boxes called *bundles*. They include ten packs of cards, a set of locations, a twenty-sided dice to keep track of your life total, and a novelization of the set's storyline. The novels vary wildly in quality, but they were what got me into reading and eventually writing. Sometimes I forget how influential this card game has been on my life.

The section next to the packs is enclosed in a glass case. There are some more packs in there, dating back to the first decade of the game, well before I started playing. The prices of many are well into the triple digits.

A few rare cards are also on display. I recognize them, but only from online card lists; this is my first time seeing any of them in person. It's wild thinking about the journey those cards must have made to end up at Cascade Games. Someone had to have opened them in a pack over twenty-five years ago, perhaps before I was even born. How many decks or collections have they been part of? Did they win games in a cafeteria for some kid in the '90s? Or did the owner hide them away until they gained value decades later? Are any of my cards fated for a game store display case in the future?

"Having a moment?" Noah snuck up on me while I was distracted.

"Just taking it all in."

"I think you might have ogled those cards more than you ever ogled me." Noah elbows me in the side, and my face flushes a little red.

"Well, they're part of a turn one win combo, so your competition's stiff."

"Outshined by cardboard once again," Noah says with dramatic flair. "Now why don't we find you a starter deck?"

Starter decks are pretty self-explanatory. They're cheap, pre-made decks designed for new players so they can start playing the game right away. The cards in them tend to be weak, so if you bring one to a tournament, you're almost guaranteed to get crushed. It'll be something I can build off of, though.

The supplementary product is all mixed together and is packaged differently now than it was eight years ago, so I rely on Noah to find what I need. He nudges around boxes and pulls out one that's bright red with a bulky kobold automaton on it. The name on the deck says, "Red Aggro," a declaration so perfectly blunt I let out a short laugh when I see it.

"What?"

"Nothing, I just wasn't expecting the name. I swear the old starter decks weren't so straightforward," I say.

"I guess there's been a push recently to familiarize new players with game terms right off the bat."

I look over the box, but the back provides nothing but a brief description of what Red Aggro is: overwhelming opponents with cheap creatures and direct damage spells. "Is Red Aggro any good right now?"

"Not really. Blue Control, Gold Sacrifice, and Green Ramp are the meta right now, and I don't see much red at all."

The meta is essentially what's currently popular. If Red Aggro isn't part of the meta, then few people are playing it because the power creep of new decks has left it behind. Getting wins with it will be an uphill battle. But sometimes that also means people aren't expecting it, and surprise can go a long way in a game like Adamant. My games against Noah last night went poorly in part because I didn't know what to expect, either from his deck or mine.

I don't know how much of my current collection I can use, so I'll need to add some newer cards to it to improve my deck. I'm strongly tempted to buy a broad selection of packs from recent sets just so I can see what all I've missed. The responsible choice is to just buy stuff from the *most* recent set, which will remain legal in Standard longer.

"What's the newest set?"

"The Apocalypse Codex."

A suitably ominous set to jump back in on. I find a bundle of the set easily and grab it. There's no guarantee I'll get anything useful out of it to add to my starter deck, but half the fun of Adamant is testing your luck with booster packs. "I think this'll be a good start."

Noah grabs three booster packs of the set for himself, and we go to the counter to pay. I expect us to head back to the apartment immediately, but instead Noah takes me to the back of the store and we claim a table.

The first thing I do is open the starter deck so I know what I've got to work with. I'm immediately struck by how strong the creatures are, especially for how little they cost to play. They've got more abilities than I'm used to and fewer obvious drawbacks. More than one would've been completely busted a decade ago, and now they're sitting in a starter deck.

The kobold depicted on the front of the box is the first card I see in the deck. It's a legend—a uniquely powerful card you can only have one copy of in play at a time. They represent significant characters, objects, and locations in the lore of the game's setting. Its name is "Brig, Overloaded," and it deals damage to players even when blocked. I'm pretty sure I'll keep it around.

Most of the creatures in the deck are automatons. Red has always been heavily themed around automatons and artificers. Its locations are called workshops, ranging visually from simple forges to complex magical factories. The hints of anachronistic technology prevalent in red appealed to me as a kid, and they still do. I like imagining my games of Adamant as me sending an army of automatons after the knights, mages, and beasts of my opponents.

"I haven't actually looked into any of the starter sets. How is it?" Noah has been patiently sitting in the chair beside me.

"I like it so far. I don't remember starter decks being this solid. Or maybe everything else has gotten so much stronger that this is what weak cards look like now." I'll need to do some research when I get home.

"Everything's gotten wordier at least," Noah says.

Checking out the starter deck is fun, but it's getting harder for me to ignore the bundle on the table. I tear off the plastic wrap and take the lid off the box. Ten packs of cards are neatly tucked in it, along with a wrapped selection of resource cards, the dice, and the novel.

I pull out the first pack of the bundle—the first pack I've held in my paws in close to a decade. The color is a smokey gray, with the set name at the very bottom and "Adamant" at the very top. In the middle is a closeup of an otter mage with his hood over his eyes and a maniacal grin.

Holding the pack brings back a rush of memories, and for once, they're all good ones. I remember huddling together in the card shop with Noah and the rest of our friends, ripping open packs in a frenzy. Afterward would be the curses or cheers, depending on what we got. We'd gloat about our luck or swear up and down that a dud wasn't as bad as we all knew it was.

On birthdays, I always asked for cards in addition to video games. They were a cheap gift, and I'd inevitably end up with a whole stack to open. Piles of discarded wrappers were left in my wake, cards shoved into boxes or tucked neatly into my deck.

My excitement to open packs now is as great as it was when I was a kid, but my approach is far more restrained. I open the first pack carefully, parting the seam with a claw. Once the cards are free, I examine them one at a time rather than jumping to the rarest card in the back.

Adamant cards are divided into three rarities: common, uncommon, and rare. Commons make up the bulk of a pack, along with a few uncommons and a single rare. Since I haven't been keeping up with Adamant since I quit, almost every card is a total surprise to me. I give most of my attention to the red cards, to see if any would be obvious additions to my new deck. Anything that catches my eye I slide to the front.

The rare in my first pack turns out to be the otter. The card's art depicts a larger scene, and he's actually standing underwater, with chains binding his ankles to a heavy stone. He can't attack or block, but he creates shadow token creatures under certain circumstances. It's a blue card so I doubt I'll ever have a deck for it, but I enjoy how the art matches its mechanics. It's flavorful, and I've always been a sucker for that; it's the writer in me.

I set aside the cards in a tidy stack and then move on to the next pack. Again, I take my time, though I pass over any cards I've already seen. The second rare is a relic card. Relics can be played with any kind of resource, so there's a chance it'd have a place in my deck. The card depicts a magic tome and has a lot of small text, which I have to read three times before I fully understand what it does. As complex as the card is, I'm not convinced it's actually good. It doesn't seem to have a place in an aggro deck.

Noah starts opening his own packs with more haste than me. He's seen the set already, and can only be surprised by pulling something valuable or useful. And he does just that with his third pack. He waves a fearsome creature made of vines at me, making the card dance in front of my face. I grab his wrist to read the card, then nod in approval.

"I'm not looking forward to facing that," I say. I can already tell it'll be tough to deal with in duels.

Noah pulls back. He's wiggling in his seat and grinning wide. "Dude, I've been debating buying this card for almost a month. Last time I checked it was thirty bucks! I think you might be my good luck charm."

"Just don't start pulling my tail." I joke, but it's happened before. A classmate in middle school misread a fable and became convinced yanking on fluffy tails would ward off the devil. She ended up panicking when a math problem on the board came out to 6.66 and pulled so hard on my tail I thought it'd come right off. She had to attend a species sensitivity discussion after school because of that.

I finally pull a red rare on my ninth pack. It's a legend named Ancelot, the Prolific. Whenever a nontoken automaton of mine is destroyed it creates a generic automaton token, I guess to represent him immediately replacing the old one or reusing its materials or something. It also boosts the strength and defense of my automatons. The card itself is strong, a shoo-in for my deck, but the art holds my attention just as much.

Ancelot is a white snake with golden markings and bright red eyes. He's laboring over a kobold automaton, tools held in both claws and his tail. His gaze is intense, but he also has a subtly eager smile, like he knows he's moments away from success.

"Found a new boyfriend?"

My muzzle twists, and I quickly look around to make sure no one else is near us. We're alone. "I was just making sure I'd read the card right." I'm a terrible liar when I'm flustered, and somehow this Adamant card has done that to me. I can't help being attracted to reptiles.

"Sure you weren't imagining all the things that tail could do to you in bed?"

"Not in public!" I hiss in a somewhat joking tone, before smacking him under the table. His soft middle cushions the already-weak blow. There's no one around us, thankfully. I wouldn't expect anyone in the store to call me a slur if they overheard I was gay, but I'm cautious out of habit. That's why my pride keychain's never seen the light of day and why my earring is a simple green stud.

"Fine, I'll save it for the apartment." He returns to organizing his small stack of new cards, wiggling in satisfaction. I wish I had a zebra card to tease him right back with. Maybe the store has basketball cards and I can find one of his old crush.

I return my cards to the box after going through my last pack. "Are you good with us heading back now? I want to start upgrading the deck." It's all I can think about, really. I'm idly considering which cards I want to switch out and which ones from my old deck would work well with it. I still don't know which cards have been reprinted recently enough to be legal in Standard, though.

"Sure."

We gather up our purchases and leave. I haven't even known about this place for a full day, and I can already tell I'm going to become a regular. Adamant's got its hold on me again, and I'm accepting it with open arms.

We narrowly avoid a light drizzle as we arrive back at the apartment. Back home. That's gonna take a while to get used to. Thoughts of Jay try to creep in, but they're held off by my desire to deck-build.

I lug the heavy bin that holds my Adamant collection from my room to the dining table and set it down on it. I spread the contents out on the table. I sort of had it organized before I quit. All my rare cards are in a binder I've had since middle school that's beginning to fall apart. The rest are in boxes, divided by color and rarity. A worn, plastic deck box holds my old aggro deck, protected in sleeves with a gear pattern on them.

At a glance, it all looks very impressive, but the vast majority of it won't be of any use to me right now. Still, there's comfort in the memories they bring, which all pre-date my relationship with Jay. If I'm lucky, I'll be able to use Adamant to bookend the period of my life he dominated.

But I don't want to think about Jay right now, or the fact that at this time yesterday I was silently packing my things while he awkwardly flipped between avoiding me and trying to help. I just want to think about Adamant and how I'm going to enhance this starter deck I got.

I take out the starter deck and spread the cards so I can see everything in it. Then I grab the bundle I bought and separate out the cards my deck can use: red and relics. From my smaller pile, I pull out the cards I feel might actually have a place in the deck. I stick to cheap creatures and anything that boosts automatons. Ancelot is in the pile, of course—but only because it'll make my deck better, not because I think the character is handsome.

Aside from Ancelot, I end up adding five more cards to the deck, mostly creatures that are straight-up improvements over existing ones. It's a pretty good haul considering the fact I pulled them at random.

I have to go through the old cards next. I take out my original aggro deck and spread it out. Old and new lay side by side, showcasing eight years of change in the game. I haven't played the new deck, but I feel my old one is stronger. It has more rares and uncommons, as well as the advantage of being tweaked over the course of years and proven in local tournaments. But the new one can surpass it. I just need to buff it and figure out the meta.

"Ah, the old bane of my existence," Noah says. He's holding Mr. Wiggles, who appears quite content with the pampering he's receiving. His tail sways lazily over Noah's arm, and he gives me an aloof look, like a bored king taking in his subjects.

"I remember you beating it plenty."

"Not nearly enough. When I started playing again, I was *still* on edge whenever I faced a red deck. It took me years to recover." He gently rocks Mr. Wiggles, but the cat meows once and he immediately stops.

"That'll be me when I go against any control deck." Control decks are the polar opposite of aggro in a lot of ways. They play defensively, countering threats while they build up an advantage of resources and cards to secure victory. They can fizzle your momentum and leave you waiting for an inevitable loss. They weren't my worst matchup, but they were the least fun to play against. A lot of things have changed in Adamant, but I don't see that being one of them.

I pull up the official Adamant card database on my phone. I'll have to search each card from my old deck individually to see if they're legal in Standard. I start with the rares, since they'll have the biggest impact on the deck's power.

"If you're putting all this effort into improving the deck, does that mean you're gonna join me at Friday Night Adamant?" Noah asks. He's not trying to hide his excitement, and I almost say yes just to keep him happy.

"Not right away. I want to ease back into the game so I can get a hang of all the new stuff, and throwing myself right into tournaments won't help."

"FNA's still as lax as it was when we were in high school."

"I'm sure it is, but I'm also sure I'd make an ass of myself if I went to one right now. I'd have to stop to look at every card and ask about a whole lot of keywords and probably fuck something simple up." And normally I'd be able to get over that easily, but the breakup has my mood all over the place so I don't want to risk tarnishing one of my only sources of escape left.

Noah doesn't respond right away, instead scratching Mr. Wiggles behind the ear. "Well, when you're feeling up to it, just tell me."

"It'll happen sooner rather than later." I hope. I feel like I'm suddenly relying on that a whole lot right now.

As expected, I'm not having much luck with my old deck. None of the rares have been reprinted since I stopped playing. A couple of uncommons have, but only one fits well into my new deck. Not all aggro decks play the same, and my pair have enough minor differences to not be one hundred percent compatible. While it's bad for my wallet, it should prove to be a fun change, something to discover.

Mr. Wiggles grows tired of being coddled and squirms until Noah lets him down. He starts to leave, but then becomes entranced by Noah's tail and stalks it like prey. Noah notices and flicks his tail about, playing a risky game of chicken with the cat that ends in a startled chirp and a win for Mr. Wiggles. Both wander off afterward.

I replace all the locations in my new deck with ones from the old. They're functionally the same, but I'm nostalgic for the older art. With that done, I take all the sleeves off my old deck and put them on the cards of my new one, to protect them from wear and tear.

Checking the legality of my entire collection—even just the red cards—would be a tedious waste of time. Instead, I look up decklists online to see if any of them have cards I recognize.

No deck ever has a definitive list. Even if ninety percent of the deck is universally agreed upon, there'll always be intense arguments over what the other ten percent should be, both online and in person. There's rarely a wrong answer. Everyone's meta is different, and a card that makes the deck dominate in one area will be dead weight in another. Until I've figured out what my meta is, I'll have to stick to my instincts.

Deck analysis has apparently improved over the last eight years, because I find a site that lists all cards common in Standard-legal Red Aggro decks as well as the percentage of player decks they've appeared in during tournaments over the years. This latter feature proves to be quite useless though, because there are barely any Red Aggro decks listed at all. I can see exactly when the meta shifted against it, because there's an immediate drop in card usage. It's not just a low-tier deck, it's a no-tier deck, which doesn't bode well for me. I may have to get used to losing a lot if I want to stick with it, which I do.

No familiar faces await me on the few decklists I find. If I want to improve my questionable deck, I'm best off buying the remaining cards individually, but that can wait for later, once I'm certain the shine of playing Adamant won't wear off. I don't think it will, but it's only been a day.

I put away my collection, leaving only my deck on the table. "Hey, Noah!" I shout.

"Yeah?" His voice echoes from his room behind me.

"Want to help me test the new deck?"

I hear the cheetah getting out of his chair before I hear his response, and I'm already smiling.

I swing at Noah with everything I've got—a half dozen automatons and Ancelot. I've kept his creatures at bay with direct damage spells all game, and the two big plants he's managed to keep alive aren't enough to fend off my swarm. No matter what he does, he's going to take lethal damage. He knew that at the end of his last turn. Rather than concede, he assigns his two creatures to block, making sure poor Ancelot gets wrecked in the final moments of the match.

"Why are you so mean to my poor snake?" I ask with a chuckle, already collecting my deck.

"Because he's a jerk, and maybe if I flatten him enough, you'll take him out of the deck to protect him," Noah says.

"I like the card, but I'm not *that* obsessed." Though I already want a second copy to increase my odds of drawing it.

Noah laughs. "I haven't played this much Adamant in one weekend since high school."

It was all we did some weekends. Us and all of our friends would hit up FNA on Friday, then have a sleepover at someone's house on

Saturday, and not disperse until Sunday afternoon. We'd play video games and watch movies, too, but mostly it'd be Adamant. Game after game after game, playing whoever was available on whatever surface we could find. So many close calls with spilled drinks and stray feet.

"I thought this was how college was going to be. But then..." But then Jay. I don't finish the thought out loud, but I'm sure the loss of my smile gives me away.

"Better late than never." Noah aims his broad smile right at me, and part of mine comes back. "Is the new deck treating you right?"

I nod. "About as well as it can, all things considered." The deck's not terrible, but Noah's outclasses it in every conceivable way. There were times when having a slightly better version of a card might have tipped the game in my favor, though. "But just you wait. Once I get it all decked out, you're gonna wish you never got me back into the game."

"I can't believe it only took you a day and some wins to get cocky again. I've created a monster!" Noah says, melodramatically.

"Oh come on, I'm not that cocky."

"I *guess* Cedric's cockier."

"Who?" Our group back in high school didn't have a Cedric.

Noah's eyes go wide. "Oh! Cedric is a friend. Forgot you haven't had a chance to meet the group I play with now."

To my dismay, it actually stings a little learning Noah made a whole new friend group in the four years we grew apart. All I did was gather loose acquaintances who I lost the second Jay and I broke up.

"They're all coming over next Saturday, so I can introduce you then," Noah says. "Guess I forgot to mention that, too. We made plans to hang out here almost a month ago, before, uh, you know." He doesn't say it, but I'm stuck thinking it. "Anyway, it's nothing fancy, just food and games. Really chill."

"A get-together sounds fun. Cedric plays Adamant, then?"

"Yep! Everyone coming does. Roy will be there, too, and a couple others I don't think you've met before. It'll be just like the old sleepovers, but with booze. And also no one sleeping over. And probably no one staying up until five in the morning." Noah stops talking, and looks like he's trying to remember how else the party won't be like a high school sleepover.

I shake my head at his tangent. "I'm looking forward to it, really." I'm good at meeting new people, I've just been terrible at turning those meetings into meaningful friendships lately. A part of me is worried this'll be a repeat of Jay's friends, that we'll all talk and hang out once a month and our connection will never grow beyond a thin, nearly invisible strand. But I can't go into this party expecting the worst. I've been plagued by enough bad changes in my life. I'm finally overdue for some good ones. I wonder what kinds of decks they play.

Chapter 3 (Zach)

After a weekend filled with change—both good and bad—Monday feels like a jarring return to my old normal. I give myself plenty of time to get into work. I've got a decent idea of how long the walk should be thanks to the visit to Cascade Games, but I'm taking a slightly different route today. I go around campus instead of through it; too many memories of Jay can be triggered there.

Going the long way doesn't add much to my trip overall, so I arrive outside Tabitha's Treasures with time to spare. I feel I've worked here long enough to comfortably state there are few if any treasures in this place. Inside, the store looks like it's been struck with a tidal wave of junk. The aisles are an eclectic mess of bookcases, cabinets, shelving units, old display cases, and stacked furniture.

There's little in the way of order, so the store has become a maze. The titular Tabitha—an elderly cormorant who owns the place—is a firm believer that the store can never have enough product and buys more with such reckless abandon I'm surprised she hasn't bankrupted herself a dozen times over. She hits up locker auctions, estate sales, yard sales—anything where she thinks she can score a lot for cheap. At most, I only see her once a month; her grandniece Elizabeth serves as the manager and is set to inherit it once Tabitha passes, which the old avian casually mentions a distressing amount. Though I guess it'd be nice to face the inevitable with such calm acceptance.

Elizabeth is at the counter up front when I come in. She has on a loose, flower pattern blouse. Her black feathers have a faint iridescent green shine to them. Round glasses are perched atop her thin, flat beak, held on by a colorful band that wraps around the back of her head. We do a quick hand-off before she heads upstairs to the office for the rest of the day to make sense of her grandaunt's finances and recent purchases. I don't envy her job; she always looks worn out when she leaves after covering my breaks.

Quiet country music plays through speakers scattered throughout the store. The radio stays on the same channel year-round, aside from a month-long break in December for non-stop Christmas music. In the four years I've worked here, I haven't heard it play any other stations. I don't mind it, though the holiday music can be a bit much a couple of weeks into the season.

I can still remember when I thought I'd only be putting up with the Christmas music once. I don't know why I had such lofty ambitions for myself. I hadn't made any meaningful attempt to find something else at that point. Hadn't made any progress writing, either. I just didn't seem like I *should* have been here any longer, that's all. But then one year became two, then three, then four. It was routine. The last routine I've got left now that Jay and I are through.

I don't want to be behind this counter all my life. The job isn't stressful; it just doesn't lead anywhere. Ignoring that used to be easy. I'd shrug it off and lie to myself that things would change soon. Haven't been able to do that since the fights with Jay. Now it's *his* voice reminding me of how little I've done with my life rather than my own or my parents'. That hits harder.

The lack of anything to do eventually pushes away my self-loathing. Business is slow on weekday mornings. We get bored retirees mainly, who look around and reminisce but don't buy much. Towards the evening there'll be people wandering in looking for deals on things they can't afford new. They tend to treat me better overall and buy the most. On the weekends, things change up, and we get a mix of curious tourists looking to ogle our small-town wares—they buy less than the retirees—and art students from CWU in search of raw materials, who are the second-best customers despite their meager budgets. There are very few regulars, though sometimes a customer will act familiar enough that I assume they've been in more than once, even if I don't remember a thing about them.

Two hours in and we've only had two customers. I grab the cordless phone and start to wander. I keep an ear out for the bell of the front door, so I can return if a customer does show up. With how messy the store is, I always manage to find something new when I look around. Could be it was hidden behind something that recently sold, or got picked up and dropped off by a customer who reconsidered it. Could be brand new, as Elizabeth throws up stock in the morning before I get here. Some stuff I just forget about and then rediscover. Other things I overlook for months, only for them to catch my eye by chance.

It's impossible to take in everything walking down the aisles; there's too much. Shelves overflow with junk. I glance to my left and see a chaotic assortment of kitchen stuff: novelty cookie jars, salt and pepper shakers, teacups, gravy boats, candy dishes, and more. A wooden dish rack is filled with decorative plates I'm too nervous to browse through, and a china cabinet has so much glassware the doors don't fully close. Gaudy chandeliers crowd the ceiling above. My ears twitch as the tips brush against dangling plastic beads.

If an earthquake struck right now, I'd undoubtedly be crushed beneath a mountain of knick-knacks and curios. I contemplate that more often than I'd like to admit.

My aimless journey leads me to the closest thing the store has to a toy section. The vast majority of it is aging stuff for younger kids. There are whole shelves of unsettling dolls in various states of dress, with faded features and missing tails. A few have been crudely altered to change their species, adding patterns and trimming features. A wolf becomes a cross fox thanks to a heavy coat of black and orange paint that's chipped in places to show the original gray beneath. A donkey has their ears clipped and a mane drawn on to become a horse.

My parents never went that far with my toys. Some of my action figures were foxes and wolves, but I had a lot of cats and lizards and dinosaurs, too. I sigh. *Paleo Force* better not have awakened my reptile interest. Best not to dwell too much on the origins of my sexual preferences.

We've got board games in the store, but only the classics; stuff like Landlords, Lexiko, and Sleuth. Boxes are falling apart and the remaining pieces are sealed in plastic baggies on the verge of being antiques themselves. I don't think I've ever rung one up. You can grab brand new copies from Hillmart or online from Boreal for barely more than you'd pay here, and at least then you'd be guaranteed to have everything.

Mixed in with the board games are playing cards, tarot cards, and baggies of other card games. I've never given them much thought before, but with Adamant on my mind I take a moment to look. Lo and behold, one of the baggies actually has Adamant cards in it.

Curiosity gets the better of me. I open the bag and skim through the cards. I recognize about half the cards as coming from sets that were brand new at the time I quit the game. The others must be from sets that came out immediately after. My best guess is the pile comprises a couple of decks, part of an unorganized collection. There aren't any rares and a lot of the cards are in rough shape; water damage, bent edges, marker scribbles changing them to proxies of better cards.

I begin thinking about where the cards came from, just like I had when I saw the valuable rares in the case at Cascade Games. I doubt Tabitha knows a thing about card games—the price label on the baggy refers to them simply as "cards" after all—so they must have been from a locker or something a local donated. We don't get much of that since there's an actual thrift store just a few blocks away, but Tabitha's never been one to turn down free junk.

If someone my age or younger were getting rid of cards they'd either pass them to a friend who still played or ditch them at a card store. All I can think of when I see the cards is a parent tossing out their kid's old toys. Jay's parents did that when they found out he was gay.

He'd gone home for dinner to celebrate the winery taking him on full time when his internship ended. His parents had never fully accepted his career choice, so the night started rough—his father considered working with wine to be effeminate, and his mother always went along with everything he said. Jay had been drinking to make the visit tolerable and when a lawsuit about providing services for gay weddings came up, the only counter he could think of to his father's ensuing diatribe was to out himself.

In Jay's own words, his father looked like his son had tested positive for cancer. First he'd been convinced that Jay was lying; then he decided going to college turned him gay. He eventually settled on blaming the winery, as if his preferred choice of liquor had made all the difference in him wanting to fuck me instead of a woman. His mother left the room once the shouting started, and Jay didn't see her at all before inevitably storming out and driving home drunk. Considering the circumstances, I never really had an opportunity to be pissed at him for being so reckless.

Jay called them a week later in the hopes of having a civil conversation with them, but was promptly disowned. We later learned they'd already thrown out all of his old belongings by then. Everything he'd left behind was tossed, from little league trophies to kids movies. In a lone act of rebellion, his mother had kept their family photos, but they were hidden in a box in the attic.

I'd known that coming out didn't always end well, but Jay's was the first bad one I'd had personal experience with. My parents had been accepting enough, and Noah's had been so supportive they'd offered to take me in if things went bad when I came out. Jay had known they wouldn't be happy, but he hadn't expected them to erase him from their lives without hesitation.

Was that when things had changed? We went out less in the months that followed and fucked a lot more, but I'd always felt things went back to normal after that. We didn't talk about his parents or what had happened; it became an unwritten taboo. Being queer means spinning a wheel to determine if your family loves you or hates you when they find out, and even if you expect the worst, it can be devastating if it becomes reality. Far too often we have to create brand new families with others who've survived the same trauma. And for a while, I thought that's what I was going to be doing with Jay, even if I was still on cordial terms with my own parents.

Two years later his father had an *actual* cancer scare and a "vision" from God telling him to seek forgiveness. He called Jay in the middle of the night and rambled on about past mistakes and not giving him a chance and a lot of other things that sounded like complete gibberish. Jay, confused and completely unaware of what his father was going through, had accepted the apparent apology. Within a week, his father's cancer went into remission. His father considered the coincidence to be proof his change of heart was divinely ordained, and he started reconciling with Jay. It's going to be a long process, one I'll no longer be able to help with.

Am I really not going to be able to go an hour without thinking of Jay? I know it's only been a few days since we officially broke things off, but emotionally I feel like I've been going through this for months. Adamant's the only thing that's been able to distract me. Well, that and hanging out with Noah. I fret less about the new ex when I'm with the old one.

But I can't worry about Jay so much. I remember the cards in my paws and give them my full and undivided attention. There doesn't seem to be anything valuable in the stack, and most of these cards probably aren't Standard legal anymore either, but they tempt me. Maybe it's nostalgia for the older cards or the chance to add stuff to my collection from the period I wasn't playing as a means of catching up on something I missed out on. Maybe it's just to grow my collection in general, regardless of if I put the cards to use.

Someone cared about these cards in the past, played them enough to wear a few down. Who knows when anyone else will stumble through the clutter and buy them. What's the harm in giving them a good home?

The whole stack is cheap—neither Tabitha nor Elizabeth knows enough about CCGs to price them—so there's little to dissuade me from nabbing them. I bring the stack up to the counter and ring them up for myself. Technically I'm not allowed to do that, but the bosses trust me so I'm given a lot of leeway. That's one advantage to being the senior-most employee in a place no one stays at for more than a year.

The day slows down again after my surprise find. A couple of college kids stroll in and scour the place, chatting as they wander the aisles. Based on their conversation, they're not looking for anything in particular. They leave without buying anything, my existence essentially ignored. After them comes an antelope who spends almost an hour looking through jewelry, bewildered. I don't envy him. Not all jewelry is species-neutral, and we've never bothered organizing ours. There's no point, since they get moved around more often than anything else in the store. He settles on a turquoise necklace which he insists so firmly isn't for him that I start to have doubts.

Elizabeth is gone by five, and I close up shop at six. It's an easy task. All I have to do is close out the register and make sure nothing's on the floor in the aisles; at least nothing that isn't supposed to be there.

Normally I head straight home, and I'm about to do that when I remember Cascade Games is only a block away and still open. I just got new cards, but not enough to sate my desire for more. Adamant's helping fill the void left behind by Jay, so I put little effort into resisting its allure. I take a left instead of a right, and soon I'm back in Cascade Games.

I head straight for the card games. I stick with booster packs because I don't want to spend much, settling on three from Unearthed Lore, the set that came out before The Apocalypse Codex. They'll still be useful for a while, and I'll get to see all brand new cards when I open the packs. I also check out the supplies section. I want a new deck box to replace my aging plastic one; something nice, like Noah's. Luckily for me, they've got a red one in stock, with the color's crescent gear symbol in black on the front. Each color has a unique symbol, which is used to represent the specific aether produced to play cards associated with them. I scurry out of the card section before I spend any more money.

The tables in the back of the store aren't empty like they were yesterday. Two guys are in the middle of a game of Adamant. One is a beaver rapidly tapping his paddle tail against the back of the chair as he looks at his hand of cards. The other stops me in my tracks.

He's a stout snake, not quite chubby but not quite fat. His scales are milky white with a few honey-colored splotches scattered about. His eyes are a piercing red, focused more on his opponent than his cards. I can't see the state of the board, but I know he's winning. He looks almost bored, as if the game's already been decided and the beaver hasn't realized it yet. He also has a passing resemblance to Ancelot.

I don't know how long I stare at him. Pulling my gaze away is a struggle, and it's a miracle I haven't been noticed yet. What I'm doing is rude and also a little reckless. If he sees and guesses I'm gay, a torrent of slurs could be headed my way. But I don't want to believe the snake is hateful. I also don't want to believe he's straight, though the odds are against me on that one.

I get ahold of myself and head to the counter. My eyes wander, and I feel my face warm up as I spot the snake's tail coiled around his chair in a near-constant state of motion. Jay always flicked his tail when he was nervous. Perhaps I'm wrong about his guaranteed victory.

When I leave the store, I let out a sigh that turns into a faint whine. I feel guilty getting so riled up when I haven't even gotten over my breakup yet. Countless nights with Jay swept aside in favor of fantasies about that snake's tail slithering over my body before I slide into him from behind. I'm hard, and that makes it so much worse.

As I walk home I steadily get over myself. Fantasies are what I need right now. They give me hope there'll be someone after Jay, even if a large part of me just wants my lizard back. It doesn't matter that the last few months have provided ample proof we just aren't meant to be together. So I think, *To hell with it*, and let my mind wander to thoughts of snakes and coils.

New routines form faster than I anticipate. I wake up, go to work, go home, hang out with Noah, fall asleep, and then do it all again the day after. As the week progresses, I feel more and more like I'm back in my freshman year of college. A lot of TV, games, and chatting, with work replacing classes. I almost forget Noah is still taking classes himself, as they all happen while I'm away, and he rarely talks about them.

Noah and I have a lot of catching up to do, and it's happening in short bursts. One of us will spontaneously remember something from a couple of years ago and ramble on about it as if it just happened yesterday. It might be an incident from a night out with friends or a movie we really liked. Or hated; going to movies was one of Jay and my default dates, so I've seen almost everything that's come out in the last four years.

Talk of Jay is avoided as much as possible. Noah catches on quickly that I change the subject whenever a conversation is heading towards something I strongly associate with Jay. He's patient with me. He always has been, but he's never had to put up with me being in this bad of a place before. My own memories feel like a minefield, and I can only imagine he sees that in the way my mood flips so rapidly. I'll find a way to pay him back one day.

The only times he gets stern with me are when my confidence cracks and I start blaming myself for my failed relationship. But even then, I'm not completely convinced by his encouragement. If you watch a sure thing crumble to pieces, you're bound to believe you didn't do enough to protect it. It's like the cards I found at the antique store, like anything at that store really. Quality of goods varies, but how much of the wear and tear is a result of neglect, and how much is just inevitable? Until I figure out exactly what went wrong with Jay and me, I fear I'll never feel comfortable entering another relationship.

Chapter 4 (Zach)

I think on and off about Adamant all week. I've poured through every Standard-legal red card multiple times in search of ways to improve my deck. Others with far greater analytical skills than me have already explored every possible way to create this kind of deck in the current environment, but searching on my own is fun. It also helps familiarize me with new keywords and the general state of the meta.

I can see how Red Aggro has grown weaker in the last two sets. The color red shifted from an automaton and relic focus to a random chance focus, with lots of cards based on dice rolls. In the lore, it's meant to represent the trial and error of invention, with artificers taking risks in the hopes of making breakthroughs while also suffering the occasional catastrophic backfire. It's always been a minor theme in red, but they brought it to the forefront for Unearthed Lore and The Apocalypse Codex.

Random chance can be a fun mechanic, but it's inconsistent, and more likely to slow an Aggro deck than benefit it. Red Aggro decks in the current environment are relying predominantly on efficient, low-cost cards from older sets since they haven't gotten anything useful from the new sets.

When I look online, I see far more players complaining about random chance cards than praising them. That amount of flak tends to get noticed by the game's developers. Of course, the bulk of the design work for the next couple of sets should already be done by now, so who knows how long it'll be before the game is able to respond to the backlash.

Even with all my reading, I still feel a little lost. Eight years is a lot to catch up on, and it's not like there's a detailed guide anywhere for me to look at. The Adamant fandom is spread across countless forums, online articles, wikis, and chat services. When it comes to Standard, everyone's attention is on the present and the future, not the past. Sure, I'll see people mention infamous banned cards I've never heard of, but speaking their names is the entirety of the argument or reference. For those who were playing when they were around, that's good enough, but I'm left looking up the cards and having to guess what made them so oppressive. Sometimes a card isn't banned because it's good on its own, but because it creates an overpowered combo with a completely different card, one that might not be banned along with it.

But I was lost when I first started playing Adamant, and I had far fewer resources at my disposal back then. One day I'll know every keyword and famously overpowered card again, and when someone goes off about a set being weak or broken, I'll be able to nod in agreement as if I'd been playing all along.

Besides, when I'm obsessing over Adamant I'm not thinking about Jay, or my dead-end job, or what I'm going to do with my life, none of which I have the energy to confront right now.

I come close to changing my mind about going with Noah to Friday Night Adamant. It starts shortly after my shift ends, so attending wouldn't be a problem. I even bring my deck with me to work, just in case. But sitting around the antique store gives me a lot of time to think, and I realize I still don't feel comfortable enough to duel strangers yet, not in a tournament setting. I'll be able to play plenty of Adamant at the party tomorrow night, and hopefully that'll be the confidence boost I need.

I cross paths with Noah on the way home, only a block away from the shop. I think of how we must have been close to bumping into each other every Friday night for the last couple of years. If I'd gone north once instead of south, would we have reconnected earlier? Would having him back in my life have made a difference in my relationship with Jay? I wish I could stop coming up with new what-ifs.

"Sure you don't want to come, Zach?" Noah asks as we greet each other.

Again I almost reconsider, words of acceptance on the tip of my tongue. "I'm good. I just want to relax after work tonight." Mostly the truth. Adamant relaxes me, even the losses. All I'm going to do when I get home is be lazy.

"I'll see you in a bit, then. Wish me luck—and keep Mr. Wiggles out of trouble!" Noah laughs, heading off towards Cascade Games.

"No promises!" I yell back. Mr. Wiggles does what he wants and has shown no interest in listening to foxes, especially ones trying to shoo him away from their fluffy tail. As far as I can tell, he just thinks of me as a new toy that's arrived at the apartment.

When I walk through the front door, Mr. Wiggles gets up from his spot on the couch and scurries over. He looks up at me and lets out a very long and mournful meow. Usually that means he's hungry. Or that he wants attention. Noah swears he meows differently for things, but I'm pretty sure that's just him trying to play up his alleged feline connection, and that Mr. Wiggles simply meows because he can. The cat's food and water are fine, though, so I just walk past him to my room. He follows and meows some more, but quickly gets bored and switches to batting at my tail. He leaves when I hold it out of reach, denying him fun. We're both going to have to put up with being bored tonight, at least until Noah gets back.

The day of the party is the first time I really feel how small the kitchen is. Spread over the counters and stovetop are two pizza boxes, a large bowl of chips, soda, beer, and Noah's small collection of hard liquor. There are also paper plates, plastic cups, and napkins taking up even more space. We had to move around appliances to make room for it all, but I can't imagine us being able to host more than the small group we'll be having over.

"This'll be enough, right?" I ask.

"Huh?" Noah's voice comes from further than I expect. Turns out he'd been on the far side of the living room, not by the dining table.

I lean out of the kitchen. "We have enough food, right?"

The question seems to catch him off guard. "We should be fine. Unless you're planning on wiping out a whole pizza by yourself."

I'm pretty sure I'd go catatonic before I could finish the last slice. "No. Are you?" It's a terrible comeback and doesn't even make sense, but it's out before I can think much on it.

"Ah damn, you got me. I was gonna roll one up and eat it like a burrito." The first thing that comes to mind is the mess such a stunt would make. "But seriously, we'll be fine. Worst case scenario I'll run over to the QuickStop down the street and snag more chips."

I hear two quiet knocks. "I think someone's at the door?"

"That's gotta be Roy," Noah says as he hurries to the door, reaching it before I do. "He's too polite for his own damn good sometimes."

I do my best to remember Roy. He was Jay's roommate our freshman year of college and part of our quad. He's a snow leopard and bisexual–he figured that part out the last year of high school, though I never heard the details. He's not quiet, he just holds back a lot. Him and Noah even dated for a few months. None of us were ever really sure when the relationship began or when it ended, and the two cats seemed to think keeping it a secret was hilarious.

Our whole quad had originally planned to stick together after freshman year, but then Roy had grown close with a few others in his major and decided to find a place with them instead. We still hung out as a group a lot our sophomore year, but I didn't see him much after that. Whether that was because he spent more time with his other social circle or because I fixated on Jay, I'd rather not ruminate on.

When the door opens, the first thing I notice about Roy is that he's wearing the same glasses as me. Aside from that, he doesn't look much different from the last time I saw him.

"Zach, it's great to see you!" Roy swoops in and gives me a tight hug that squeezes my reply out as a raspy squeak. He swiftly rubs his face against my muzzle. "It's been too long!"

"It has," I say, after I've caught my breath. I'm struggling to come up with anything that isn't: "Sorry I haven't talked to you in six years."

Fortunately, there's another guest behind Roy, so introductions will buy me time to think of something. The newcomer is a plump, white and chestnut brown pinto horse. He's got a white stripe down his muzzle and a platinum blonde mane that goes down to his shoulders. "Dude, you must be Zach!" He gives me a firm side hug with a hard slap on the back.

"Yep," I choke out. My glasses have bounced off my ears and slid to the edge of my snout. I take a moment to nudge them back into place.

The horse takes a step back, a wide grin on his muzzle. "Name's Cedric."

All I can do is nod to that because he already knows my name. The four of us grab beers and head back into the living room. I end up on the couch in between Roy and Cedric while Noah brings over a chair from the dining table.

It's been a while since I've had to introduce myself to new people, but I fall back into it fairly easily. Sometimes giving a person a solid question to latch onto is the best approach. "So, Cedric, how do you know everyone?"

The horse tips his beer towards Noah. "All thanks to Professor Spots here." The nickname gets a snort from Roy and seems to fluster Noah, oddly enough. "He was my tutor three years back. My grades were slipping, and Coach said I'd lose my scholarship if I started failing out of shit."

"Football?" I ask. Right away I wish I'd guessed wrestler. His shape seems better suited to it.

"That's what everyone guesses. Not sure why." That gets another snort from Roy. "Track and field, baby! I was a pole vaulter." Cedric mimes his hoof leaping over his beer.

"Show him the picture," Noah says with a mischievous grin.

Cedric pulls out his phone, flicks a finger across the screen a few times, and then turns it to me. On the screen is a photo of a horse arching his body over a horizontal pole. His red CWU tank top is pulled up a little, showing off his abs. Even though the mane and patterns match, I have trouble believing it's actually Cedric in the photo.

I know Noah and Roy want me to ask the obvious question, but I'm not about to be baited into being rude. Instead, I stick to being genuinely impressed. "Damn. So, did Noah, uh, help you keep the scholarship?"

"He got my grades up, but I lost the scholarship anyway. I broke my leg real bad at practice and missed the season, and by the time it was all healed I was a bit out of shape and getting back into peak condition just wasn't worth it. Besides, I liked all the free time I got while I was away. Got to hang out with my frat brothers a ton, sleep in, go out, catch up on games. Felt like I somehow accomplished more despite hobbling around on crutches. The meets were fun, but that shit takes up your whole life, and I didn't see myself making a career out of it so why miss out on the best years of my life, ya know?"

I haven't been part of a team since little league, but I do have experience feeling like I wasted a few years dedicating myself to something for nothing, so I can see why Cedric wanted to get out of it.

"And if you were still leaping around all the time, you wouldn't be here to play Adamant right now," Noah said.

"Exactly! Professor Spots started getting really chatty about the game and showed me how to play in between study sessions. Was great for when we didn't have time to fuck."

Noah almost chokes on his beer while Roy laughs in the seat beside me. For a second, I wonder if I'm being messed with, but Noah's definitely blushing, and I've already gotten the impression Cedric isn't the type to make things up for the hell of it. Of course, I also didn't think he was gay a few seconds ago.

I look at my roommate, who hasn't quite recovered yet. "You two were a"—I press my pointer fingers together—"thing?"

"We never dated," Noah says.

"Just had fun when we got pent up. You know how hard it is to find dudes into other dudes around here. It's not like Chimes is ever packed," Cedric says.

Chimes is the city's only gay bar, but it's also a sports bar and right next to campus so even on a good night you're lucky if a third of the people there aren't straight. Most folks are better off using hook-up apps than bar crawling on this side of the state.

I hear the faint rumble of a purr come from Roy. He used to do that whenever he was particularly proud of himself. I glance over before he even starts talking.

"You know, Noah's slept with all three of us at one point or another." Noah's eyes are already widening. "I wonder how he thinks we all compare?" He may only have a slight smile, but the sporadic purrs tell a tale of smug feline satisfaction in the chaos he's about to cause.

"Shit, you're right! Who's best in bed?" Cedric casually asks. I don't know if he's just going along with Roy's ploy to embarrass Noah, or if he thinks it's seriously a good idea to ask.

Noah slouches in his chair. "Well Roy's at the bottom now."

"Cheers for bottoms!" Cedric raises his beer and chugs most of it.

"He said I'm at the bottom, not I *am* a bottom."

"Nothing—*urp*—wrong with being a bottom." Cedric wipes his mouth. "Though it's hard not to blow my load laughing when the dude riding me says shit like 'yeehaw.'"

"Something I *never* did," Noah insists.

"You were too busy purring."

"Dude!"

"You rumble like an engine once you get going," Roy adds.

"Oh as if you didn't purr just as loud when we fucked!"

"Yes, but mine are soft, like a massage. Yours almost threw me off once."

"They did not!"

"If you didn't have those love handles to grab onto, I'd have tumbled right off the bed."

"They come in handy," Cedric says matter-of-factly, gesturing at Noah with his beer. A second later he seems to realize there's a pun in there and lets out a giggling whinny.

I stay quiet during the back and forth about their sex lives, doing my best to avoid laughing at how flustered Noah is getting. It's been years since I was last in the middle of such a casually gay conversation. Most of Jay's friends are straight. They're tolerant and accepting, but they aren't the kind of people I ever felt comfortable discussing, well, gay stuff with.

"Zach?"

I look around before settling on Roy, who I'm pretty sure just said my name. "Huh?"

"I was asking you about how hard Noah purrs during sex. On a scale from moped to rocket engine."

I finally crack, muffling my laugh with the back of my paw and trying not to spill any beer. "God, it's been so long." We never fooled around after we stopped dating. Getting back together with Noah—even just for fun—had never occurred to me. I guess I'd decided that when it was over, it was over, that there wouldn't be any do-overs. It's the same way I'm feeling about me and Jay, and that thought kills my laughter hard. I won't have a breakdown at the party. "Really I just remember the chirps."

Noah shoots me a look of betrayal, but I know it's exaggerated. There's no way he didn't chirp while fucking the other two.

And I'm right, because my comment leads to a flurry of stories about how adorable the noises he makes are. It takes a while, but Noah's eventually able to divert talk away from himself. It helps that I lay off him, and Cedric just goes with the flow of conversations, seemingly eager to talk about anything at all.

"Roy, when's Vera gonna come to one of these things?" Cedric asks once we've exhausted our ways to tease Noah.

My confusion must be obvious, because Roy directs his attention to me first. "Vera's my girlfriend."

"Another hospitality major?"

"Nah. We met at a bar three years ago." Roy looks past me at Cedric. "And she's still not interested in Adamant. Deck builders are her least favorite board games, and she's convinced Adamant will be just like those. But there's such a huge difference between building a deck from random cards in a board game and crafting a deck in a CCG."

"One day she'll see the light," Cedric says.

The sound of claws on fabric startles me, and something furry brushes against my ears. Mr. Wiggles has jumped onto the back of the couch. The cat hurries over to Roy and immediately starts rubbing against him. He's showing as much love for the snow leopard as he usually does Noah. "Hi, Wiggles," Roy sighs.

Cedric leans in behind me and tries to pet Mr. Wiggles, but his fingers only reach far enough to brush against the tip of the cat's tail. "Having fun with your stalker?"

Roy sighs louder. "Wiggles is fine." He scratches the cat behind his ear, earning thunderous purrs.

"Stalker?" I ask.

"Mr. Wiggles is fond of Roy, that's all," Noah says. His smirk implies otherwise.

"I'm telling you, he's gotta think Roy's some sort of cat god or something," Cedric says. "Seriously. If you were a little itty bitty kitty and you saw a giant version of you walking around on two legs and wearing fruity polos, wouldn't you want to earn their favor?"

"My polos aren't fruity."

"There's a banana on it."

"That's the company's logo."

"I rest my case."

There's a knock at the door, harder than Roy's from earlier. Mr. Wiggles bolts, scampering to the safety of Noah's room. Noah's up before I can even think of grabbing the door. It'll be a while before I think of the apartment as mine and remember I'm technically a host right now and not a guest.

I hear greetings at the front, and soon another round of introductions are made as a deer and an otter come over.

The deer is a dark shade of brown with a spot of white on her neck and the bottom of her muzzle. She's shorter than me, but sturdy, in a way that makes me think she could pick me up and throw me across the room if she wanted to. She has on a touch of black eye coloring and her lips are painted the same color. The red leather collar around her neck has diamond-shaped studs on it.

The otter is almost the same shade of brown, though she's leaner and taller than the deer. She's got on jeans and a white shirt, much plainer compared to her companion. I spy a leather bracelet on her tail painted a few shades of purple and orange.

"So you *do* exist," is the first thing the deer says to me.

"I certainly hope so," I reply.

Noah chimes in. "Sienna's just being mean because I've mentioned you a lot but never had you over."

Because I cared more about Jay than maintaining even my closest friendship. Every day I feel like I have more to make up for.

"The professor's been holding you back because he knows I'll talk your ear off about old shit. No one else has played the game for, what, longer than three years, Roy?" The deer looks past me.

"I've been playing three and a half," Roy replies.

"See? No one to get excited whenever they reprint an old busted card or rework one. Oh! Meet my otter!" Sienna wraps her arm around the otter and nudges her forwards, prompting a quiet squeak.

"Babe!" the otter whines, her eyes darting to the floor before returning to look my way. "I'm Blair."

"Nice to meet you."

Sienna and Blair each grab a beer, and we all get pizza. I focus my attention on the three guests I've never met before. Not getting to know people while I was still with Jay was a mistake I won't make again. To my relief, they all seem nice.

Sienna's as boisterous as Cedric. The pair enthusiastically discuss the Lumberjacks, the football team over in Seattle, going on about the draft which I guess happened recently. Again, I've never been into football. I know of a couple of Lumberjacks players off-hand, but that's only because they won the Federal Bowl a few years ago. It felt like everyone in the state suddenly became a football fan after that.

Blair—Sienna's girlfriend—is the quietest out of all of us, but once she does talk she talks a lot, and the otter seems somewhat sheepish whenever she realizes that.

As fun as it is to finally just hang out and talk with people again, Adamant is never far from my mind. I've only played Noah since getting back into the game, and I'm eager to see how I fare against other players and decks. So when Noah suggests we start playing, I'm the first to toss my plate and grab my deck.

There's not going to be any organization to our games. This isn't a tournament—not even a casual one—just games between friends. Future friends, in my case. I shouldn't be getting ahead of myself, but building a new social circle will go a long way towards helping me get past Jay and everything else going wrong in my life right now.

Sienna volunteers to be my first opponent. We claim seats opposite each other on the far end of the table. Her deck sleeves have a grinning, three-eyed goat face on them set in front of flames, like a scene from a heavy metal album cover. As she shuffles, I catch glimpses of red and blue cards. That's enough information to narrow down the potential theme of the deck. Spells and relics are the main areas where red and blue overlap. Either she's playing a deck where she gets bonuses for casting lots of spells, or she's playing a deck centered around relics. Those aren't the only ways to build a red/blue deck, but they're the most likely.

Not for a second do I consider the possibility her deck will include *both* themes. On her second turn, she plays a creature that creates something called a *bomb token* when it comes into play, which she represents with a dice. The bomb is a relic that can be sacrificed—purposely sent to the discard pile—in order to deal damage to any attacking creature. You can also make a gamble by sacrificing it to roll a dice for a chance to either deal that damage to an opponent if you roll evens or yourself if you roll odds. I'm not sure if she'll bother testing her luck, but the first ability is strong enough to destroy nearly every creature in my deck.

I'm getting ahead of myself. She may have played the only card in her deck that can produce mines, and it's simply a speedbump to slow an aggro deck like mine. On my turn, I attack, and she blocks with the creature; both deal lethal damage to each other and are destroyed. On her turn, she plays a spell that creates another bomb token, confirming my worst-case scenario.

I'm not going to give up on a game only three turns in, even if the matchup no longer seems in my favor. A lot can happen over the course of a game.

As I look across the minefield Sienna's creating across from me, I notice her resource cards are familiar. The archives—blue's locations—all have a gloomy feel to them; there are trashed libraries with books scattered about and crumbling scrolls covered in overgrown vines. While my workshops are vibrant factories, hers are smashed or cobbled together.

"Your archives are from Forlorn Whispers, right?" I ask once I recognize their set symbol.

"Yep," Sienna says, grinning. "The set had just come out when I started playing, and I love the aesthetic."

"You really have been playing for a while. I only started a couple sets before that."

"Adamant's hard to give up. I've taken a few breaks, but I never stay away for long."

"Wish I could say the same. Just coming back after not playing for eight years."

Sienna whistles. "Damn, you missed some good sets, then. Red was so good two years back they had to ban three cards in Standard to get players to build literally anything else."

"Fuck." Banning a card or two to deal with a deck isn't unheard of, but three is extreme and means something major was overlooked during the design process. Then again, there's a big difference between a design team playtesting a new set and a few million players actively searching for a broken combo.

I can't break through the wall of mines Sienna's built up so I hold my creatures back for defense. The situation's bleak, but there's nothing I can do. At the very least, I'll be able to see more of her cards and have a better feel for how her deck works. After a brief stalemate, she plays a legendary creature that can sacrifice the mines to deal damage to me without having to flip coins. I make one last attack because I can and then fall under a barrage of mines.

"I wasn't fast enough," I concede. I'm smiling, and not just to be polite. Learning how a new deck works in real-time is exciting, victory or not. I'm already thinking of ways I could tweak my deck to better defend against mines and relic-heavy decks in general.

"My starting hand was pretty damn good, too," Sienna says. Then she grins. "Though usually I start lobbing mines earlier."

We're still waiting on the others to finish their games, so we talk. Sienna wasn't kidding when she said she wanted someone to reminisce with about how Adamant was a decade ago. We share which decks we played when we first started out—she was aggro before she branched out—and what our early playgroups were like.

"It was my three older brothers for the first couple years. Mom made them teach me." Sienna's idly shuffling her deck. "They all got bored of it eventually. I tried getting into a group at school, but most of them were shits who didn't want to play with a girl so I had to bully my friends into learning. Never could get Vera to bite, though. She's Roy's girl."

I see the snow leopard's ears twitch at the sound of his name.

"Don't worry, we're not shit-talking you, fluffball," Sienna says. That gets Roy's ears to flatten and makes Cedric laugh so hard he burps.

"So then you met Roy and," I flick my paw, "everyone else through Vera?"

She nods. "I got to hear all about the new man of her dreams after their first date." She clasps her hooves together and rests her chin upon them. "'Oh Sin, he's got the fluffiest tail, and the nerdiest glasses, and the cutest polo.'"

"What has my polo done to earn such scorn tonight?" Roy asks. I can't help but notice Mr. Wiggles has come back out of hiding and is laying under Roy's chair. The cat really is obsessed with him.

"It knows what it did," Sienna says with what I hope is mock seriousness.

"Is this something you and Cedric planned? Am I gonna get like a dozen polos for my birthday this year?"

"Ooh, thanks for the idea!"

"Please don't do that. I don't have the dresser space for it."

"I attack you for twenty, dude."

"And Vera will—wait, twenty?!" Roy's attention is immediately back on his game, and so is mine.

Roy's playing a gold deck, while Cedric has a white/green one. Cedric's side of the table has ten dice, all with the two side facing up. He's running tokens, then.

"You blocking?" Cedric asks.

"Where'd those even come from?"

Cedric points to a card on top of his discard pile. "I played it while you were defending your polo's honor. So, you gonna block?" He's got a shit-eating grin on his face.

I see that Roy only has two creatures to block with, so a lot of damage is going to go through, probably enough to take him out now. Roy looks at his hand and groans. "No."

"Victory!" Cedric pumps his fist.

We switch opponents, chairs scooting in and out as we take new seats. Now I have to play Cedric, who's still ecstatic about his win.

I don't have to guess what kind of deck he's running since I saw a glimpse of it in action already. Lots of tokens and some way to boost them. What I won't know are the support cards, the things that'll deal with threats or give him the aether to get tokens out faster. It's like heading into a competition only knowing the star player of the opposing team. Knowing how to counter them is important, but you can't just shrug off everyone else.

Cedric plays fast and messy. Only a few seconds pass between him drawing a card at the beginning of a turn and tossing something into play. His locations are jumbled together and everything else is spread out. That makes it harder for me to keep track of what all he's got in play, but I don't think he's doing it on purpose; it's too chaotic to be a strategy.

Since both our decks are fairly straightforward, we have plenty of time to talk during turns. "You mentioned you were in a frat earlier; which one?" I didn't hit up Greek Row that often, but there's always a chance one of the parties I went to was at his place.

"Upsilon Eta Alpha!"

Nope, I haven't even heard of it.

"We get called Farmhouse a lot."

Now *that* I've heard of, so I nod in acknowledgment. "Are you studying agriculture then?" All I know about Farmhouse was that they have a lot of farmers. Or maybe just farmer's boys. Honestly, I never hung out with enough frat boys to learn the differences between the fraternities or why any have the nicknames they do.

"Sort of. I'm majoring in craft brewing."

"You can get a degree in that?" It sounds like a joke a beer-loving frat boy might make, but Cedric sounds more sincere than amused.

"Yep! It just started in like, 2015. The professors have their shit together, though, so it feels like it's been around forever. Fuck, I should've brought over a couple growlers of the ale I brewed for a final. I've got a good feeling it's gonna get me an A."

"Damn, that sounds really cool." I shouldn't be surprised that you brew beer in a craft brewing degree, but here I am. It's even sillier since I remember Jay making wine as part of his degree. "What made you choose craft brewing, though?"

"My buddy Cameron. He was a senior in the frat while I was a sophomore; just this huge hulking moose who was on the football team. He was a great mentor, got me passionate about beer." I'd like to think I can tell the difference between admiration and horny, and it certainly sounds like Cedric's fondness for Cameron went beyond his taste in booze. "His parents run a brewery so he knows everything about beer. He talked up how different each kind of beer is, what goes into making them, where they all came from. A lot of the other guys sort of shrugged him off whenever he'd talk about it, but that shit stuck with me. He must have noticed, cause he's the one who recommended I check out the craft brewing degree. Before that, I was still undecided. If it wasn't for Cameron, I'd probably have ended up nabbing a communications degree. Wouldn't have mattered much if I stuck with track, but—ha, you know!" He lets out a belly-shaking laugh. "Done."

I was so engrossed in Cedric's story that I missed him producing a flurry of tokens and ending his turn. It's not the swarm that took out Roy, but it's going to stall my assault on his life points for a bit. Fortunately, I draw a damage-dealing spell that manages to destroy three of Cedric's tokens and slow him down.

You can never underestimate the importance of luck in a game like Adamant. Building a deck properly will affect your odds of drawing the card you need and knowing when to use a card will ensure it's effective, but neither matters if your draws are bad. Luck of the draw can lead to frustrating losses and dramatic finishes, depending on which side of the table you're on.

"It's awesome everything worked out for you. And your major sounds really cool."

"It is!" Cedric plays another creature but isn't able to produce any more tokens on his turn. If I can keep up my momentum I'll win. "You went to CWU, right?" I nod. "What major?"

"Lit." It's Creative Writing specifically, but that always creates more questions so Lit is my default answer. Some people have trouble understanding how you major in writing. The rest always wanna know 'what you're currently working on,' and that's even worse.

"You a teacher like Noah?"

I can't fault him for the default answer. "Nah, not good at that sort of thing. I just write stuff when the mood hits." Which it hasn't for years now. Why am I even calling myself a writer anymore?

"Cool. I suck at writing. That's what Noah helped me with. Numbers are nice and easy once you memorize the rules. And you can get right to the point with them. When you do that in an essay you get a lot of notes in red ink about needing to add more words or paragraphs or shit like that." Cedric's still smiling.

"I'm the opposite. I suck at math, but I've got a way with words." So I've been told. It's been a long while since I last believed that.

"And a way with cards. I think I'm boned."

He is. I plow through the few defenders he has left and wipe Cedric out before he can create a token army. The win pushes away the writing anxieties that had tried to creep in, and I'm back to just thinking about Adamant and the party.

The other games end shortly after ours, so I don't have much time to talk with Cedric before I'm moving to face Roy. Mr. Wiggles has followed him, lurking under his chair. "I know they're all giving you shit for it, but I do think it's cute he keeps following you around."

Roy shakes his head and leans down to pet Mr. Wiggles, who meows at him. "It's a well-recorded phenomenon that certain feral species bond strongly with their sapient counterparts. Or sapients with a superficial resemblance to them."

"If you gave him glasses and fluffed up his tail, he'd be your clone," I say, provoking a round of laughter.

"We did that once," Sienna says. "Neither of them was amused by it, but we got some cute pictures."

Two different phones are shoved my way, and our games are delayed until I can see the entire album of Mr. Wiggles being forced to cosplay as Roy. Sienna's right; the pictures do look cute, especially the ones of Roy reluctantly holding Mr. Wiggles in his arms and glaring at everyone out of sight.

The diversion I accidentally caused has given Roy plenty of motivation to defeat me, but I think it was worth it.

Roy's playing the one color I've yet to go up against in any form with my new deck: gold. Gold has a very decadent theme, befitting the color used to represent it. Their locations are called *palaces*, and most of their creatures are nobles, pirates, and powerful merchants. It tends to focus on making players discard cards, weakening or destroying creatures, and stealing cards in play. I didn't see enough of his cards when he was playing Cedric to know what to expect.

The first creature Roy plays, Debt Collector, has an ability that allows him to deal one damage to an opponent and gain one life whenever a creature dies. Since gold has a lot of ways to destroy creatures, it also has a lot of ways to gain boons from their destruction. One damage doesn't seem like a lot, but it adds up. The same is true with life gain. Each point will basically undo an attack from my weaker creatures.

Roy gets a second copy of Debt Collector out followed by a legendary creature named Grand Duke Konstantine. I recognize the name from when I last played Adamant; they were just a lowly alchemist in the lore back then, though. Now the gray wolf is sitting on a lavish throne, and every time Roy gains life, they can deal one damage to a creature.

Well fuck. Now whenever a creature dies I'll lose life, and Roy will gain life. Konstantine's ability will then trigger, dealing damage to a creature. Most of my creatures don't have enough defense to survive that damage, meaning they die and the cycle will start up again. The combo is good in general, but devastating against my deck.

"Ouch," is all I can think to say as I look at the state of the board.

"It's a bit of an uneven matchup, honestly." Roy has a sympathetic smile on his face.

"Every deck's bad against something." Roy's probably struggles against Noah's and maybe even Sienna's. As the game's shifted wildly in Roy's favor, there's not much else I can do but chat. "What got you into Adamant?" I don't remember him ever mentioning the game. Then again, Noah and I couldn't have played more than once or twice in the dorms, so he wouldn't have had a reason to bring it up.

"Sienna bugged me into learning because she thought that'd finally convince Vera. Of course, she wasn't interested, but by then I was hooked and needed more people to play with, so I bugged Noah to start up again. Just a happy little chain reaction. Like this."

Roy plays a creature and then immediately uses its ability to sacrifice it to draw a card. His two copies of Debt Collector deal two damage to me in response, then gain him two life. Konstantine dutifully deals one damage to a creature of mine, which dies. By the time Roy's run out of viable targets, I've lost three creatures and eight life. Every point of damage I dealt to him has been regained and then some.

To my credit, I actually manage to dismantle the combo before finally losing the game a few turns later, unable to recover from the initial blow.

"I needed that win after getting leveled by Cedric," Roy says. He leans back for a second, and Mr. Wiggles leaps onto his lap. The cat's tail smacks Roy a few times in the face before he convinces them to sit. He adjusts his glasses and sighs, reluctantly petting the cat.

"Mr. Wiggles, I don't think I'm good enough to face you," I laugh. The cat looks my way when I talk, but quickly returns to wanting Roy's attention.

I leave Roy and Mr. Wiggles to face my next opponent, Blair. Her deck sleeves have tropical fish on the back and she shuffles her deck with exceptional care. "I've only been playing for a few months, so sorry ahead of time if I play slow."

"Don't worry. I haven't played in years so I'm not much faster." A bit of an exaggeration, but I don't want her to feel uncomfortable in a casual game.

I expect her to have a simple deck that's easing her into the game, like my aggro deck or Noah's ghost deck. Her deck is blue and gold, though, and her first few plays have me dumping cards from the top of my deck into my discard pile. The effect is commonly referred to as *milling*—in reference to the first card in the game to do such a thing, Automated Mill—and takes advantage of the fact you lose the game if you no longer have any cards in your deck to draw.

The only way to directly counter milling is to use cards that replenish your library through your discard pile, but that's more of a gold and green thing than a red thing. But to win through milling, Blair needs to get rid of nearly sixty cards in my deck, which takes time. When she's not milling my deck, she's using gold cards to destroy my creatures and blue cards to return them to my hand. It's not quite enough to stall me, and her life total is shrinking faster than my deck.

"So I take it Sienna got you into the game?" Blair's shyness means I need to be proactive in starting conversations, which I'm fine with.

Blair lets out a short laugh and nods. "It was part of our tradeoff."

"Tradeoff?"

"We both agreed to try out something the other enjoyed. Sienna went to a few plays with me in Seattle, and in exchange I learned how to play Adamant. Honestly, I didn't think I'd like it, but I thought it'd be worth it for the chance to see a play in person and not just a recording at the movie theater." Blair shifts the cards around in her hand.

"Well you're still playing months later, so I'm guessing that's a good sign?"

She laughs again. "It was a lot to begin with, but Sienna's patient and a good teacher. And it's a nice way to spend time with each other after work if we're not in the mood to watch anything on TV."

"Sounds like Noah and me." Blair gives me a small smile, and I suddenly realize I made our friendship sound like a relationship. "Are you both still going to plays, then?"

"Not often, but she's stuck to her half of the bargain. Occasionally I pick plays I think she'll like. Tragedies keep her interest better than dramas and comedies. They're not my favorite, but it's all about balance and making sure both our needs are met."

Something Jay and I should've been doing. I don't think we ever tried introducing each other to anything. When we did stuff together, it wasn't a new experience for either of us. We saw movies we would've seen even if we weren't dating and watched shows we both already liked. I didn't teach him to play Adamant, and he didn't teach me the differences between wines. When we did speak about our passions, it was rambling, us venting something meaningful without expecting anything more than a nod or polite vocal support. It wasn't any deeper than talking to a coworker about what you did on the weekend.

Were we really just existing with each other the last six years? That can't be right. No matter how many mistakes we made, there were still passionate moments, and losing him still hurts. I know I could've done better—*we* could've done better—but that doesn't mean every aspect of our relationship was a failure. The sex was good, for one.

The moment of brooding prompts me to throw my thoughts at the game, and the next couple of turns are quiet. Blair isn't milling my deck fast enough, and I clear away the few obstacles she throws in my way. Half of my deck is still safe by the time I win.

We have a few minutes to chat while we wait for the others to finish up, and I manage to learn Blair works in Cascade Parks and Rec. I politely avoid asking her if it's anything like that comedy show from a few years back. I suppose not, since she mainly mentions paperwork and conferences.

Noah's the only person I haven't played yet tonight, so we face off next. Our game doesn't feel any different from the ones we've been playing all week, with me having a strong start but inevitably running into the wall that is Noah's better creatures. I lose, but I'm convinced I've been making Noah fight for his victories more lately. A few more changes to my deck and maybe we'll be evenly matched.

We start up a second round of games, not knowing if we'll have the time to finish them all. At this point, I care less about how my deck's doing and more about the fact I'm actually hanging out with new people for the first time in what feels like years. It's the best hangout I've had in recent memory. Cedric, Sienna, and Blair all seem fun, and reconnecting with Roy has been great. At last, I'm breaking free of the isolation I'd unintentionally imposed on myself.

We do manage to finish every game, but it's closing in on midnight, and we're all yawning and making questionable plays. My victory against Noah is thanks in part to him overlooking a location card that slid beneath another and failing to play a creature one turn earlier, denying him a blocker.

Once our decks are all put away, we say our goodbyes.

"Fuck, that was fun," I tell Noah after everyone has left. I collapse on the couch, and he takes a seat beside me. I don't think either of us has the energy to clean the place quite yet. There's no reason we can't put it off until tomorrow.

"Having an even number of players for once is great."

"Ah, so that's why you got me back into Adamant."

"You seem hooked so I guess my diabolical plan worked."

"Is that what you actually do all day when you say you're going to classes, get people addicted to card games?" I tease. "You just stand in a shady alley on campus in a trench coat, snickering as you pass a starter deck to a wide-eyed freshman with no idea what they're getting into?"

"If only it was that easy! Pretty sure I'd just get called a nerd."

"Well you are one."

"You're nerdier than I am; you've got glasses!"

"You're the professor in training."

"That means I'm a professional nerd. You're just a nerd for fun. Definitely puts you a few steps below me on the hierarchy."

"So there's a hierarchy now?"

"Yes, and if you don't watch out the theater nerds will soar right past you."

I don't even have a retort to that. I just laugh, and soon Noah does too. Once I'm done I lean over and hug Noah. The cheetah's surprised but accepts it. It's pleasant how soft he is.

"I know I keep saying this, but thank you so much for everything, man."

"It's only been a week; don't thank me yet," Noah laughs.

"It's been a *very* good week." My eyes start to water, but I hold back tears.

"I'll do my best to keep them good, then. Think you're ready to start coming to Friday Night Adamant with us?"

After tonight, there's no way I can say no. I feel more comfortable playing against others now, and I want to see how my deck handles the local meta. "Sure. Like you said; I'm hooked."

Noah bounces a little in his seat, and I half expect an ecstatic chirp. He reigns himself in, though. "Hell yeah! I swear it's usually chill. Sometimes you get jerks, but most of the players are just there to have a good time. And the place doesn't smell, either!"

"I'm already convinced." Though I appreciate the reassurances. "I miss FNA, and I'm not about to turn down a chance to hang out with you more."

"Then it's a date!" Noah slaps me on the back, and my face suddenly feels a little warm. Am I blushing? Just because he joked about FNA being a date? I mean, he had to be joking. But what if... no, I'm grasping at straws in a desperate attempt to find meaning in nothing. We've just rekindled our friendship; I refuse to ruin that.

But when I look over at Noah, with his big smile and twitching tail, I'm struck with feelings I haven't had since I was a nervous teenager coming to terms with his sexuality with the help of his best friend.

Chapter 5 (Reeve)

The curve of the line isn't quite right. I click the undo shortcut on my pen and try again, drawing a new line on the screen of my tablet with a flick of my fingers.

Still not right. Too straight.

Another click, another line.

I make an angle, not a curve.

Another click, another line.

It's jagged.

Another click, another line.

Not even close.

Another click, another line. Another click, another line. Another click, another line.

I stop.

I flip the pen between my fingers so the tip's facing up to keep myself from trying again, from failing again. A quick break will help me regain my focus. The curve of a blade shouldn't be hard to draw. I've done it a thousand times before. It's not even the hardest part of this piece. I managed the anatomy of the bear wielding the sword just fine. His scars, his muscles, the bits of damaged leather armor that don't quite fit to show off how he's had to make do with gear taken from others. Does that even come across well, though? Are people going to think he's been the target of an enlarge spell and outgrown it? That he's too dumb or wild to wear proper armor? That I was lazy and didn't want to draw the full outfit?

Now the bear's stance looks awkward. His legs shouldn't be so far apart. And maybe his left arm should've been angled differently. Higher. No, both arms should've been. *God, even his eyes are too far apart, what the hell have I been doing?*

I set down the tablet pen too firmly. I shouldn't be rough with it; they're expensive to replace. A minute ago I felt like this piece was going somewhere, but now I'm seeing flaws everywhere. I can't keep at it, not with that attitude. I'll just end up trying to redo half of it and then ruin the piece completely. I'll work on it later when I've calmed down. Maybe.I shift in my seat and cause it to wobble. I sigh and look behind me. My heavy tail is wrapped around the legs of the chair, three coils deep. I reach down and grasp a white and amber coil. When I give it a tug, it barely budges. I must have constricted the chair once I started making mistakes. I carefully wiggle my tail from the tip to the base to loosen the death grip it has on my chair.

Snakes tend to get stereotyped as having whip-like tails, but the tails of pythons like me are mostly muscle. *And fat, if I'm being honest.* I've always been a little thick. So really my tail's more like a club. One that's crushed its fair share of chair legs and end tables. At least that only happens when I get distracted and anxious, and I've never hurt anyone with it before.

I grew up watching PSAs that warned me about the strength of my tail and how being reckless with it can injure or kill people. So many had silly names that almost seemed to detract from the seriousness of the content, like "Constricting Catastrophe," "Tragic Tail Tales," and "Danger: Breathless!" I remember sitting in a classroom for the species-specific health period, surrounded by anacondas, boas, other pythons, and anyone else with constrictor ancestry. We'd joke around by seeing how loud we could all hiss in unison and block the aisles with our slithering tails. It was somewhat comforting being with so many snakes.

When the videos or slideshows started there'd be snorts and muffled giggles. None of the PSAs had great production values. Invariably they'd involve a young snake with a non-reptile friend. They might be wrestling or simply playing around, but eventually the snake would wrap their friend in their tail and tragedy would strike—broken arms and ribs were a staple. By high school, they'd added the dangers of drinking to the mix, with sloshed snakes crushing cans with their tails before accidentally crushing a hand.

Those presentations were important, but I can't remember anyone taking them seriously past elementary school. Then again, I've heard they're not nearly as intense as the ones venomous species have to sit through. Keeping my tail in check sounds so much easier than dealing with venom.

With my chair out of danger, I look back on the drawing. It still hasn't gotten any better in my mind. Why did I think this would be an easy piece? It's for my portfolio; of course I'm going to be more critical about it than usual, even if it's only a sketch of an action pose. This is the stuff I show to prospective clients, the stuff that's supposed to represent what I'm capable of. A real artist could've knocked out two in the time it's taken me to fail with half of one.

No no no, I can't think that shit. It's my parents who don't think I'm a true artist, not me. Their idea of art is centuries-old museum pieces or modern art they believe is dumb but know sells well. I'm not Picasso or Michelangelo so the commission work I do is a hobby at best in their minds, a phase they thought I'd grow out of before I graduated high school. It doesn't matter that it pays my bills; it needs to be buying me a house or earning headlines or becoming part of a collection. I'm not sure they'd support it even if it was doing all of those things, though. They have a very restricted and conventional view when it comes to careers.

I should return to the sketch. My heart isn't in it right now, but working freelance doesn't let me take mental health days off even if I need them. If I don't finish this today then I'll fall behind on the work that makes me money and lets me live on my own. I pick my pen back up and try again to draw the sword.

I don't know how much more time I waste with the sketch. A shrill ringing from my phone wrecks a line and forces me away from the tablet. It's Dad. I gave him a unique ringtone that's loud and annoying so that I instantly know he's the one calling. I've been expecting the call, but I'd hoped Mom would make it. Not that she ever does. Or that it'd be much better.

I pick up the phone and answer. "Dad."

"Hey, Reeve." He sounds cheerful, but he's good at faking that. I wonder if he learned that at his job or if he's always been that way. "How've you been?"

"Good." Maybe not today, but I have been in general. I didn't put enough conviction into it, though, so I'll have to watch out for him turning that against me.

"Good, good." There's a pause. He could be putting something away since he probably just got home from work. He could also be giving me an opening to talk about how well things have allegedly been, as if he just called to catch up. I refuse to give him ammunition. "So, what time were you planning on driving over?"

There's the real conversation. I got him to get to the point quicker than usual this time. Not sure if that's a good sign or a bad one. "When are we meeting up?"

I hear a faint sigh on the other end. Intentional. I have to come across as the one starting shit, not him. "Your mom and I are trying for noon. We were hoping you'd come up earlier for breakfast, though."

Breakfast and an interrogation. I love Mom's food, but it's not worth the chat that'd come with it. "Even without traffic, it's still a two-and-a-half-hour drive to Spokane; I'm not heading over that early."

"You could come the day before and stay the night. We always have a spare bed for you, and your mom would really appreciate it."

Invoking Mom's name hasn't worked on me in years. She isn't as bad as Dad, but she rarely sides with me on anything. "I have other obligations; I can't stay away for that long."

"I think you can make time for a memorial for Christ's sake."

"I *have* made time for that." I feel my tail coiling back around my chair, the wooden legs pressing into my scales. "Maybe if you'd asked earlier, I could've planned for it." Dad won't fall for that lie, but I don't care. All that matters is I'm being nice and visiting Ty's grave with them, which I'd do on my own if I could.

My older brother died four years ago. He'd moved a few states over to Colorado right after college because he wanted to be somewhere he could hit the slopes most of the year. He used to text me random pictures of snow-covered valleys, mountain passes, dense forests, and towering cliffs—anything of nature he thought looked cool.

It sounded like he went out into the wilderness every weekend, regardless of the weather. He liked to joke about how good he'd gotten at reviving his car in snowstorms and how he'd never had to call a tow truck, unlike coworkers who'd lived there their entire lives. He was working on his car when he died, struck on the side of the road by someone who'd lost control during a storm. I've tried reminding myself he died somewhere beautiful, the sort of place he wouldn't mind spending his final moments, but it always makes me cry.

Ty was the one person in my family I was close to. I love my sister and my parents—even with all the crap they put me through—but Ty was the one who believed in me without question and who I could talk to about anything.

All I remember of the summer after Ty's death was his funeral and the endless stream of condolences from family friends I didn't know and relatives I'd never met. Flowers and cards filled our home. Mom would break down, crying. My niece and nephew were too young to understand what had happened to their Uncle Ty and none of us knew how to answer their questions.

I nearly forgot to sign up for my fall semester classes at CWU. I just couldn't bring myself to care during the first few months that year, barely attending classes or doing work. My roommate, Yuri, struggled to get me back on track while also giving me room to grieve. By the time I pulled myself together, my grades were beyond recovery. I failed three of the five classes and had to take a summer semester to graduate on time. Dad's hellbent on making sure I don't forget that.

My relationship with my parents changed after Ty's death. Dad had made me get a business degree I didn't want, but he'd left me alone for the most part. I think he just assumed I'd embrace it after four years, especially with him and Mom paying for the whole thing. Ty was the one he'd dumped all his ambitions onto, the one who was going to climb the corporate ladder and become the sort of person who owns two homes and a vacation spot in the Caribbean. I was just the happy little accident who could afford to be mediocre.

Once Ty was dead, my parents suddenly became interested in what I was going to do for a living after college. Art wasn't a valid answer, of course. They didn't accept it when I was able to rent a place in Cascade on my own with the money from art commissions, or when I did my first book cover. The extra revenue I get streaming Adamant Online games on Vista would never sway them, either. As far as they're concerned, conventional success is all that matters. If I'm not getting a salary and working at a desk then I might as well not be working at all. They act like I'm constantly on the verge of ruin and that my future would be secured if only I listened to them. It's a frustrating mix of genuine worry and a rejection of my agency.

"How about staying for lunch, then? We haven't seen you since Christmas." Dad's not giving up.

"I can see if I have time for it, but no promises." Not a yes, not a no, just something noncommittal so he'll drop the subject.

"It'd be nice to have a chance to sit down and talk with you. Work's starting a brand new internship program, and I think you should look into it."

That's blunter than usual. Either he's tired or he thinks he can throw me off guard and get me to listen to his spiel. Well, time for me to be blunt right back at him. "I doubt I'd do well in that kind of environment."

"And what kind of environment is that?"

"An office."

"Then what was your degree for?"

To please you because you said getting an art degree was pointless and getting none at all was life-ruining. I'm not going to have that argument with him. Not now, not ever. "It's come in handy with my commissions." I feel like I'm getting better at bullshitting him.

"Reeve, that art stuff is a great way to spend your free time, but it's not a job." No anger, just pity, and fake pity at that. It's Dad's approach to arguments. He'll pretend to be sympathetic or disappointed but never raise his voice. It worked on me when I was a kid, and I'm sure it works in the office as well. He talks a lot about how well liked he is at work, how he's the office mediator. It's a shame he's never used those diplomatic skills in our relationship.

We've debated my art so much I already know how the conversation is going to go. He'll start with me not having good health insurance and ask what I'll do if I get hurt and can't draw. Telling him how much I've managed to save up won't help. He'll ask what happens when people stop buying art, as if it's just a fad that'll vanish any day now. What about retirement? A 401k? If I'm paralyzed and can't draw? Sometimes he comes up with new concerns, but this time...

"What about insurance?"

Yep, it's the same conversation. At least he knows not to invoke Ty's name during it; I hung up on him the one time he did. I'm not in the mood to argue with Dad right now, so I give one-word answers to whatever questions I don't ignore outright. It's all so tedious and aggravating. Like always, I wait him out.

"Dad, I've got work to get back to. We can talk about this next week." I know I'm risking a renewal of the conversation by referring to my art as work, but I'm annoyed and feeling bold. Thankfully, he doesn't take the bait.

"Alright. See you then. Love you." There's a pause before the last part, almost like an afterthought. I got to him a little, then. Good.

"Love you." Our words are formal, not passionate.

The mood to draw has left me completely. My drawing will have to remain an unfinished sketch, which I might work on tomorrow. Saturday's supposed to be my day off, but even those aren't guaranteed as a freelancer. For now, I've got Friday Night Adamant to think about.

I'd love for FNA to cheer me up tonight, but that isn't likely, and not just because of Dad's call or the anniversary of Ty's death coming up. I go alone, so FNA is just a few games against people I see every week but know nothing about. The only friend I made at college was Yuri, and he left Cascade after graduation. The handful of people I've met online through my art aren't local. Most aren't even in the state.

The alternative to FNA is only playing online, and it doesn't have the same feel. Being able to see and read an opponent's face is almost as important in Adamant as it is in poker. Little things can give away that you've drawn the card you need, from a smile to a wagging tail. And if your hand's shit, hiding disappointment can be hard.

I power down the tablet and lean back in my chair. My entire collection is neatly organized on a shelf within reach of my computer; that way I can easily grab cards to show off while streaming. Long felt boxes hold cards separated by color and rarity. My rarest cards are in binders. The bulk of the cards are ones I've either bought or received as gifts over the years, but a large number used to belong to my brother.

Ty got me into the game, I'm sure so he'd have someone to beat. But when I started getting good he wasn't bitter. Our time playing Adamant didn't overlap long. He stopped while at college and never got back into it. Even then he was always willing to listen to me ramble about the state of the game and how things had changed. When he died, I got what was left of his collection. I kept every card, from the twenty-five cent commons to the old rares I could've sold for hundreds of dollars. There's still a part of Ty in them all, memories I can never sell.

I've only got a single Standard-legal deck put together. It's Blue Control, the result of tweaking and updating the same deck for close to a half decade now. I've added and removed other colors and overcome the banning of important cards. I've always managed to make it work, no matter how much the meta has changed. Never underestimate how much a boon knowing your deck inside and out can be. While there are still decks that can overpower me, few can catch me by surprise. A single game is more than enough to give me a feel for what I'm up against and change my approach if necessary. And I research every deck that gets talked about online, from the tried-and-true classics to the experimental fads. In most cases, I know more about an opponent's deck than they do and could probably play it better, too.

Reminding myself of my skill hasn't been enough to improve my bad mood. Moping at home won't do me any good though. At least if I'm moping at FNA I'll be winning games and probably some packs. My mood needs to be better before tomorrow, when I stream. Viewers won't stick around if I'm silent. Otherwise, they're just watching high-level Adamant play in a void. But I'm always off this time of year, and I've still got a conversation with my parents looming on the horizon.

Things will improve in a week or two. That's just how it is.

Chapter 6 (Zach)

I thought I was hooked on Adamant after playing with Noah, but the party leaves me completely obsessed. I dream of Adamant that night, a chaotic string of games that don't make any sense and rarely have winners or losers. While playing Roy, his deck shifts from gold to green to white, my dream aggro deck smashing through each one in quick succession. Against Cedric, all of our cards become labels on beer bottles, which he casually drinks one by one until we're both left with nothing. Sienna's tokens go off like fireworks, singing my fur in a way that seems cartoonish, even to the sleeping me. Blair is only sort of there, hiding in my peripheral vision and playing cards when I'm not looking.

Noah is nude in my dream. I try to be polite and avert my eyes, but he's everywhere I look. There's a point where I give up and give him my full attention. The sight of him distracts me from our meaningless game, which plays itself as we talk about the past. At least that's what I think we were doing. It's all a jumble when I wake up, my mind on my morning wood. I awkwardly head to the bathroom to take care of it.

As casual as the party was, it also provided me with valuable information on how my deck plays against others. I spend the next few days tweaking the deck as best I can with the cards I have. I don't want to invest too heavily in new cards that might work well in the meta of my social circle but not the meta of the game shop. I also don't want to change too much of the deck at once, since I've just started getting a feel for it. Having a deck at peak performance is meaningless if I can't accurately guess what I might draw or what an ideal starting hand looks like.

I put most of my energy toward putting together a side deck. A side deck is an optional set of up to fifteen cards you can swap into your main deck in between games. You usually fill it with cards that target decks you're weak against, ones too specialized to have a place in your deck full-time. In theory, it's meant to ensure one or two decks can't dominate the meta. In reality, effective solutions don't always exist for every deck.

I consult online decklists to see what others are including in red side decks. There's not as much to go off as I'd like, but it's better than nothing and gives me some direction. Noah's deck has been giving me more trouble than I expected, so I add two damage spells dedicated to dealing with the large creatures my swarm is defenseless against.

The rest of the side deck is a little harder to figure out. I add cards that deal small amounts of damage to a lot of creatures to counter other swarm decks like Cedric's, but beyond that I'm clueless. Once I've played a few games at FNA, I'll know exactly what my side deck needs.

On Friday, work drags on. The shop is busier than usual, and I'm mostly stuck at the front while customers lose themselves in the maze of aisles and junk. I answer the few questions I get as best I can, but without a recorded inventory of the shop's stock I'm not much help. All I can do is direct people to where I think stuff might be, which rarely pleases them.

Fortunately, most customers seem intent on wandering around without interacting with me, and the worst I deal with is an older gentleman who decides to spend twenty minutes telling me the history of a watch brand that went out of business decades before I was even born. I've got plenty of experience tuning those spontaneous lessons out while politely feigning interest. People like him mean well, but sometimes I just don't have the time to listen.

As soon as six hits, I'm out the door. "Zach!" I turn at the sound of my name and spot Noah already waiting at the end of the street for me. I jog over and we start walking to Cascade Games. "How was work?" he asks, always a few steps ahead of me.

"Fine." I rarely describe it any other way, even when things are bad. I'm never in the mood to go into detail about work. "Spent most of it thinking about FNA."

"Ha! I'm glad I've given you something to look forward to on Fridays now."

"Hey, I've always looked forward to weekends!" But he's right. My attention has been squarely on tonight, not tomorrow or Sunday. More importantly, it hasn't been on Jay. At least not as much as before. The grief is still there, but I'm getting better at shutting it out.

Cascade Games is the busiest I've ever seen it. A room has been opened up in the back, and it turns out that's where FNA is held. People are spread out across four long tables, some playing games while others chat. The group ranges from teens to adults, just like it was when I was playing back in high school. Adamant has an older audience on average than other CCGs like Gardemon, but most players start young.

Noah and I signed up for the tournament online a few days ago, at his suggestion. At the card shop in Wenatchee we could just show up and that was it. Having even a dozen players was rare there, though. Here they like to know ahead of time how many players they'll have so they can prepare enough food and figure out the brackets beforehand.

The players will actually be split between four eight-person brackets tonight. Everyone will play four rounds, best two out of three. Players with the best records will earn rewards in the form of free booster packs and a special promo card. I don't care about the rewards, though. I'm just here to play Adamant and have fun.

The familiar sight of Roy and Sienna brings back good vibes from the party last weekend and holds back my lingering worries of playing with a bunch of strangers.

"Zach, good to see you here," Roy says, nuzzling my face with his muzzle in greeting.

"After last weekend I just had to play more." I scan the room. "Are the others here?"

"Cedric's not into tournaments. He likes things to be chill."

"And they don't let you drink outside the cafe because of the kids," Sienna adds.

"Yeah, that might be the main reason," Roy admits with a laugh. "He does drop by sometimes to hang out."

"And what about Blair?" I had to think for a second to remember her name.

"She works a lot of late Friday nights and is a bit too shy for the tournament scene. I've told her it's not that bad, but I'm not about to push it on her," Sienna says.

We talk about how our weeks have been as we wait for the tournament brackets to be posted and the first games to start. Noah mentions his finals and being excited for a short break before he teaches during the summer semester. Roy had to deal with two of the industrial washers at the hotel he works for breaking down on the same day. I learn that Sienna works for the Forest Service, which is currently preparing for fire season.

I—on the other hand—have no stories to share. Nothing ever happens at the antique store. There are very few terrible customers, no obnoxious coworkers, and my one boss is so hands off I almost forget she's there. I don't even have any interesting items to tell them about, since I give everything little more than a passing glance. I feel inadequate compared to the others, who either already have careers or are currently training for one. They didn't mean it, but I'm reminded why I go out of my way to avoid conversations about jobs. When I'm inevitably asked about my week, I simply say it was uneventful, and we move on.

During lulls in the chat, my gaze drifts to others in the room. That's when I spot the white and amber snake who looks like Ancelot. He's by himself, finishing off a slice of pizza while looking at his phone. His tail is slithering under the table behind him.

I feel the urge to walk up to him and start a conversation. But what would I even say? We obviously both like Adamant, but aside from that the only connection we have is me ogling him, which I can't exactly be open about. Instead, I bite my lip and hope we'll sit near each other during a game and get a more organic means of introduction to each other.

The staff gets the room's attention and posts the first round's matchups. I'm going to be at the second table, section four, against someone named Reeve. I wish the others good luck and head to my seat. I'm pulling my deck out when I hear the chair across from me screech, and I look up. It's the snake.

Two weeks haven't jaded my childish crush on him. This close, I can see his individual scales; there's a shine to them, even brighter than Jay's were. His eyes are a gorgeous red. Size-wise, he's right in between Jay and Noah. Too big to be chubby, not doughy enough to be plump. He's sturdy, is what he is.

I've been staring too long. I look down at the table and then up again, as if for the first time. He's brought a plastic playmat with him that depicts a magical library. I assume it's from an Adamant card, but it's not one I recognize. Then again, I'd probably only recognize a fraction of the cards. His card sleeves have an image of a tome on the back—the symbol for blue—and so does his deck box, a faux leather pouch held closed by a fancy metal clasp.

The accessories alone make me feel woefully unprepared to play him, but our matchup has given me the perfect excuse to talk with Reeve, and I'm not about to miss out on it. "My name's Zach; nice to meet ya." I hold out a paw for a shake.

Reeve freezes in place and then looks at me, as if confused as to why I'm here. "Uh, Reeve." His voice is soft. It's very different from Jay's confidence or Noah's energy. I like it.

Reeve makes no move to shake my paw though, so I awkwardly pull it back and scratch an imaginary itch on the back of my neck. It's hard to shake the feeling I'm intruding on his personal space just being here. He's probably just shy. Or maybe he came straight here from a long day at work like I did. Though mine was more long in the "felt like it took forever" sense, not the "exhausted me" sense.

My thoughts are getting jumbled. I really am crushing hard on this stranger.

Reeve glances towards my deck and his eyes widen. "Red Aggro." He's not guessing what my deck is; he's declaring it, and I hear hints of surprise, maybe even dismay, in his voice. Whatever it is, it's not positive.

"Yeah, it's always been a fave of mine." Why do I immediately regret saying that?

"Sure." Reeve's barely said a word to me, but his tone has become increasingly distant. I feel like everything I say is inexplicably making him uncomfortable, and because of my dumb crush, it's really getting to me. The illusion of Reeve I so carelessly put together has shattered within minutes, and I have only myself to blame.

But there's still a chance things will improve once we've actually begun to play. I just need to watch what I say. "I just started playing again recently after a long break, so sorry if I play a bit slow." Surely he'll appreciate the warning.

He does not. I hear a faint sigh come from him, but he doesn't say a word. Maybe I'm better off shutting up for the time being.

We finish shuffling our decks in silence and then cut them. My opening hand is acceptable, so I keep it. Reeve's obviously isn't, because he mulligans, which is when you shuffle your deck and draw a new hand. You have to place a card from your new hand on the bottom of your library, though, so there's some risk in the move. A dice roll later and Reeve is going first.

He drops an archive and plays a spell called Hasty Browse. It lets him look at the top card of his deck and either discard it or put it back. He can then draw a card. He opts to discard the card, a fairly cheap spell. I guess he's hoping to draw something better. I can't know for sure though, because he's practically expressionless throughout his turn.

On my first turn, I get a creature out. When I try to get another out on my second, Reeve plays a spell card that negates my creature card, sending it right to my discard pile. Blue always has plenty of cards with *negate*—the official term for stopping a card before it comes into play—and they're a cornerstone of control decks. My cards are cast aside as quickly as my attempts at conversation. With how cute the snake is, the dismissive nature of his deck and personality both compound in a way that flusters and frustrates me.

I manage to get a second creature out the next turn, but Reeve swiftly plays a spell card that returns my first to my hand. I try to play it again the turn after, and it's also negated. Unfortunately, I start drawing more locations than creatures, slowing my deck to a grinding halt. Meanwhile, his stalling pays off as he plays a creature called Ascended Ritual. The art depicts a series of glowing magical symbols in the shape of a bird. Its strength is equal to the number of spell cards in Reeve's discard pile, which is already four. So that's why he was willing to discard the Hasty Browse card earlier. It also has flight, which means only other creatures with flight can block it, something my deck sorely lacks. The creature is likely his primary win condition, one exceptionally strong against my deck.

Reeve had to tap all his locations that turn to play the creature, though, which means he won't be able to negate anything I play on my next one. Ascended Ritual has high strength but low defense, if I draw a direct damage spell, I can take it out before it gets even a single attack off. My paw hovers over my deck once Reeve ends his turn, and I will myself the luck to pull what I need most.

I draw a workshop, which I have an excess of. Well shit.

I get another creature out and hit Reeve for one. On his turn, he plays a second Ascended Ritual and another Hasty Browse, putting a fifth spell card in his discard pile. His first Ritual can now attack and swings at me for five damage, and I've got nothing to block it. Just like that, I've lost a quarter of my life in one hit.

I expect Reeve to lighten up now that he's taken control of our game and gained a solid lead. If anything, he's gone from aloof to irritated. I've never seen someone look so low-key miffed while winning.

The direct damage spell I need still doesn't come, and all I can do is toss out a couple of creatures who can't even block the Rituals. He doesn't play anything the next turn and hits me for ten, taking me down to five. At this point, he has the game won. There's nothing I can draw that'll take both Rituals out at once.

In the face of inevitability, I keep playing. I play a creature, attack for an insignificant amount of damage, and promptly lose on Reeve's next turn. My first game back at FNA and it's a crushing defeat against a quiet grouch I think is hot. Adamant has changed a lot in eight years.

Now that Reeve's beaten me, I hope maybe he'll mellow out and be willing to talk. I just have to show him I'm not a sore sport for losing. "Good game."

"Uh-huh," he says as he gathers up his cards. I've got the strangest feeling he's disappointed in me specifically. Maybe he craves a challenge and is pissed he got a relative newcomer instead?

Reeve opens up his deck box and pulls out what I assume is his side deck. He swaps out cards with swift precision and shuffles his deck, ready to begin again. I race to catch up, fanning out my side deck and looking over everything. Aggro decks are traditionally strong against control decks, but Reeve is completely outclassing me. I set aside the stronger damage spells right away. Is there anything else that'll make a difference, though? I don't have any way to stop his spells or get rid of them once they're in his discard pile, so taking out the Rituals is my only option.

As I look over my side deck, I feel the gaze of red eyes upon me. I'm beginning to wish he wasn't so handsome. "Sorry," I say, hastily swapping out cards I hope I don't need for the ones I definitely do. Decks are shuffled and cut, and the second game begins.

Since I lost, I go first this time. My starting hand looks good, but I thought the same thing last game and got my ass handed to me. My mind chooses the worst possible time to wander and I ponder what the pattern on Reeve's rump looks like. The thought leaves me half-erect, and I quickly squeeze my legs together to hide my arousal, despite the fact Reeve would literally have to duck under the table to see it.

I drop a workshop and a creature, pass the turn, and try my best to focus on the game and not how attractive this complete stranger is. Reminding myself he's more than likely straight only makes me bitter in a way I haven't been in years. For me, one of the worst parts of high school was not being able to casually flirt with other guys. Everyone else in school could choose someone of the opposite sex and at worst be laughed at if they expressed interest. I'd have risked being beaten up if I'd done that to a guy I wasn't certain was gay. And since no one at Wenatchee High was running around with a pride pin on, I had to assume everyone was straight.

Being with Jay meant I didn't have to think about that for six years. Now that I'm single again, the era of endless unrequited love has returned with a vengeance in the form of a rather handsome snake. *One who hates you*, I think, as my second creature is negated.

Reeve doesn't play a location on his turn or the next. His poker face cracks, letting more annoyance through than usual. The snake's bad draws may be just the thing I need to get ahead. I get a few automatons out, only losing one to a negate. Then I draw Ancelot.

It's weird, looking between the snake on the card and the one sitting across the table from me. They're not identical, but the resemblance is still uncanny. Reeve has enough locations available to negate any card I play this turn, so there's a huge risk in playing Ancelot. But the snake's sacrifice wouldn't be in vain; it'd use up one of Reeve's negates, increasing the odds he won't have one available to handle spells I throw at any Rituals he plays. If I can't stop his spells, I can at least make him waste them.

"I play Ancelot, the Prolific," I declare, tapping a few workshops and placing the card onto the field. I look at Reeve, waiting for a response that'll send the creature into my discard pile or right back to my hand, but he's just staring down at Ancelot. Maybe he hasn't seen the card much and is trying to read it to see what it does. He suddenly averts his gaze to nowhere in particular. I guess he's decided Ancelot isn't a threat. Or he's seen through my strategy and is saving the negates for my direct damage spells. Ploys within ploys are a bit too complex for me, so I continue swinging at Reeve with my growing swarm.

Reeve's luck doesn't improve; it just gets worse in different ways. He starts getting locations out, but his plays are sloppy compared to the first round. He wastes a negate on a creature worse than

Ancelot, denying himself a way to stop me from zapping the one Ritual he plays out of existence with a spell. Even with his bad start, he shouldn't be struggling this much against me right now. Could his first win have been a fluke? Having only played him twice, I can't really be certain of the kind of player Reeve is.

I rapidly wear Reeve down and win without taking a single point of damage. He doesn't say a word, avoiding eye contact with me as he scoops up his cards and shuffles them. I was planning on checking my side deck again to make some changes, but I feel like delaying the final round will only annoy Reeve more, so I just go with what I've got.

In the third round, we only speak to declare our plays. All life has drained out of the game, leaving it bland and mechanical. I feel like I'm playing against a particularly good AI. The strangest part is Reeve looks, I don't know, somewhere else entirely. He's playing well—the game's becoming a repeat of the first—but I don't get the impression Adamant is his priority right now. He reminds me a bit of how Jay would get after an argument. It didn't matter if we were watching TV or fucking, he'd offer up only the bare minimum of interaction, as if he was on autopilot.

I lose, though not quite as badly as last time. The cards I swapped in helped, but they were as vulnerable to Reeve's pile of negates as the rest of my deck.

"Disappointing," Reeve says under his breath. He packs up his deck and his playmat and leaves our table without saying another word.

"Good game, I guess," I say to no one. I came here expecting to lose, not to be quietly belittled by a stranger I had a shallow crush on. No, that I *still* have a crush on. Being an ass isn't enough to make my horny brain stop thinking about Reeve in a positive light, which honestly concerns me. If I can't get over a jerk I don't know, then how the hell am I ever supposed to get over Jay?

It's extra frustrating because Jay's the last person I should be thinking about right now. Tonight's supposed to be all about playing Adamant and having fun. A single awkward interaction can't sour the whole night, but it reminds me once more of how much harder it is to date when you're gay. It's hard to not get a little bitter when already rare heart flutters immediately lead nowhere. I didn't exactly throw away a good thing by leaving Jay, but it *was* a rare thing. Dating can be like deciding on a card to discard in Adamant. Sometimes you have to set aside a solid card that's not doing you any good at the moment, and hope you draw what you need before time runs out. I return the swapped cards from my main deck and side deck back into their proper places and spend the next few minutes thinking about what I should swap out in various situations.

To my great relief, my next matchup is Roy. I meet up with the snow leopard at the whiteboard with all the names on it, and we head to our table together.

"How'd you do in the first round?" Roy asks once we've sat down.

"Lost two to one."

"Hey, still got that one win in, though!"

"Yeah, but it felt like a fluke. The guy was aether-screwed early on and never recovered." And acted strangely, but maybe I shouldn't bring that up.

"What deck was he running?"

"Blue Control."

Roy nods. "Ascended Rituals, then?"

"Yep. I couldn't keep them under control because everything I threw out got negated."

"Control's a real bastard right now if you don't have ways to clear cards out of their discard pile or block fliers. Pretty sure the only reason Ghosts is in the current meta is because it's a hard counter to control. It rips up your opponent's discard pile and always has enough fliers to throw in the path of Rituals."

No deck's invincible. There's always something a deck is weak against, and that weakness spawns a deck, which spawns more decks designed to beat *it*, and so on. Since control is part of the meta, I'll undoubtedly be facing it a lot in the future. I either have to get used to losing or find a way to adapt. Adamant's in a constant state of flux, after all.

Playing Roy at FNA doesn't feel any different than playing him at home. We chat about Adamant as we play, which gets me thinking about Reeve again.

"Do you know Reeve, the white and amber snake here tonight?" I ask.

"The python?" I can't believe I hadn't figured that out already. I guess his coloration threw me off.

"Yeah. I played him in the first round."

"Rough. He's probably the best player here. He's an Adamant Online streamer, too, apparently. I'm impressed you scored a win off him," Roy says.

"He sure wasn't. Is he always a bit of an ass?"

Roy looks up from his hand and raises a brow. "He's never seemed like the most sociable person, which is odd cause he streams and all, but I've never had a problem with him. What'd he do?"

"He was quiet, but not in a shy way, more of a 'please go away' way, I guess."

"Maybe he had a bad day?"

"Maybe." I'd love for that to be the reason, but it doesn't sound like Reeve's had many of those before, otherwise there wouldn't be so much doubt in Roy's voice. All I can do is hope the next time we meet he's less caustic towards me.

I'm a little distracted, and Roy's gold deck is still solid, so I lose the first two games I play against him, giving him the win. Getting swept doesn't bother me, though. I've managed to confirm where I'm weakest against his deck, and I already have a couple of ideas for how to deal with him next time. The hardest part will be finding room in my side deck. I've got limited space and have to include cards to handle multiple decks, not just Roy's and Reeve's. After a few weeks, I'll have a good feel for the deck composition here, which will help me decide which decks I most need to prepare for.

We played slow since we were talking, so there's little time between the end of our round and the start of the next. We congratulate each other on the games and part ways.

My third opponent of the night is a heavyset wasp with a gold deck fairly similar to Roy's. He's not very talkative, but he's polite, and that alone does a lot to turn the night around for me. I pull off a win in the first game, then lose two in a row. We have a cordial chat that mainly consists of bringing up various plays from our games before we move on to round four.

My final opponent is a bat who I'm pretty sure is still in high school. He's playing a white/green deck, and I immediately suspect tokens. I was able to beat Cedric's token deck, so I should have a chance against whatever this kid is running. But he doesn't play tokens. Instead, he plays a white exploit card that makes it so I have to pay two aether for each creature I attack with. That slows my momentum considerably. My deck doesn't have any way to get rid of exploits so I have to endure it.

Then he drops a unique location card called Temple of the Fallen God. It comes into play with a bunch of counters on it, which can be removed by paying aether. When no counters remain, he can create a 20/20 legendary avatar creature with flight. It's a ticking time bomb I'm not sure I'll be able to outrun.

I do my best to pick away at my opponent's life total with direct damage spells and the few creatures I can afford to attack with. Meanwhile, the bat's playing spells that prevent damage or stop my creatures from attacking. He's also played a relic and a spell that can remove counters from cards, which, of course, he's been using on the Temple.

I've gotten my opponent down to ten life by the time he removes the final counter from Temple and creates his game-winning token. It utterly crushes me in one attack, and I can't help but laugh. The bat's clearly proud of his ridiculous combo going off.

We check our side decks in between games, and I swap cards in to the best of my ability. Luck isn't with me in the second game, either. The bat gets his event and his Temple out again, and I'm doing less damage than before because I'm drawing fewer direct damage cards. When the kid inevitably creates the avatar token, he crushes me again. Oh well.

The bat's respectful in victory, more so than Reeve was. He doesn't stick around to talk, running off to see how friends are doing. That gives me plenty of time to reorganize my deck before the officials declare the round over and start tallying up the final standings.

I find Noah and the others already hanging out near a wall.

"Yo, how'd you do?" Noah asks me as I approach, beaming.

"Terrible," I laugh. Out of ten games, I only won two, yet I don't feel discouraged. I've thrown myself into an environment I've been out of for years, and I won't catch up overnight. Half the fun of Adamant is figuring out how to beat your opponents.

"I unfortunately had to wail on him a bit," Roy says, adjusting his glasses like a damn cartoon villain.

"What, couldn't take a fall and give him some wins?" Sienna nudges Roy just hard enough to make him nearly lose his glasses.

"That'd go against the very spirit of the game," Roy insists.

"Dork." Roy winces, as if expecting another nudge from Sienna, but she simply chuckles at him.

"I think I'll survive the thrashing he gave me," I say. "I went against a similar deck the round after and got a win off it, so I've already got some ideas as to how I'll defeat him later."

I played the worst out of our group, with Sienna only having one more loss than win. Roy and Noah both had more wins than losses tonight, with Roy coming out one game ahead. He revels in fake humility, which gets us all smiling and holding back laughter. I'd forgotten how much of a pleasure he is to be around. Sometimes I can't believe I went so long without close friends.

The top three players of the night are brought to the back of the room to get their prizes. I'm not surprised that Reeve is among them. It doesn't look like his mood has improved at all since we played, despite the fact he placed second overall. Roy seems to think he's the best player here, so maybe he isn't happy with anything but first? I know people can get hyper-competitive in card games the same way they can in sports.

The win-loss records of the top three are written on the white-board behind them. As the store official passes out their prizes, I check the scores. Reeve only lost twice. If not for me, he'd have tied for first. I know he lost to someone else as well, but it's hard not to feel like I'm the one he'll want to blame.

But Reeve doesn't glare at me dramatically or swear revenge. He accepts his prize of a few packs and a promo card and then leaves the store without so much as glancing in my—or anyone else's—direction. As the only platinum fox and one of the few canids here, I'm not hard to miss, either. Even Noah sort of blends in thanks to a large jaguar who was also playing.

Maybe I dodged a bullet avoiding his hypothetical ire. But as he leaves, I can't help but sneak a peek at him, taking in his rear and slithering tail. Sometimes I wish I weren't so easy.

Chapter 7 (Zach)

It's a brisk night, hovering right on the edge of t-shirt weather. My longer fur saves me from needing to bundle up, and I suspect Noah's padding does the same for him. He isn't complaining about the cold at least on our way home.

"This walk's a whole lot nicer when someone else is with me," Noah says.

We're passing through campus, because I can't think of a good way to tell Noah about all the bittersweet memories of Jay the place brings back. I have fewer of the campus at night, at least. I simply pretend I'm somewhere else and keep my eyes off the brick buildings in the shadows. Talking to Noah helps.

"Is that a hint to pick up my pace?" I'm joking, but I swear every few minutes I have to rush forward so I don't fall behind. I'll have to start jogging in my free time if I want to keep up with him.

"Oh no, I wouldn't think of pushing you after your horrendous loss to Roy tonight. Few ever recover from the onslaught of that spotted menace!"

"If I fall, just roll me into the canal and remember me fondly."

"I'll try," he says, and we both laugh. When we get ahold of ourselves, he looks toward me, smiling. "You had fun, right?"

"Of course I did. The shop's great, the games were great, the people were"—I think of Reeve—"mostly great."

Noah notices my little addition to the last bit and stares at me with feline curiosity. That's as blunt as any actual question. Holding back will get him guessing and assuming things are worse than they really are. Who knows, maybe Noah's had an experience with Reeve that'll explain how he was acting tonight.

"Do you know anything about Reeve, the snake who got second?"

"The python?" Everyone but me is a snake expert now. I nod. "He's quiet and stupidly good, I guess. Why?"

I tell him about my first round against Reeve, obviously leaving out the part about how I'm crushing on him.

"Maybe a fox with an aggro deck pissed him off once?"

"Dude, what are the odds he's faced another fox with an aggro deck? Have you ever seen any other foxes at FNA before?"

"Probably?" He bites his lip and looks away, squinting. "Sometimes a red fox drops by. And a fennec, I think."

"Yeah, I doubt he's got a vendetta against foxes." He'd better not. My dick's not desperate enough to overlook a speciesist.

"I'm sure it's nothing, then. And it's not like you'll be facing him every week. The player pool's big enough that it might be months before you sit across a table from him again."

Noah's right. By the time we're matched up again, he'll have forgotten why I annoy him and we can start from scratch. Until then, I can silently admire him from a distance, maybe even get over my dumb crush entirely.

The first thing we do when we get home is grab beer. I haven't gained a taste for Cascade, but I have grown fond of an evening buzz on the weekends. It reminds me of college, when friends and a little liquor were more than enough to make me forget about homework, tests, and my uncertain future.

Noah sits on the couch, and I plop down next to him. We find more to say about FNA and Adamant, much to my surprise. Me still being eight years behind on the game helps. Before long, I'm setting my empty beer bottle down on the floor in front of me.

"The last couple of weeks have been really good to me, all things considered," I say. I'm not actually drunk enough to ramble on about my feelings, but the beer's as good an excuse as any to. "I kind of feel like I've done more in the last two weeks than the last two years." I let out a sad laugh.

"I'm sure it's not that bad." Noah's wrong, but I appreciate the sentiment.

"Really, Noah, I didn't do anything with myself while I was with Jay. I think..." There's a lump in the back of my throat, and I have to force the words out. "I think maybe us breaking up really was for the best." I've heard the saying "the truth hurts" all my life, but never before have I truly felt those words. Nothing could've saved the fragile relationship Jay and I had both stubbornly hung onto. We could've delayed the inevitable for a few more years, but that's all it would've been, a delay. We should've realized things wouldn't work right after college, maybe saved ourselves four years of lost time. Ultimately, making mistakes was what we most had in common. Thinking about it makes my eyes water.

Rather than lie and tell me I'm wrong, Noah slides an arm around me and pulls me in close. He's soft, like a pillow. "You did the right thing. Both of you. It's a lot harder to accept something's wrong than to pretend it's right."

I nod in his embrace. It's taking everything I have to hold back the tears. If I say anything right now it'll come out as a sob. A part of me is still maliciously trying to take all the blame for what happened, despite all the evidence to the contrary. It cruelly takes the form of Jay's voice, adding a bite to his words and demanding to know why I fucked everything up.

"And hey, you'll get through this," Noah continues. I can see him out of the blurry corner of my eye, smiling. "You're all settled in, and now you have to deal with me chirping away on a nightly basis."

He actually chirps, and I laugh. I take the moment to wipe away the hint of tears. "I missed the chirps. Fuck, dude, I missed all of you." I lean over for an awkward side hug.

"Not gonna say there's a lot of me to miss?" he smirks.

"There is, but I'm not gonna be a dick about it." My mind wanders. "God, this is gonna sound pitiful, but the thing I miss most right now is the sex. I haven't gone this long without it in years." Sex had been the last good thing about the relationship. Just thinking of the things Jay can do with his tail alone flusters me.

"If it makes you feel better, I haven't had any for close to four months now." His eyes tilt upward in thought. "Yeah, four months. New Year's party."

Jay and I made a big deal about doing something for New Year's, but instead just drank cheap champagne while watching the fireworks show in Seattle on TV. "Cedric, I assume?"

Noah looks shocked for a moment. "Almost forgot he told you."

"It didn't seem like much of a secret."

"Only because he's never been discreet about it." Noah shakes his head and laughs. "But yeah, it was Cedric. We still hook up now and then since neither of us is in a relationship right now. It's a whole lot easier than cruising. And safer."

"So you've never considered making things permanent?"

Noah snorts. "Cedric and I have a lot of fun, but going serious has never crossed our minds. I can't really imagine a romantic night with him. It's all too casual. The last time he gave me a blow job he belched afterward."

I clamp my muzzle shut with both paws, but it isn't enough to hold back my laugh.

"The worst part is, I can't even tease the bastard about it. It's one of his favorite stories to tell!"

I've only met the guy once, but it's not hard to imagine him boasting about it with no provocation at all. "And yet you're going to give all that up?"

"Don't worry, I know he's gonna be the frat boy of someone's dreams one day."

"And you'll be the hunky professor of someone's dreams, too."

"Can't say I've got many wanting to take up private lessons."

"Well they don't know what they're missing. I remember having a lot of fun when we were young." Maybe that's nostalgia speaking, but I'm not in the mood to sour my own good memories.

"Zach, I assure you I'm a lot less clumsy than I was eleven years ago." Fuck, it really has been that long, hasn't it? "I'm a lot better with my tongue, too."

I nearly choke. "You weren't bad with it back then." Overeager, maybe, but not bad.

"That's a lie and you know it. When I gave my first blow job to Cedric he asked if I'd practiced lapping up milk. We actually stopped, and he gave me one real quick to show me how it was done."

"Sounds like he was doing some tutoring of his own," I snicker.

"Too bad there aren't any finals for cocksucking."

"What, do you want one?"

"Are you offering it?"

Am I? It'd started out as a joke but jerking off hasn't been a replacement for sex. I'm too spoiled to go back to just my paw, and I've never had the courage to buy a dildo. Even though we haven't fucked in almost a decade, I'd feel comfortable with Noah. "I, uh, maybe?"

Noah's mouth opens a little, his grin replaced with surprise. "Really?"

"Never mind, I shouldn't have said that. You've done so much for me already." I'm saying words as fast as I can think them.

"I mean, if you really want to have a go at it again for old time's sake, I'd be down." I realize he's blushing.

I haven't thought about Noah in a romantic way since we broke up. After our fling, we went back to being friends, and that was that. I didn't have any horny dreams about him, I didn't pine for him, I didn't seek out porn to fill a cheetah-shaped gap in my heart. The breakup was the polar opposite of what I've been going through with Jay now. But as I sit beside Noah, his arm still around me, I start to wonder how it'd feel to straddle him again.

"It could be... fun." Damn, I'm a smooth talker. No wonder Jay wanted to get into my pants. "We can do blow jobs. Ya know, to ease back into things."

"It hasn't been *that* long since I got fucked," Noah says. His smile's back, wider. He hasn't stopped blushing, and I think I am too. "But I'm fine with whatever you want to do."

In the heat of the moment, I'm not even sure what I want to do. Everything, I guess. "Same."

"Wanna head to my room, then? Unless you want to risk me popping the air mattress."

"You're not that fat," I say.

"That's not what I meant!" He tousles the fur on my head. "My fat ass isn't the threat, it's my claws." I forgot cheetahs don't have retractable claws, so he has to file his down just like I do. Even then, they don't completely lose their edge. I was taught sewing skills at a young age so I could fix all the holes I made when not being mindful around my clothes.

"I haven't popped it, so why would you?"

"You weren't being railed on top of it." Noah's playful smile pinches his cheeks.

"Your bed it is," I squeak.

I toss our empty beer bottles away and follow Noah to his room. I've gotten a glimpse of it before, but now I really take it in. He has two bookcases full of textbooks, biographies, and histories with such similar names they all jumble together. His focus is on Roman history, so of course there's plenty of books about specific emperors and the empire's rise and fall. He also loves local history, about as far as you can get from ancient ruins and continent-spanning empires.

His dresser is heavy and old, and I remember it from his bedroom in high school. It has all the knicks I remember, from claws and falls and rough moves. The top is cluttered with charging cables, loose change, and some more books. He's still got his basketball signed by the zebra from the Seattle Supersonics.

The bed isn't made. Mr. Wiggles is curled up on a jumbled mound of sheets, king of his comfy little mountain.

"Time to go, Mr. Wiggles." Noah scoops up the cat, who meows in protest and looks longingly towards the bed. He gently places them down on the floor outside the room and shuts the door before they can dart back in.

"Protecting him from our sinning?"

"No, protecting us from him." A little paw pushes under the door, bats around, and then withdraws. "If we don't keep him out, he'll jump on the bed and start demanding pets, which is really awkward when you're thrusting away at someone." The paw returns, a foot to the left of where it was before. I hear a meow. "Oh come on, Wiggles, you've still got the couch. He'll give up in about ten or fifteen minutes."

I watch the paw vanish again and turn back to Noah. "So, what now?"

It's weird, doing something that feels both familiar and unfamiliar. Noah and I have had sex before, but that was years ago, and we've slept with others in the meanwhile. We aren't going to be fucking on a pile of sheets and pillows on the floor of his bedroom, paws clamped over our mouths to muffle the growls and moans so the rest of the house doesn't hear us. There won't be the hesitation of not quite knowing if we're doing something the right way, how something might hurt or feel surprisingly good. But there'll be the hesitation of not quite knowing what the other wants now. I guess that won't matter much if we stick to blow jobs.

I don't know how his preferences have changed, if at all. I'm not even sure I remember them. We tried everything when we were young. Learning how to have sex was like being handed the menu in a restaurant and only finding food you'd never had before. We looked up gay porn online to serve as a guide, but that only helped so much. The closest video we found that matched our situation involved a red fox and a white cougar, and it's not like they were narrating why they were doing certain things. So we practiced, and experimented, and had plenty of failures that still embarrass me. Hopefully, I won't be adding tonight to those memories.

"Since I was gloating about my tongue work, why don't I go first and put my money where my mouth is." Noah waggles his brows in the dorkiest, cutest way imaginable. It's easy to say I only dated Noah because he was all I had back then, but he truly did come close to capturing my heart. It's just he's funner as a friend than a lover.

"Sure." I pull off my shirt and drape it over Noah's computer chair. It'd feel rude just tossing it anywhere. I undo the button of my pants and unzip them, hesitating before I take them off. Once I shed my boxers, I'm standing nude before Noah for the first time in years.

I've always considered my appearance to be average. I'm not muscular in any way—no abs or biceps to show off—but I'm not huge, or even chubby. I sometimes get compliments when my winter coat comes in and I fluff up, but I don't have people tripping over themselves to flirt with me, male or otherwise. I don't mind being average. My personality's my biggest strength, anyway. It's what won over Noah back in high school, and Jay back in college. I can only hope it'll help me find someone else.

"I see you're as handsome as ever." I watch Noah's gaze look me up and down, lingering low.

"Didn't you used to say I looked like someone spilled ink on an arctic fox?"

"That's a compliment, Zach. I could've said much worse."

"Do tell."

"I could've said you look like someone cummed all over a silver fox."

"Christ, dude," I laugh.

"You were the one who asked. You've got no one to blame but yourself."

I've never had foreplay go in this direction before, even during our last brief relationship, and it's oddly refreshing. I'm craving intimacy, but I don't want something that reminds me of Jay. I need new memories, a reminder there's life after the lizard I was so convinced would be mine forever.

"Okay, now you owe me that blowjob, Professor." I speak in as sultry a voice as I can manage, flicking my fluffy tail back and forth.

Noah's face scrunches, and I'm certain he's trying to hold back a laugh. "Keep calling me that and I'll leave you edging as I go through one of my lesson plans. You'll be stuck feeling awkwardly horny about the Year of Five Emperors for the rest of your life."

"What are the odds anyone will bring whatever that is up?"

"One hundred percent, because I've got *carte blanche* to talk about history whenever I want. I'll start talking about the Praetorian Guard, and suddenly you'll remember my tongue running up your shaft and have to cross your legs to hide the erection."

My treacherous mind starts filling in the blanks and my cock stirs, peeking out of my sheath. I'm not convinced his plan will work, but I'm not about to risk being horny for history. "*Fine. We don't have to roleplay,*" I tease.

I take a seat at the end of the bed and spread my legs. I start thinking about someone hot to coax my cock out of my sheath, and the first person who comes to mind is Reeve. Despite my issues with the snake earlier, it gets a bit of a rise out of me. I suppose it's better than thinking about Jay. Noah's paw swoops in to do the rest.

He gently runs a blunt claw up and down my cock. I shudder. It's not any different than what I've been doing with my own paw, but it's undeniably better. There's intimacy in this, in having another person care enough to pleasure you.

He wraps his paw around the base of my erect, quivering member. "It's bigger than I remember. Good thing I've got such a hearty appetite."

I chuckle, which quickly becomes a stifled moan as my cock shakes in Noah's loose grip. He leans over and wraps his lips around the tip of my cock, then slowly takes it all in. The sensation of his lips traveling down my shaft is wonderful. He retreats back up, then down again, before finally bringing his tongue into play. I moan as he teases my length with steady motions. I'm clenching the edge of the mattress with my paws, doing my best to avoid leaving holes in it, all while Noah rhythmically works his way up and down, up and down, up and down.

For the first time in two weeks, Adamant isn't on my mind. Jay still is, because part of me can't help but compare Noah to him, but Noah's doing a fantastic job of making the comparison a positive one. I'm not surprised Cedric keeps hooking up with him.

Noah's careful approach leaves me in a blissful state that feels like it'll never end. But I can't hold back forever. "I'm—*mrrmph*—almost there," I warn. Noah keeps his mouth around my cock and picks up the pace. My restraint collapses, and I arch my back, my eyes shut and my head aimed at the ceiling. A series of frantic thrusts release my load into Noah's mouth. My grip on the mattress loosens, and I unclench my teeth, panting.

Noah pulls back and wipes his lips with his thumb. He's got a wide grin on his face. "Better, right?"

I nod without putting any actual thought into the question. I'm not going to remember the precise details of a blow job from that long ago. Even the last one I got from Jay exists in my mind as a series of broad sensations—his tongue flicking out, over and over, along with extra mouth movements.

"Cedric's a good teacher."

"I'll make sure to tell him that next time I see him." He winks. I try to groan, but the lingering euphoria of the blow job makes me moan instead. "You ready for a little tit for tat?"

A blow job's about all I can pull off right now. I'm afraid I'd fall asleep if Noah mounted me. "Sounds good to me."

Noah strips without any of the hesitation I had, letting his clothes clutter the floor. There's nothing to hide his curves now, and the cheetah has a lot of them. His belly hangs over his waistline like a furry tidal wave frozen in place. He's the opposite of Jay in so many ways.

My long muzzle means Noah's round middle doesn't get in the way of the blow job. I always knew I was pleasing Jay by the way his tail snapped around and how he moaned. With Noah, it only takes a few sucks to get him chirping, and the purrs follow shortly after. I can feel his whole body rumbling as he purrs, his elation vibrating me. I grab a hold of Noah's love handles so I'm not shaken off him. I try to imitate Noah's tongue movements, but his endless purrs make it hard to tell if it's making a difference.

The purrs are only interrupted once when Noah tells me he's about to blow. I keep at it, accepting the full load just like he did. I'm less graceful pulling away, though, and cough a few specks of cum out. Better than a burp, but it still gets a rumbling snicker out of my friend.

"Cedric's right," I say, wiping my mouth. "Those handles of yours really do come in handy."

"And here I was just about to praise you." Noah wiggles backward and lays down, purring as loudly as ever.

I crawl onto the bed and lay beside him. After being on my feet most of the day and being on my knees for the last few minutes, it feels good to be on my back. "So I did good?"

"Of course you did good, Zach." Noah turns and rubs his face against mine. "I'll have to tell Cedric he's got competition."

"Why do I get the feeling he'd start sending me texts gloating about how long he edged you?"

"Oh, it wouldn't just be texts." It's hard to tell if Noah's joking while he's purring in between every word, and I'm not sure I want to find out in this case.

"I think it's cute you two do the whole friends with benefits thing. That's nice to have out here."

"There's no reason we can't have the same thing. So long as you have fun."

It *was* fun, and it gave me warm, nostalgic feelings. "I think I'd like that. Cedric won't mind, right?"

"Dude, you saw him at the party. When he finds out, he'll either want to compare notes with you or set up a threeway."

"As fun as it might be to say I've done that at least once in my life, I don't think I'll ever be ready to see what he's like in bed."

Noah only laughs, his purrs intensifying. It's amazing how soothing the sound is. I close my eyes for a moment to focus on the rumbling and don't open them again before falling asleep.

Chapter 8 (Zach)

The music in the shop is unbearable. It's shaking the shelves and rattling the product, adding an undertone of clattering to the heavy bass. Strobe lights reflect off porcelain and glassware. People pack the aisles, laughing and dancing. They grab glasses off shelves and drain them of beer I don't remember them being filled with. The same song has been on repeat since the party began. Nothing about this party makes sense. It appeared when I looked down at my phone to check a message. No one gave me the heads up about it, but I'm sure they've got permission. And even if they don't, I'm not paid enough to disperse parties.

I'm doing my best to ignore it all when I spot the lizard in the crowd. I see his tail first, flicking to the beat of the music. Then everyone around him parts to give me a clear view. He dances with his hips, keeping his upper body relatively still as everything below twists.

Light shines off his polished scales, like it always does when he's fresh out of the shower. He's never polished them before, though, has he? No. It takes too much time, and he doesn't like the smell of the polish. Two years ago I bought him a jar of scale polish with a nice, citrus scent to it. The woman in the beauty department had insisted my "girlfriend" would love it. Jay had smiled when he opened the present, but it was his polite smile, as was the hug he'd given me afterward. He placed the jar in the medicine cabinet, and that's where it stayed, unopened. Maybe he was just waiting for me to leave to use it.

I'm not ready to talk with Jay yet. I hurry out from behind the counter and open the front door. I'll stay outside until the party's over. No one's buying anything, so it's not like I'm needed.

When I pass through the door, I end up in the living room. Normally I'd consider that convenient, but now I'll have to walk all the way back to work to close the shop up when the party ends. God, this has been such a weird night.

Something's off about the furniture in the room. It's wrong, but it's right, and I suddenly realize I'm not in Noah's living room, I'm in Jay's. At least he's at the party and not here. But someone else is.

Reeve is sitting on the couch in front of a long table that looks just like the ones at the game shop. I guess Jay has been doing some redecorating already. He's nude, his fine scales so smooth and glossy that he resembles a polished marble statue. A half-foot tall Adamant deck is on the table in front of him, and he seems to be playing against no one. The hand he's holding is jumbled, with cards periodically falling from it.

When the snake finally sees me, his eyes narrow. "You again?"

"Sorry, I didn't mean to come here." It's not my fault this is where the door led. How did it even bring me here?

Reeve stands, and I avert my gaze to be polite, though I sneak frequent glances. He has the sturdy build common among constrictors. The ones I've seen in porn tend to be burlier, though, like they belong in a strongman competition. Not that Reeve isn't handsome.

"Did you come to screw me?" Reeve hisses and tosses a card onto the table.

"Of course not!" I blurt the words out as fast as I can, but they can't hide my erection. I'm thinking of how it'd feel to lift the heavy base of his tail and run a paw over his ass and thigh as I slide in close.

Reeve begins circling the table and tosses two more cards onto it. They land with the precision of a casino dealer. "Sure. Sure sure

sure." No matter how many cards he hurls at the table, his hand never diminishes in size. "I'm not stupid. You're here to screw me like you did at FNA. Just fuck me right in front of everyone!"

Now I'm naked, too, my cock at full mast and impossible to hide. I've never had such a conflicting hard-on in my life. I wish I knew why he was so pissed off at me. There's no way I was the first person to beat him in Adamant. "Don't worry, I'm leaving."

Reeve throws the rest of his cards onto the table and storms up to me. He gets in my face, red eyes staring straight into mine. I should be moving, but I'm not. "Leaving, huh? I don't think so."

His tail slithers up one of my legs, the tip inches away from my cock. He leans forwards and kisses me, his tongue flicking into my mouth.

I jolt awake. The memories of my dream are fading fast, but Reeve's kiss refuses to leave. I feel his tongue dancing over mine in the same way Jay's used to. I've woken with throbbing morning wood, and it's a miracle I didn't go off in my sleep.

I'm so transfixed by the dream it takes me a moment to realize I'm not in my room. I'm in Noah's, on his bed, completely naked. I frantically toss the bed sheet over my shame before I notice I'm alone and let out an embarrassed sigh.

Last night really happened. I know it was only blow jobs, but that's still a lot more intimate than most friends get. And yet as wonderful as being with Noah was, Jay and Reeve were the ones to invade my dreams immediately after. My arousal isn't from Noah—though remembering how he worked me over certainly isn't making me any less horny—it's from Reeve. Dream Reeve, who even when idealized by my subconscious remained a jerk.

I slide to a sitting position on the edge of the bed. Why do I feel so guilty? Jay and I are over, as much as that still hurts to admit. I can do whatever I want with whomever I want. Maybe it's who I played around with that's getting at me. It wasn't serious, we made that clear both before and after, but what if I change my mind? Our last relationship didn't work out but we remained friends, and that was all the way back in high school. We've both matured and changed since then. Things might be different a second time around.

My shoulders slump. I'm trying to jump into a new relationship too soon—that's where the guilt's coming from. I told the truth last night when I said it was just for fun, but now my head is throwing out a dozen what-ifs to get me to reconsider.

It'd make such a romantic story to tell, wouldn't it? Two childhood friends opening up to each other as teens and then eventually realizing they were destined for each other as adults. The kind of story where they both walk out on some shallow fling and meet up by chance at a meaningful location to declare their love and kiss. The camera pans out and the screen fades to black as a perky love song plays over the credits while people clap.

A gay version of all the straight romance movies and books I grew up on. It's a lovely fantasy, but not one I should be forcing upon Noah.

It's still too soon after Jay. I fear my craving for love will lead me to see illusionary relationships wherever I look. That's probably why I'm crushing on Reeve and having dumb horny dreams about him, even though he was distant and rude the only time we met face-to-face. Even though he's *gotta* be straight. It's like I'm back in high school when I fantasized about the crocodile on the wrestling team pulling me under the bleachers and coming out to me before we make out. Not every dream can become a reality.

Noah deserves better than to get caught up in a rebound relationship. I won't hurt him like that. I take a deep breath. His scent is all over my fur, a lingering mix of shampoo, deodorant, and his natural musk. Familiar scents are always comforting, and I've come to associate Noah's with support and safety. And it should stay that way.

It takes some effort to will my cock back into its sheath. I try thinking of bland things at first, like work and the weather, then switch to Adamant. That seizes my attention better than anything else, distracting me from the last stubborn thoughts of Noah's purrs and Reeve's ass. I change back into my clothes once I'm presentable and leave the room.

I follow noise to the kitchen, and this time I'm not surprised to find Noah cooking breakfast shirtless. He's pushing around scrambled eggs in a skillet. Two paper plates with toast sit on the counter beside the stove. He looks up at me with a wide grin that instantly makes me feel better about the night before.

"Morning, Zach," Noah says.

"Morning. Uh, sorry for passing out in your bed last night. It'd been a long day, and I guess the blow job was enough to knock me out." My tail droops, and I scratch behind an ear.

"No worries. I didn't last much longer myself." Noah cuts up the fluffy mass of eggs with his spatula. "And it was cozy waking up next to someone again."

"Thanks again for last night. It was fun." I hope my face is better at conveying my gratitude than my words because they sure as hell seem to be failing me right now.

"It really was. If you're ever in the mood for it again feel free to ask. I can't guarantee I'll always be up for it on short notice, but our libidos are bound to overlap every once in a while," he laughs.

"I'll keep that in mind." The blow job I gave him last night didn't awaken any buried feelings in Noah, and he seems content to be friends with benefits, much to my relief. It'll be easier for me to fend off desperate thoughts knowing for sure he's also treating the whole thing casually.

Breakfast is simple, but good. Mr. Wiggles takes a seat at the table with us, staring at our plates but never daring to go after them. Noah says he taught him not to jump on the table by hissing whenever he did. Wiggles usually hissed at him in return, but always backed down. I chuckle when I imagine the two felines hissing at each other, ending in Noah's triumph over his much smaller foe.

Noah retreats to the bathroom after breakfast to freshen up since he'll be on campus studying until late afternoon. It's odd knowing he's still going to school four years after I graduated. I can't imagine having to spend so much time on a degree.

Without Noah around, I'm left to my own thoughts, which isn't a good thing these days. I don't want to believe I'm living my life from one distraction to the next, but it's starting to feel that way. At least Adamant is a *fun* distraction to fall back on.

I've been improving my deck little by little, but FNA highlighted how much work still needs to be done. A tweaked pre-made deck can't stand toe-to-toe with the meta. That was true even back in high school. I need better cards, more practice, and knowledge about the decks I'm going to be facing week after week.

Then I remember Roy mentioning the online version of the game. I hurry over to my computer, head to the official Adamant website, and easily find the download for Adamant Online. Once I finish installing it and create an account, I'm met with a long series of tutorials designed to teach brand new players how to play Adamant. I appreciate that they exist, but it's a little aggravating having to trudge through the absolute basics since I've been playing as long as I have.

Eventually, I'm freed from tutorial hell and left to my own devices. Ironically *that's* when I find myself in need of guidance. The main page is promoting a host of special events, half of which mean nothing to me, and quests I can do for rewards. When I spot the "Play Game" button in the corner, it brings up far more formats than I was expecting.

I ignore all of that for the moment and go to the tab labeled *decks*. Completing the tutorial unlocked five starter decks, one for each color. I'm pleasantly surprised to discover the red deck is an exact copy of the physical pre-made deck I bought.

Adamant Online's UI is a bit daunting for me, so I back out and hunt down beginner guides. Most of the ones I find are meant for players brand new to Adamant, but they still prove valuable. I learn I'll unlock even more starter decks just by playing the game, and that most of the bundled product comes with codes to get free packs online. For once I'm thankful for procrastination, as the packaging for my bundle is still sitting on a storage bin in my room. I dig out a card with a long code on it and redeem it in Adamant Online for more packs. I also enter a bunch of other promo codes listed in the guides.

The packs and starter decks have netted me a respectable virtual collection. I open the red deck and spend time tweaking it. The end result isn't an exact replica of the one sitting in a deck box beside me, though it comes pretty damn close. There are tokens I can use to gain specific cards, but I decide to save them until I've got a better idea of what my final deck should look like.

With my deck complete, I throw myself into the online queue. My opponents vary considerably in skill. A lot of them are using variants of the starter decks, which are okay but not on par with the meta I've faced either at the store or with my new acquaintances. But it doesn't take long for me to see takes on the decks I've quickly become familiar with. While victories against the starter decks are nice, losses against the meta decks benefit me so much more. I'm getting a better feel for which cards are the biggest threats to my deck specifically, the ones that either dismantle my strategy or I have no consistent way to stop. I'm reaching a point where I can recognize the moment the game is over for me, even if the end takes another three or four turns to arrive. Now I really do feel on the cusp of regaining the level of play I displayed back in high school.

I play Adamant Online on and off for most of the afternoon. It's easy for me to throw my full and undivided attention into the game. Adamant is something I'm good at, something I'm beginning to feel I could even be great at if I put the time into it. And what else is there for me to do? Work is a dark pit I'm too afraid to pull myself out of. My writing is only theoretical at this point, a dream to think about on another day. And the less I think about my relationship status the better, as it's a volatile mess of regret and desperation.

I know it isn't healthy to ignore your problems, but lately it feels like this game is one of the few things keeping me sane. Whenever my mood dips, Adamant pulls me back up, so I might as well embrace my rekindled hobby. And hell, the game is already helping me meet new people and get out more. Maybe it's the key to stabilizing my life right now.

Chapter 9 (Zach)

The frequent lulls at work give me plenty of time to mull over my deck. I sit behind the register on a wobbly stool no one will ever buy and search Cascade Game's website on my phone. The store has everything I need and their prices for individual cards are reasonable. My finger hovers over the add to cart button.

I've only been playing Adamant again for two weeks, and I'm already caving in to my desire to buy specific cards for my deck. There's a voice in the back of my mind telling me there are better things to spend my money on than more cards, but it comes from a source of obligation, not conviction. It's just something I'm sure I should be thinking, even if the likelihood of me listening to it is close to zero. Since Adamant has rapidly become my primary form of entertainment and socializing, I know I can justify the purchases. All I'm doing is directing the money I'd normally spend on movie tickets or video games to Adamant instead. And I'm not draining my bank account, either.

If anything, buying individual cards is the responsible way to play Adamant. Buying packs and bundles is gambling at its core. I could buy a hundred packs and maybe only score a couple of cards I really want. I might get lucky and pull a valuable card I don't even need, which, unless I bother selling it, there's not much of a point in having it.

In high school, I couldn't afford to buy cards that often. I traded if I wanted something, or borrowed cards from friends who had what I needed but weren't using it that night. Younger me would be jealous I'm casually ordering cards to pick up from Cascade Games while at work. To be fair, I'm also jealous of the younger me who still thinks he'll figure out his life in college.

When I leave work an hour later and head down the street, I turn right to go home, but then I stop myself as I remember I've got the order to pick up, but then I only take one more step before stopping again. It dawns on me that I didn't have to catch myself trying to walk towards the old apartment tonight.

It's such a little thing, but it almost overwhelms me. I should be happy—I *want* to be happy. I'm putting my old life behind me and moving forward, and even the muscle memory is on my side now. But it's not the walk home I've been missing most, or even the apartment. It's Jay, who I'm running away from in my dreams yet can't stop thinking about. No matter how many times I tell myself I'm making progress, I still get struck with spontaneous bursts of memories that leave me reeling.

I fend off my anxieties with Adamant and arrive at the game store. I tell the seahorse at the front my name, and he retrieves my order from behind the counter. The order is a grand total of five cards, each protected within a slim plastic sleeve. Though it's a small purchase, five cards can have a major impact on a deck. For now I've settled on obtaining additional copies of cards that have helped the deck out most.

There is a single luxury among the purchase, though. I walk away from the counter and carefully flip to a copy of Ancelot from the bottom of the pile. It's a rare foil version that reflects the light as I hold it up. Ancelot shines beautifully, like Reeve did in my dream a couple of nights ago. Just thinking about it is enough to get me a little hard, so I put the card away and adjust my pants.

As I'm not in any rush, I look for a place to sit down and begin switching the new cards in. I brought my deck to work with me so I could think about potential changes during my downtime. Staring at it for half my shift was probably the main reason I decided to buy the new cards. Editing the deck only takes a couple of minutes.

The sounds of an Adamant game nearby break me free of my deckbuilding daze. One of the players has a quiet, yet familiar voice. I know who it is before I even see the white and amber back of his head. Reeve is a few tables away with his back to me.

I know our time at FNA together was awkward, but I'm immediately struck with fanciful delusions. Maybe he was having a bad day and will greet me with a friendly smile. Maybe he'll apologize for his rudeness, and we'll start over from scratch, forming a lasting bond of mutual respect.

Or, more sensibly, he'll scowl at me.

The game ends in Reeve's victory, if the frustration on the face of the otter opposite him is anything to go by. The second the otter stands to leave, I stand as well. I need to figure out if the snake's attitude towards me has changed at all, or if I'm just going to have to accept he inexplicably dislikes me. The latter might be for the best, honestly. I can't crush on an unobtainable jerk forever.

Reeve has swiftly put away his deck and switched to working on art. It's an excuse for me to reconsider and leave him alone, but even as I think about it, I'm moving forwards. My heart's pounding. When was the last time I was so nervous? The first thing that comes to mind is when I asked out Jay. And six years later when he said we needed to talk and the last vestiges of our collapsing relationship fell apart.

All I'm doing is asking a guy to play a game of Adamant. Why is my body acting like this? I don't have to look far for the answer. It's because I've thrown together this mental image of Reeve based entirely on desires that can't be reciprocated. That's enough to freeze me in place with doubt. If I'm going to play Reeve, it needs to be for the right reasons. Not because I'm attracted to him, not because I want him to like me, but because he may be one of the best local players, and I want to prove myself.

I walk around the table and stand beside the chair the otter vacated. "Hey, would you be willing to play a game of Adamant?" I ask.

Reeve looks up from his tablet, and his eyes widen a little. The ensuing silence makes me wonder if I asked aloud or just thought it.

"Sure." His response is sudden but hesitant. I feel like I somehow guilt-tripped him into accepting.

"Thank you." I take a seat and we pull out our decks. "So, do you want to play best of one or best of three?" I ask.

"We can play until you're bored," he says.

Until I leave in a huff from losing too much, he means. Crushing other players can't be the only reason he's hanging out here on a Monday night. He could do that in Adamant Online from the comfort of home wearing nothing but his boxers. Or maybe he prefers briefs. I squeeze my legs together and silently chastise myself for so readily letting my thoughts wander.

"That might take a while. Since I got back into the game, all I've wanted to do is play. Practice makes perfect." I grin. My life is a mess right now, but I've always defaulted to outward positivity, no matter what. It prevents people from worrying about me and makes them happy. Well, it makes most of them happy.

Reeve lets out a whisper of a scoff that comes out like a sharp exhale. I can't tell if he did so out of amusement or disdain. He's hiding himself in too deep a layer of apathy.

The first game begins and ends with barely a word. It feels better than any of my losses against Reeve at FNA, but it's still a loss. Most of the cards I try to play are negated or bounced, leaving my side open for him to slam his beefed-up rituals into. Victory's not a breeze for him this time, though. I spent the weekend going against plenty of ritual decks like his online, and I know how to blunt their impact. Rather than playing cards as soon as I draw them, I strategically hold back so he uses his turns dealing with the threats in front of him and not the ones yet to drop. If I think he might be able to negate something, I'll play a weak card first to serve as a decoy, ensuring the safety of the stronger card I play right after. Reeve shows hints of hesitation in his plays. His turns slow a little. It isn't enough to beat him, but my improvement is undeniable.

He doesn't comment on it. He stares at me when he thinks I'm not looking, probably trying to read my expression to guess what I've got in my hand.

I thank him for the game and challenge him again. I lose again. I challenge him for the third time, and lose for the third time, but I make him fight for that third win. I destroy the first ritual he plays and force him to scramble to take care of all the creatures I'm getting out. We trade damage back and forth, both reduced to single digits. I throw everything into a last-ditch attack that seems to have a chance of success, only for him to clear away enough attackers to survive and swing at me for lethal damage the next turn.

It's the first time I've felt like Reeve really had to try to win.

Reeve doesn't gather up his deck right away. "Why are you playing Red Aggro?"

The question is so unexpected my mind goes blank for a moment. "Because I've always had fun with it, I guess."

"So you just like throwing a bunch of cards on the table?"

I remember the Reeve from my dream, shouting at me and throwing cards. I don't necessarily feel *déjà vu*, just the fear of it. Then the implication of his words hits me, and I'm annoyed. "I was doing more than just that."

"Play, tap, attack. Play, tap, attack." Reeve turns a card sideways with two fingers, over and over again. "That's an aggro deck."

It can't seriously be my deck that's making Reeve cold towards me, can it? Every archetype has its fans and detractors, but I'd hoped he was above that. "Negate, bounce, draw. Negate, bounce, draw. That's a control deck."

"You forgot the part where I attack and win."

"Those feel more like an afterthought with control." Fuck, why am I arguing with him? If he didn't hate me before, he's sure as hell going to hate me now.

"I don't have to put any thought into them when I'm facing a brainless deck."

"Aggro's not brainless." Walking away would feel more childish than continuing our impromptu debate. "You have to know when to hold back cards you could easily play to keep your opponent off-guard. You have to know which creatures you can afford to sacrifice and what threats to focus on. It's not exactly playing chess, but there's legitimate strategy involved."

Reeve looks down at his cards and taps a finger. "That almost sounded genuine until I remembered you're running around with a glorified starter deck."

"I've tuned it quite a bit," I insist.

"You can't tune a broken piano."

"Well I'm doing the best I can with what I've got." I've never gotten defensive about a deck before, and I'm feeling borderline embarrassed. High school me had more self-control.

"No, you're not," Reeve says, sternly. "How many locations are you running?"

"Twenty... something?" I haven't thought about that at all, and now I feel like I've been ambushed by an exam I didn't study for.

"You don't know, do you?" He lets out a sigh so loud I swear it's fake.

"All my cards are cheap; I didn't think messing with the locations was important."

"Location allotment is fundamental to *any* deck. It doesn't matter if you're running a bunch of low-cost cards or a bunch of high-cost cards, you need to have a good aether base for a deck to be effective." He taps two fingers extra firmly on the table in emphasis with the last word, and I flinch. He stops tapping and holds the offending hand in his other, as if to restrain it. "Count your locations. You've probably got twenty-four."

There's a newfound energy in his voice, and his simmering apprehension has faded. I'm not sure how our argument managed to transform into a lecture, but I guess that's better than devolving into a shouting match. I go through my deck and separate the location cards. "Twenty-four," I say when I'm done.

"Thought so. The first thing you should've done is take two of them out. That's two more spells you could be drawing instead."

I start to complain about how it won't matter if I draw those spells if I don't have a way to play them, but I stop myself. How many times have I ended up hoping for a creature and drawn a location instead? I haven't exactly gotten aether-screwed that often. "Yeah, yeah that sounds smart."

"It *is* smart." Reeve's eyes keep dodging mine, defaulting to the cards on the table. He must be pouring through his vault of Adamant knowledge to figure out where to dunk on me next. "Spread out your deck. I want to see what you've done to it."

I don't question him; I just do it. I lay it all out before him, separating the unique cards while overlapping the copies. When I'm done, Reeve glares at the result.

"I thought I might be missing something, but nope." He's tapping again. "Your deck doesn't have a direction. No, it's trying to go in too many directions at once. You've got most of an aggro deck, pieces of a midrange deck, and about half an automaton theme going on. It's a miracle you beat me at all last Friday."

Well, he remembers me at least. "I got close last game, too."

"Hoping for flukes to happen isn't how you win games."

"I play Adamant because it's fun, not because I want to beat people. Winning is a nice bonus, but I don't need to win all the time," I say. I'm worried he's about to start ranting about how winning is everything and that I'm a filthy casual or something. Maybe I want an excuse to stop feeling attracted to him.

"Even if you don't care about winning, you can still give your deck a fighting chance. It's not just low tier because of the current meta, it's low tier because it's half-assed."

Hearing such harsh words about my deck is hard, but he's got a point. The deck is a mess, and having something a bit more solid would be nice. I wasn't lying when I told him just playing the game is what I enjoy most. I'm like that with any multiplayer game. Having more close games and a regular chance of winning would make it more exciting, though. If I'm losing, I want my opponent to have to fight for their win, and maybe even learn something from it. Or at least I want to make sure they can't brag as much after.

"That's fair. And how would you go about fixing it?"

"I don't know. I don't play red."

"You knew how many locations I should be running, though."
"That's basic stuff."

"Well, I gotta start somewhere."

The tapping stops. "You need to choose a focus. Aggro or mid-range?"

"Aggro. I prefer speed to heavy hitters." Faster decks have always served me best, especially against control decks. I'm not about to admit that to Reeve, though. I don't want him to think I'm tweaking the deck to counter him specifically.

He nods, but he's still reluctant to look me in the eyes. "I assume you want to stick with automatons since you added Ancelot?"
"Oh, um, yeah." He's the last person who needs to know Ancelot's in my deck because I think he's cute.

"Then if you really want my advice, take these out for sure." He nudges Brigs and another large creature away from the deck. "Get rid of anything that isn't a fast automaton. You're not getting the full potential out of Ancelot if you've got creatures he can't interact with. If you do that and add some more removal spells then maybe you'll pull off a few more surprise wins. Don't expect a miracle, though. Red Aggro isn't anywhere close to being in the meta." He admits that with a quiet sigh.

I look at my deck and mentally remove the cards that need to go. About a dozen. I've got some work ahead of me, then. "I'll be happy if it plays even a tiny bit better. And thank you for the help. I honestly appreciate it."

"Sure. This is a one-time deal, though. I've got better things to do than fix decks all day." Reeve hastily puts away his deck and his drawing tablet. He tries to push his chair away from the table, but it barely budges an inch. He freezes and lets out a deep sigh. A few seconds later the chair scoots back without issue and he stands. I guess he backed into his tail or something. Jay did that when he wasn't careful.

"Are you often here Monday nights?" The horny part of my brain managed to get a word in and now he's probably going to think I'm a stalker.

"Sometimes." He answers fast enough I'm certain he's lying. Last Monday and today weren't a coincidence; they're routine. Now the question is what I should do with that information. I tested my luck approaching him tonight and the outcome has been one I would never have expected. To come again could be tempting either fate or Reeve's patience. It's something I'll need to think about.

"I'll see you at FNA, then," I say.

"Sure."

Reeve leaves at a brisk pace, and my eyes follow him until he's out of sight. It's going to take me a while to unpack what just happened.

Chapter 10 (Reeve)

I can't get out of the store fast enough.

My tail drags behind me on the sidewalk, protected from scrapes by a worn leather sleeve. It makes an unpleasant sound that reminds me of sandpaper. Keeping my tail raised is usually second nature to me—it's considered the polite thing to do and prevents it from getting dirty—but I'm dealing with too much shit right now to care. The streets aren't crowded so I'm not a tripping hazard, and the ground's dry enough. I'm fine with wiping a bit of dust off my tail when I get home.

That fox won't leave my head. I've never seen him before last Friday, and now he's suddenly everywhere. Well, the same place on two different days, but what are the odds he'd show up tonight *and* have his deck with him? The only people who ever ask to duel me are the ones already here for the weekly Miniatures Mayhem event the store runs. Apparently a fifteen-minute game against me is refreshing after moving around armies and rolling dice for two hours. If the fox had been with them, I would've noticed. Worse yet, he might have noticed me noticing him.

I hiss under my breath. I tend to be a lot better at maintaining my composure, but something about that fox just... just fucks me up. His fur is gorgeous. The white and the gray blend so well together and remind me of rain clouds rolling in. I didn't know foxes could have a pattern like that. Could he be a hybrid of an arctic and a silver fox?

It doesn't matter, I shouldn't be thinking about him at all. Crushing hard on people has never ended well for me.

My senior year of high school, I thought I'd found the love of my life. Someone I barely knew dragged me to a party and hooked me up with a husky named Mac. He attended the private Catholic school and, in his own words, was desperate to be anywhere he could be his real self. So we hung out and opened up to one another, using the loud music to disguise any conversation that might get a slur thrown our way. The party was tolerable, not tolerant. We both experienced our first kiss that night in the laundry room of an unfinished basement, my back against the door so we'd have fair warning if someone tried to wander in. Meaningful moments in life aren't always as glamorous as TV lets on.

Our relationship felt like a forbidden tryst right out of a romance novel. We'd sneak off to the edge of the city to see movies or grab food, places no one would know or remember us. We took each other's virginity in the back of his truck on the side of an empty road at midnight, then washed afterward with bottled water. I was even shyer then than I am now, but being with Mac made me feel like a whole new chapter in my life had begun.

College was a question we avoided all year. Mac was expected to attend Gonzaga, a local Catholic university, but I couldn't see him going through with it. He'd string his parents along and then come up with an excuse to attend something secular like University of Washington or Washington State. Even if we didn't end up in the same place, we could always take the time to visit each other every couple of weekends. We'd meet in the middle outside dusty towns barely on the map, eating at aging diners before dealing with our pent-up energy in private. That was the rebellious aura I'd built around our relationship.

As the last year of high school ended, Mac broke the news he'd settled on Gonzaga after all. At first, I thought his parents were forcing him to, but the truth was, they barely had to pressure him at all. I had—in hindsight, stubbornly—assumed his faith was shallower than it truly was, a ruse and a joke perfected over the years to hide his less-than-pious pursuits. He might not have been a zealot, but he really did believe in God.

I knew I couldn't satisfy his spiritual needs the same way I had his carnal ones, and while he never admitted it, I'm sure he felt the same. So I went to CWU with the broken heart of a kid dumped for the first time who didn't think he'd ever love again.

My second relationship started a month into college. The third started barely a semester later. For a while, I'd leap into relationships with anyone who showed the slightest interest in me. I wanted the passion back that I thought I'd had with Mac but couldn't even snatch the illusion of it.

I was so damn sure I'd gotten over that phase of my life until I sat down in front of the fox at FNA. He's pushing buttons I didn't know I had. I want to swipe his glasses and hold them just out of reach as he laughs and tries to get them back. I want to ask him why he pierced his ear and why his earring's green. I want him to build a proper fucking deck.

But it's pointless thinking any of that because he's obviously not gay. And if he knew *I* was, he'd probably snarl with disgust. I haven't forgotten that Cascade Games gave up on their tiny display table celebrating Pride Month after customers kept "accidentally" knocking it over. Geeks are just jocks with better grades. Different game, same toxic environment.

And even if the fox isn't secretly a raging homophobe, he's only interested in my Adamant skills, not me. He saw me place second at FNA and decided I had nothing better to do than be his tutor. His talk about not giving a shit about winning was all for show. He cares, he's just too stubborn to stick with an actual meta deck.

What am I going to do if he shows up at the store next Monday? Helping him with his deck was such a stupid mistake. *You can't leave well enough alone, can you, Reeve? You saw him trying to run Red Aggro and with Ancelot of all cards, so you wanted to find a way to make it work.* The only saving grace is I resisted telling him which automatons he should look into. I'm better off with him thinking I've only got a passing knowledge of the deck type.

There's no way he'll make it work, though. The current meta's been dissected to hell and back again, and Red Aggro has no place in it. It probably won't have a place in the meta when the next set comes out and the spring set rotation hits, either, since I haven't seen any theorycrafting online about it. Maybe two sets from now it'll be good again, and the handsome fox will have a deck worth worrying about.

I should consider avoiding the store next Monday. The fox will show up, see I'm not always there like he's somehow guessed—fuck me and my predictability—and give up on trying to leech my Adamant knowledge. We won't form a fake, shallow friendship, and I won't be stuck silently agonizing over a guy I can't have. Problem solved. Now I just have to find a way to stop fantasizing about running my claw through the fur on his chest.

I-90 heading east from Cascade to Spokane is a wonderful expanse of flat nothing. The highway stretches straight into the horizon beyond and behind me, an asphalt line crossing the state. Tilled fields surround it, making the low, gently rolling hills they cover look like sprawling sand dunes. Scattered weeds and brush offer a bit of green faded by the sun that bakes Eastern Washington but other than that, it's a borderline wasteland.

On a good day, the drive to my hometown takes me around two and a half hours and crosses half the length of the state. The scenery changes little in that time, switching between fields and arid plains. I pass within sight of the occasional small town, places I only know from worn highway signs and distant, forgettable glances. That's all they'll ever be to me, and I prefer it that way.

If I took a picture and showed it to people, most wouldn't believe it was Washington. They'd guess somewhere in the southwest, or maybe south of the border in Mexico if they realized it was a trick question and thought they were being clever. Everyone thinks of rain when they think of Washington. On a good day, someone might recognize Mt. Rainier, or they'll remember Mt. St. Helens because it erupted in the eighties. I'm sure most states suffer from that generalization, though.

Once you cross the Cascades from West to East, the whole state changes. It's all desert and farms out here. It can reach a hundred degrees in the summer and bury us in snow during winter. The radio stations dissolve into static, pop songs replaced by country and Mexican music. Every county has a rodeo, and every truck has a fading sticker of the American flag.

I've lived here all my life, and I genuinely love it, but it's hard to forget that an uncomfortable percentage of the people around me don't believe I deserve basic rights and would literally cut the state in half to deny me them.

I check the clock. It's only been fifteen minutes since I last looked, and I've still got a solid hour left to go. An hour before I have to deal with shit. Driving through the endless fields seems downright pleasant in comparison. I could always take the long way and tell my parents I got stuck behind tractors or ran into unexpected roadwork. Dad might investigate. Or he'll ask why I didn't look into my route beforehand. I've made the drive so many times I barely need the GPS anymore—why would I bother looking at a map?

No. Delaying is so damn tempting, but it won't make my visit any shorter. I miss when going home didn't fill me with dread, when I wasn't asked about careers everyone else wanted for me. And Ty's presence is all over. Mom and Dad put up almost every picture they had of him once he died. Every few feet you stumble into themed clusters; birthday parties, school portraits, family vacations, and any presentable picture that'd been on Ty's PeerList.

But even if the pictures aren't there, the memories will be. I can't forget all the Christmas mornings opening presents or the Halloweens he was forced to take me trick-or-treating. I know which table still has a nick in it because we weren't being careful fighting with our tails. I can hear the sappy music he blasted on repeat after his first college girlfriend dumped him over summer break.

Good and bad memories hit me equally in that house, and there are times when a single stray memory is all it takes to get my eyes watering. If it weren't for the holidays, I don't think I'd ever go back.

I used to assume I'd spend the rest of my life in Spokane, not because I thought it was inescapable, but because there was nowhere else I wanted to be. My friends and family were there. Then most of my old friends moved away, and my family became a reminder of overbearing expectations and lost joy. So now I live in Cascade and wonder when life will improve again.

Ty is buried on the outskirts of the city. I get off the highway and pass through a small suburb before entering the wooded cemetery. The parking lot is sparse, so I easily spot Mom and Dad and park a few spaces away.

Mom's dressed brightly, with a floral pattern sleeve spiraling around nearly the full length of her tail. She's where my brother and I got our white scales from, though we have a lot more amber splotches than her, so she's always favored colorful clothing. She has a bundle of four sunflowers with her. Dad's got on a polo and jeans, like he's ready for casual Friday at the office. His scales are the traditional brown and yellow, same as my sister. Since she lives on the East Coast, she can't drop everything and fly over in the middle of the week. It's not like the Spokane airport is the easiest place to fly into, either.

"Hey, son," Dad says.

"Hey." I'm guessing that'll be the most comfortable interaction we have all day.

Mom swoops in and gives me a side hug to protect the sunflowers. "How was the drive over?"

"Same as always." I've never answered any other way.

"We missed you at breakfast," she says.

"Sorry, it's just hard to fit everything in."

"Maybe next year you can plan a bit more in advance. Or you won't have to worry about the drive," Dad says. Yep, we peaked at, "Hey."

"We'll see." Being noncommittal is the best way to approach him. He's not the kind to push back immediately. He acts like he's backed down and then comes back later with a little escalation. He's all about disappointment and guilt, not rage. I didn't inherit that attitude, thankfully. Maybe out of spite, another way to reject his idea of what kind of person I should be.

We start down the curving path that leads to Ty's gravesite. With all the trees, I feel like we're traveling through an eerie forest. They break up the rows of grave markers and cast long shadows that offer brief spots of relief from the heat. I passed a few clouds on the way in, but they're avoiding the sun right now.

The walk is quiet. Dad's clearly busy thinking of how he's going to bring up me staying the whole day again, while Mom is holding back tears. I'm stuck in the middle, preemptively considering my responses to Dad while trying not to stumble any time I think of Ty.

The sound of the Spokane River gradually breaks the silence as we approach the very edge of the cemetery. It serves as an okay distraction, at least until we step off the path and onto the grass.

A small, rectangular plaque marks Ty's resting place. There's no denomination or decoration, just his name, his date of birth, and his date of death. Seeing his name is all it takes for a lump to form in my throat. My knees feel shaky, and I let my tail drop to the ground to keep me stable. I remember my claws shaking as I carried the casket at the funeral, marching alongside Dad and my cousins. The priest gave a speech so cold and generic, nothing but the feeling of apathy stuck with me. I watched the casket lowered and covered, listening to the river compete with the sobs. I'd cried everything out that morning before the service and had nothing left for my brother as he was buried. It didn't feel real at the time or for months after.

Looking down at Ty's grave is the only time I wish *I* had religion. I want to know he went somewhere better or that I'll at least see and hear him again, but even his death hasn't been enough to make me believe in any of that. It isn't fair. I want to curl up on the grass and cry and tell Ty how much I miss him. I want to tell him how shit things have been, and then I feel guilty whining about little things when he's dead. But the last thing I need right now is to break down in front of Mom and Dad. Any compassion they'd show would be steeped in a desire to see me come home and finally "do something with my life," because nothing I've done so far has met their expectations.

We don't talk, we just stare down in silence. Mom's sniffling, wiping tears away as soon as they appear. Dad has his eyes shut, but I see the corners of his mouth twitch sporadically as he holds back. This is how things have gone every year. We don't share memories of Ty or tell the plaque how our lives have been since he left us. We don't even really console each other, either. None of us know what to do.

Eventually, Mom crouches down and lays the sunflowers beside the grave. She keeps adjusting them, trying to make the large flowers all face upward without sitting in a heap. Eventually, she leaves them be but doesn't stand. I can see the tears running down her cheeks.

I kneel and slip my claw into hers, squeezing it tight. She squeezes back. We stand together a few seconds later.

No one says it's time to go or we've been there long enough. It just sort of happens without a word. We gradually turn away from the grave and head off, almost in unison, not looking back.

The walk to the parking lot is slow and quiet. Visiting Ty's grave with Mom and Dad never feels quite right. It's not the celebration of life or mourning of loss it feels like it should be, and I'm not sure that'll ever change. Coming alone would be more meaningful to me, and I hate that fact.

When we reach the cars, Dad turns to me. "We were thinking about grabbing lunch at Waffle Den. You're free to come if you want."

Spoken so politely and casually, almost like an afterthought. Typical of Dad. He excels at making demands sound like requests, in guilting you while coming across as reasonable. I've spent my entire life learning to interpret what he means when he talks to me. I'm not going to deal with this right after visiting Ty's grave.

Saying no immediately is tempting. Free food isn't worth getting lectured by Dad about work while Mom jumps between supporting him and asking me the most mundane questions in a token attempt to lighten the mood. The conversation will go the same as it always has and leave me furious. And the worst part is, there won't be any yelling. My family doesn't do yelling. We don't even do hissing. We'll snip at each other and smack our tails on the floor and come up with exciting new ways to be passive-aggressive, but we won't yell or hiss or bare our fangs. Mom and Dad have never shouted at me before, never cursed me out or hit me. It'd be easier to dislike them if they had. Instead, I feel unreasonable being frustrated with them over anything, big or small. I don't think it's something they do on purpose. Things just happened to work out for them like that.

There'll be more calls if I say no. Dad will find an excuse, and I won't have the nerve to let it go to voicemail. But arguing with him over the phone is so much easier than doing it in person, with Mom to back him up.

"Thanks, but I grabbed burgers on the way over, and I'm still full." I furrow my brows and put on a slight smile of false regret.

"We can always stick to appetizers," Dad says without missing a beat. Of course he'd have a backup plan. "We haven't seen you since Christmas. It'd be nice to talk."

Talking isn't going to make any of us happy. I shake my head. "I'm good, but again, thank you. I really need to start heading back."

"Honey, you just got here," Mom says. She has her claws clasped together and held close to her chest. Her intentions are more genuine than Dad's, but giving in will lead to an argument and ruin whatever happy get-together she's hoping for.

"I really gotta get back, Mom. It's a long drive and I've got work to do." Fuck. I shouldn't have used that word. I can see Dad about to jump on it.

"Have you thought about the internship, the one I told you about over the phone?" Dad asks.

The one you mentioned in passing and didn't provide any details about because you think being paid to do art is less legitimate than being unpaid to fetch coffees for rich assholes? I doubt Mom knows that part, though. "I can't drop everything and leave Cascade. I've still got months on the lease to my apartment."

"You know we'd let you live at the house rent-free. Once you have a full position in the company, rent won't be a problem." Starting strong with the compassion angle because Mom's with us. She's nodding along.

"It's not just the rent, Dad. I like Cascade. I've built myself a life there." An embellishment, but the city isn't that bad. A little bit smaller than I'd like, but I don't have the energy to start over anywhere, especially Spokane. Prices in Cascade are a lot more affordable, too.

"Have you been seeing anyone again?" Mom looks so hopeful.

"No, not right now."

"Oh." She nods. My sister's given her two grandkids, but she's always bluntly hinted at wanting more. Ty deflected all that attention away from me while he was alive, promising Mom a whole house of grandkids once he found the right girl. I think he would've been a good father. But now I'm her only hope for more, so she's gained a keen interest in me finding a partner and at least adopting. My parents are fine with me being gay—for all their flaws, they've always been tolerant of that at least—but I'm afraid that would change if I were the only one capable of giving them grandkids. I don't believe our relationship would've survived that.

I haven't even put any *thought* into kids. I don't know if I'm father material, or if my hypothetical husband would be. I don't even know when I'll have a boyfriend again, let alone a husband. Love isn't a chore on a to-do list; I can't just go out and score a guy in between grabbing groceries and cleaning my room. And as nice as it is that my parents have warmed up to the fact I'm gay, they still don't seem to understand the challenges involved. Cascade celebrates Pride Month and has a gay bar, but just last June there was a string of rainbow flag burnings that was openly praised by a couple of senators.

"If Cascade is where you want to settle down, then that's fine with us." Even when I know he's lying, Dad still sounds almost genuine. It's the little hint of reluctance he puts in his voice to create the impression he's giving in. He'll be preparing a swerve soon. "Have you been looking into full-time work over there?"

I guess he doesn't want to draw things out today. Fine. "I wouldn't be able to juggle a second job and my art."

Dad lets out a deep sigh. "You should really give it a chance. Having a stable job could do you some good."

Sitting in an office all day or working retail wouldn't do me any good. They'd both crush me in their own ways. I worked part-time in college, and every shift left me so drained that I know it isn't something I could do for the rest of my life. Going in to work stressed me out more than classes. I quit as soon as I started doing commission work, which made less but didn't drive me mad in the process. I've mentioned that to Dad in the past, but he conveniently forgets in between arguments. He's a firm believer that stress builds character, and, that if I stick with it, everything will magically click after a certain point, and I'll overcome all my insecurities. I wish he believed in my art that much.

Maybe things would be better if my sister was still in the state. She's always known how to deal with Mom and Dad, letting their little complaints wash over her while casually countering with her successes. It helps that she has a more traditional life. I don't. I never have. First I was their shy son who hid behind his tail and didn't know how to speak with anyone. Then I was their gay son insisting he wasn't going through a phase. Now I'm their shy gay son who wants to be an artist for a living and not even vaguely follow in their footsteps.

"Art is working out just fine for me. Have I ever had to ask either of you for money?"

"Not yet."

"And I've been able to secure medical and dental insurance, too." I'm sure I'd be screwed if an actual emergency came up, but they don't need to know the details. "Just trust me with this. Please."

"We do, honey," Mom says. "We're just worried about you; that's all."

And they'll continue worrying about me until I fit neatly into their idealized version of success and stability. We're stuck in an emotional stand-off where their needless stress causes me needless stress. They need to let me figure things out on my own, even if it takes longer than they feel it should and isn't anything like the approach they expect. They were on the verge of accepting that before Ty's death, but now they've unloaded all their attention and expectations onto me, and it's overwhelming. I'm not sure how to talk to them about that, either. I'm not a damn therapist.

"We don't want you to miss out on an opportunity if things don't work out. It could be a huge setback." Whenever he uses the word "if", I know he really means "when". I don't think he's waiting to revel in my assumed failure, but he should at least be rooting for me to succeed. Would it kill him to have the tiniest amount of faith in me?

"Things *have* been working out. I'm improving all the time and making more and more each year." Not as quickly as I'd like, but again, details only hurt me here.

"Son, getting by isn't enough. You need to think about your future. We won't be around forever and—"

I smack my tail on the asphalt so hard I flinch from the sound. I don't want to think about more death in the family, not here, not now. I almost yell at Dad for bringing it up, but fortunately I can't even find the words to express how pissed off I am he tried to do that. An awkward silence follows, and I know I have to be the one to break it if I want this dumb conversation to end. "I'm fine. Believe it or don't, but... I'm fine." My breathing's heavy. "Look, I need to head out so I can get back to work." I walk up to Mom and hug her. She wraps her tail around my back to complete the embrace and squeezes tight. For a moment, I'm reminded of the hug she gave me when I came home for the first time after Ty died. I didn't think she'd ever let me go then. My eyes water.

"Love you, honey."

"Love you, Mom."

Dad and I just shake. "Drive safe."

"I will."

I waste no time getting in my car and driving out of the cemetery towards the highway. I guess I won the argument this time. Though none of us ever really win them. We frustrate each other and never learn a damn thing so we can have the same argument all over again next time. It's become a twisted mockery of a family tradition. I'm glad Ty isn't here to see it.

The tears come back, and I clench the steering wheel tight. This is never going to get easier, is it?

Chapter 11 (Zach)

I've been looking forward to Friday Night Adamant all week, and my enthusiasm doesn't wane in the least as I walk into Cascade Games with Noah again. The same crowd has filled the back room of the shop, talking and playing casual games while they wait for the tournament to begin. We meet up with Roy and Sienna. I didn't realize how much I missed regularly hanging out with people.

As soon as I spot Reeve, I feel lightheaded. Our encounter on Monday only entrenched him deeper into my thoughts. When I made the tweaks to my deck, I imagined him judging each one of them, looming over my shoulder while hissing about card synergy and counters. *Just because it's a good red card doesn't mean it's good for your deck! Stick to automatons! Make sure you have enough spells!*

Thinking about it flusters me, and I force myself to look away from the python. I hope my crush on him fizzles out soon so I can stop entertaining a bunch of impossible what-ifs.

I'm as relieved as I am disappointed to see I'm not matched up against Reeve tonight. All of my opponents are new to me, but I'm familiar with their decks.

Playing Gold Sacrifice is a race to take out individual cards before their combined effects snowball out of control and wipe me out. Gold has the best removal cards in the game right now, so it's not hard for gold decks to halt my early attacks and take away my speed advantage. The best I can do is try to trade kill for kill and hope I come out on top.

Green Ramp decks are only a bit slower than Red Aggro decks. Their creatures hit harder, and they're tougher for me to kill with my damage spells, which are more geared towards smaller creatures. If I don't strike fast enough, my creatures start slamming into beefy defenders who'll survive the fight and then swing at me for lots of damage the turn after. Right now, beating them is almost entirely a matter of luck and knowing when to hold back. More often than not, my opponent drawing a bad starting hand is my key to victory against green.

Blue Control decks, the last of the best of the meta, aren't thwarting me as much anymore. As long as they aren't negated, my damage spells can pick off Rituals with reliability, and I've gotten better at flooding the field with too many creatures for them to handle.

I feel like my deck is catching everyone off guard since it's such an outlier in the current meta. No one is wasting space in their side deck with counters to Red Aggro, so they can't quite shut me down in subsequent rounds. As good as it feels to see looks of bewilderment as I start tossing down automatons left and right, confusion doesn't necessarily lead to victory. There isn't much more I can do to improve the deck with the current cards in Standard. Even with the deck at near peak performance, it's not consistently powerful enough to place in the top three at FNA. The games are closer than they were last week, with only one player managing to sweep me, but I still do a lot more losing than winning. But for now I'm having fun, and that's my priority.

When the games have ended and I'm sharing my highs and lows with the others, I look again towards Reeve as he stands at the front to accept his prizes. Despite placing first, his smile seems forced, like he doesn't want to be there. And yet I struggle to find him unappealing even then, with the light shining off his scales and his tail bunched around him.

"Got plans for the rest of the night?" Noah asks me.

I'm standing in the doorway to my room. "Not really." Though I've got a feeling I'll start playing Adamant Online if I don't find another distraction quickly.

"Do you wanna, uh, have some fun again like last week?"

We haven't talked about it the whole week, and I was beginning to wonder if it'd only be a one-time thing. Do I want it to stay that way, just a nostalgic experiment with my first boyfriend that a few close friends will tease us about? I've never had sex with someone I didn't intend to date. What if I can't accept there being no strings attached and start wanting something more? The last thing I want to do is make this awkward for Noah.

If I say no, he'll understand. The problem is, I *want* to sleep with him again. I miss cuddling and embracing and the closeness of sex. I miss waking up next to someone and knowing I'm loved. Noah can't give me all that, but I'll take what I can get.

"Yeah, that sounds like the perfect way to start the weekend." I smile, and he smiles back wider.

"I'm fine with blow jobs again if that's what you're comfortable with," Noah says.

My mind has been racing through too many embarrassing fantasies lately to limit myself to a blowjob. "Actually, I'd be down for sex. Only if you are too, of course."

Soon Mr. Wiggles is being unceremoniously ejected from the bedroom, and Noah and I are nude. I'm less hesitant being undressed around him now than I was a week ago. It still has an almost surreal quality to it, like maybe I'm only dreaming about getting back together with him, and I'll suddenly be in a classroom stressing about homework next. But we're not really back together; we're just two bachelors helping each other satisfy urges while in the safety and convenience of their home. No need to fret over hook-up apps or one-night stands with strangers from bars.

I take my glasses off and place them on his desk. The world gets a little bit fuzzy, but sight's not the sense I'm about to indulge in, and I'd rather not have my glasses rolled over and crushed while we go at it. It's happened before, and it's both costly and embarrassing. "So, what should we do first?"

Noah looks down at my crotch and smirks. "Me, probably, since you look raring to go already."

I lower a paw to cover up my cock but stop myself halfway. He's right; I'm already hard, and we haven't even started yet. Thinking about sex with Noah was all it took. If I'm this pent up, I may have to start masturbating more to keep my libido in check. "I won't say no to that. Uh, got any lube handy?"

"Same place it's always been." I stare at him. "Oh yeah, forgot this is our first time. Here, I mean." He chuckles. "There's some in the nightstand."

I saunter over to the nightstand. I slow as I pass Noah and stretch, arching my back to stick my cock out. His eyes follow it, and I see his member twitch in approval. The lube is right up front in the drawer, so I don't have to go digging for it. I apply some, careful not to arouse myself too much more lest I go off then and there.

"Are you ready to put that glistening sword of yours to good use," Noah teases.

"You're lucky I'm horny, otherwise that'd be a dealbreaker."

"Don't act like you've never railed a nerd before, nerd," he snickers.

"I make the occasional exception. Just don't toss me off with your purrs, dork."

The cheetah's smile twists for a second, and I can't help but laugh. "If y'all keep making fun of me no one's gonna scale cat mountain ever again." He turns and wiggles his rump aggressively at me.

I have to clamp a paw over my muzzle to cover up a choking laugh. "I promise I'll be nice," I say once I've regained my breath.

"You better," Noah chirps. He hops into bed and turns himself over, sliding onto his elbows and knees to present his rear.

I follow him onto the bed and immediately freeze up. My mind can't help but remember the last person I fucked. The leaner form of Jay replaces Noah. He always buried his snout in his arms when I topped to muffle the moans. I had to tilt his tail up and throw it over my shoulder to get at his hole, and if Jay wasn't careful, it'd smack me around in the process. Then I'm back in the present, with a thick feline before me rather than the lizard. Noah flicks his tail a lot during sex—at least he used to—but at worst it'll tickle my nose.

I take a deep breath and scoot forwards on my knees. I rest a paw on Noah's back. Soft purrs are already starting up. "It still only takes one touch to get you rumbling?"

"From the right person, yeah." Little purrs interrupt each word.

"How about Cedric?"

"He doesn't even have to touch."

"And you're sure he isn't your soulmate?"

"Not in this life. But God, Zach, the dude knows how to fuck." His purrs intensify.

"I'll try not to be too much of a letdown."

"Don't worry; my ass doesn't discriminate." He wiggles it while I'm inches away, and a chill runs through me. Aside from his smile, I've always thought of Noah's rear as his cutest asset. I place my free paw on his rump and get an elated chirp in response. It's so much softer than Jay's, as much due to its lack of scales as its size. If only the contrast didn't remind me of him.

I press my paw down on Noah's ass and slide my member into his hole. Every inch I push in causes a flurry of purrs and moans to erupt from Noah, along with the occasional chirp. He's far noisier than Jay, who'd only rarely growl through clenched teeth. It's been a while since I last appreciated how different two lovers could be so I kick aside all thoughts of Jay and try to give Noah the attention he deserves.

I'm fully in now, pressed right up against my friend. His purrs vibrate through my cock and into my body, massaging me. The feeling's so good I have to hold still to avoid going off prematurely. Lasting long in the cheetah is a challenge I'd forgotten about in the years since we'd last fucked. The key is to take things nice and slow.

Noah's increasingly familiar scent fills my nostrils as I take a deep breath. I pull back a little and then push back in, teasing both Noah and my dick. After a moment's rest, I do it all over again. Slow and steady is the way it has to be. Every roaring vibration freezes me in place, daring me to blow my load. Things have only just begun, and I already feel like I'm edging here.

Slower, then. If I'm not careful, this cheetah is going to turn *me* into the fast one.

I skate my paw around the globe of Noah's rump and past his love handle until I reach his erect cock. I wrap the paw around it, feeling it pulse in my grip. Noah moans. I lean forwards as far as I can. "What did I say about those purrs?"

"I can't—*ohohoh*—help it," he mutters beneath me.

"Well if I spurt, you're spurting with me."

His purrs only pick up.

As I slide gently in and out of Noah, I rub my paw up and down his shaft in unison. I don't think I'd be able to do it if I weren't going so slow, but this pace gives me a chance to play around. Anything to differentiate it from my times with Jay.

I shudder through the waves of pleasure as if caught in the breeze of a chilly day. It's so hard to resist the urge to simply let go and release my load, but I want to prolong the moment for as long as possible. I want it to dominate my fantasies so they aren't intruded upon by Jay. Or by Reeve. Lusting after one person I've lost and another I'll never have is too painful. So I take in as much of Noah's scent as I can as I make the thrust that'll set me off.

My cock throbs, and the floodgates open. My thrusts speed up. I haven't forgotten about my promise to Noah. I tease the sensitive underside of his member with my paw until I feel it jerk and pump. Noah lets out a jumbled mess of chirps and moans while I pant. I continue thrusting until we're both dry and breathing heavy.

Below me, Noah is all purrs. I look at my friend as I catch my breath, spent. Is he only a friend to me? Is there a future where this isn't just an arrangement of convenience? I find myself trying to imagine being together with Noah again. We share some of the same passions and have loved each other before. I like being around him, and the last few weeks have shown how much I truly missed him.

And that's when I remember that's all it's been since I broke up with Jay. Three weeks. Even as I fucked Noah, the lizard lingered in my mind. It's too soon, and I'm too desperate. I'm too exhausted to be thinking about something this important. I've also heard people say that the afterglow is the worst time to ponder this kind of thing. The chemicals flooding my brain feel great in the present, but they shouldn't have an influence on my emotional future.

After I pull myself free of Noah, I wipe the tip of my cock with a finger so I don't drip on the carpet on my way to the bathroom.

Noah sluggishly rolls over, revealing a smeared line of cum on his stomach. "Mmm... you're good," he mumbles, still purring.

"I'm glad you enjoyed the ride as much as I did." I try to laugh, but I'm still panting. "I'm gonna clean up." He gives me a thumbs up.

Mr. Wiggles bolts into the room as soon as I open the door, nearly tripping me, and I have to catch myself on the door frame before stumbling the short distance to the bathroom.

Noah joins me a minute later. "Nothing hornier than being clean," he laughs. His eyes are half-closed, and I keep expecting him to fall over and pass out while we wash up.

"It always gets me riled up," I joke.

We clean ourselves in soothing silence, broken only by our turns using the wall dryer to dry our crotches. We leave the bathroom nude but no longer reeking of sex.

I follow Noah back into his room. I go to pick up my clothes, but he grabs my paw instead and leads me back to the bed. "Save the walk of shame for the morning, fluff ball," he giggles.

I hesitate, before smiling. There's no harm in snuggling with the cheetah on the nights we have our fun. I'm sure it'll do me some good, and he obviously appreciates it.

The soiled sheet is tossed into a corner and we flop onto the bed, too warm to bother with the covers. After some lazy shifting around we settle into a spooning position. Noah's thick arms wrap around me, and his belly presses against my back.

My opponent has had me beat for three turns now, and I'm not sure if they haven't noticed yet, or if they're prolonging the game to pull off a flashy combo. I lean back in my chair to stretch, locking my fingers behind my head. I'm wearing nothing but a pair of red and black exercise shorts, my go-to lazy day outfit now that the weather's starting to heat up. Being able to play a few games while barely wearing anything is another bonus for Adamant Online.

I see my cards in play light up as my opponent looks them over. "They haven't changed in two turns, dude," I mumble.

The stranger on the other side of my screen checks out their hand, their cards, and then my cards again, before finally growing bold and attacking me with everything they've got. All their creatures are much larger than mine, the reason I've been stuck doing nothing and waiting for the game to end. I could block a few of them and delay the inevitable for another turn, maybe two if I draw something good and my opponent hesitates, but I can't see a path to victory. I let the attack go through and watch as the animated cards crash into my life total, bringing it into the negative. The word "Defeated" appears on screen before I'm returned to the main menu.

My games today have been about average. I've gotten quite a few wins as I go up against players either new to the game or trying out decks for the first time. My losses are more numerous. But win or lose, I feel like I'm getting a good feel for how the best decks in the meta play, and that's the kind of knowledge I need right now.

Adamant Online is so nice to have. Back in high school, I could only practice against friends or other students who brought their decks to lunch, and the skill level there varied wildly. We all had thrown together decks that ranged from pale imitations of the meta to whatever seemed cool. No one cared about banned cards or what was Standard legal. As fun as it was, the challenge of higher-level play has its hold on me. I've thought of putting together a more traditional deck online to rank up, but that can wait. For now, I'm content playing around with the unsolvable puzzle that is a winning Red Aggro deck in this Standard.

Thinking over my last few games, my thoughts inadvertently—or perhaps inevitably—drift to Reeve. Roy told me he streams Adamant Online. Considering how good Reeve is at the game and how swiftly he was able to critique my deck at the store, I assume he plays online a lot. Which means there should be recordings of his streams.

I exit Adamant Online and switch over to my browser. There's no place he could be streaming aside from Vista, so that's where I go.

Now I need to figure out what username Reeve's going by. Searching for Adamant in general is my best bet since I doubt that many people stream the game. It's not *Gun for Hire* or *Arena of Fate*.

My browser lags as close to a hundred streams appear on screen. *Well shit.* The game's more popular than I thought. I skim the rows of streams showing freeze frames of games currently in play, most of which are named after what the streamer is currently trying to do. Climbing Platinum Rank. Last Minute TAC Drafting. Standard 2021 Control.

The streamer frozen in the bottom right corner of the last one is a white and amber snake, and it doesn't even take me a second glance to know he's Reeve. Well, CoiledEquinox97 according to the stream, but obviously he wouldn't be going by his real name online.

I hover my cursor over the stream and hesitate. Why do I want to watch him? Am I genuinely interested in seeing him play more, or am I just going to ogle him down there in the corner and pretend he's talking directly to me and not a chat with a couple hundred people? It's both, if I'm being honest. Maintaining realistic expectations and not obsessing over Reeve is fine, but I shouldn't be overanalyzing every interaction I have with the guy. I click on the stream.

After a brief ad, Reeve's voice comes through my headphones.

"Looks like the opponent's risking one last big swing at me before my Rituals go off. Guess they think all my untapped locations are for show." Reeve shakes his head.

I look at his side of the board and am surprised to see he's not talking about Ascending Ritual. He's got something else in play that doesn't have any strength at all, only defense. Forgotten Ritual. I haven't heard of it before. It can't attack and comes into play with a bunch of counters that are removed whenever you play spells. Once they're all gone you flip the card and it transforms into something called Cacophonous Incantation.

"Time to make them regret everything," Reeve smirks. He's always reserved when I see him play in person, and his smug confidence online almost makes me wonder if I've stumbled upon a different white python who plays Adamant.

"First we bounce that nasty plant." He plays a spell, and his opponent loses their largest creature back to their hand. "Cost two to cast so there go two more counters from the Ritual and now it bursts." One of the Forgotten Rituals flips to become Cacophonous Incantation. It has four strength and defense, and it flies. It also deals two damage to any target whenever he plays a spell card.

"Now we play that Inquiry and draw a card. That bursts the other Ritual and sets off the first Incantation, which we'll have ping their other plant." His opponent loses another attacker. "Have the Incantations block and kill these beasts here, and there we go, no more creatures."

He turned the game around in a single turn, and it wasn't even his own. The moves he made leading up to that moment certainly helped, but from my perspective, he just went from losing to winning in a few seconds. I don't think there's any scenario in which my aggro deck can pull that off.

On his actual turn, Reeve manages to play two spells, causing his incantations to deal eight damage to his opponent. He then swings at him unopposed, dealing another eight. His opponent gets two more creatures out, but neither of them can block the flying Incantations, and they're soundly defeated the next turn.

The brief bit of action I witnessed is impressive, but I've got a nagging feeling it's not quite as solid as his usual deck. Forgotten Ritual takes time to go off, while Ascended Ritual can start attacking the turn after it's played. What if Reeve had lost the Rituals before they transformed? What if he hadn't been able to activate the Incantations as much as he did? If you don't hoard enough spells, the creature's not guaranteed to get you the win.

"You think the deck's too slow?" Reeve asks.

I jolt, trying to figure out how he read my mind. Then I notice someone in the stream chat made a comment almost identical to what I was thinking. I should've known better.

Reeve continues, oblivious to my embarrassment. "It's definitely slower than using Ascended Ritual, but you gotta remember that people tested the hell out of Forgotten Ritual when it came out to see if it was better. It wasn't, but it was still wailing on the rest of the meta. Shit, I saw one get third at FNA last night. This is a solid deck, and I see it holding up when Standard rotates."

Oh yeah, the annual set rotation should be happening soon, shouldn't it? Adamant releases four new sets every year, and every spring the four oldest sets phase out of Standard. One new set is released at the same time, followed by another new one every season, and then the cycle begins again the following spring. The process keeps the game in a state of constant flux, keeping things interesting while also conveniently providing greater incentive for players to buy more cards as brand new decks come to the forefront.

Ascended Ritual must be in a set about to leave Standard, so Reeve's getting a head start on tweaking his control deck. I should look into that and see what my deck's about to lose as well.

"'What about White Ghosts?'" Reeve reads from his chat. "Alright, I agree it's gonna get a boost next set, but I'm not sold on it running rampant through the meta like people are worrying about. Forgotten Rituals can stall almost everything that deck will be running, and when they transform, they'll be able to zap its creatures away. The deck's too close to being midrange for it to be a hard counter against me."

"'Will Gold Sacrifice survive rotation?'" Reeve grins while shaking his head. "No way in hell. It's losing half the cards that make it work and not gaining replacements. I haven't seen a single person bothering to theorycraft it. And good fucking riddance—it's a pain in the ass to go against."

I find myself nodding along as I remember the times I've gone against Roy. It's oddly comforting to know the deck has been giving Reeve as much trouble as it has me.

Reeve seems to be answering every question that pops up in chat. Temptation gets the better of me. I type a question, erase it, then type it again. A finger hovers over the enter key. I remind myself Reeve won't know who I am and press enter.

I see my question appear on the screen and suddenly regret it. Two more messages come in, burying it in the column. Maybe the chat will move too fast for him to see it.

"'Do you think red decks will do better in the next Standard?'" I shrink as he discovers my question. His smile wavers a bit. "No clue. I haven't heard much about red and only glanced over the red cards in the set spoiler. They're getting a decent dragon at least."

A flurry of messages related to red decks flood into chat, but a question about green decks shifts the conversation. Of course I worried over nothing.

Reeve slows down on the questions, adjusting his deck some before jumping back into the queue. The format he's playing only includes cards that'll still be legal once Standard rotates, and his opposition is chaotic. I see a lot of watered-down versions of existing decks right alongside wild experimentations that more often than not earn a scoff from Reeve. He tears into their strategy while he's playing, juggling his moves, his analysis, and the occasional chat question.

It's the first time I've seen him having fun while playing though. He's relaxed and talkative. And he smiles—fuck, he's got a cute smile. Before today, I thought he might not be capable of anything warmer than mild disappointment.

I watch Reeve until he ends his stream two hours later. Normally I browse the internet while watching streams, but the python gets my full—albeit jumbled—attention. I listen to his advice and theories as if it's a lecture I'll be tested on later. In a way, it is. The test will be the games I play online, at FNA, and—hopefully—against Reeve at the store.

Reeve finally gives his goodbyes and the stream flicks off. I lean back and sigh, abruptly aware of the tent in my shorts.

I've never been so frustrated with a boner before. Having a crush on a stranger is fine, but I'm starting to obsess over Reeve. I need to take a very, very long step back and stop approaching him from a romantic angle. As long as I'm rational and control my impulses, he might be able to teach me a lot about competitive Adamant. Maybe we can even eventually become friends. *Maybe.*

It's been a while since I've had to get over a crush before, but I know it's possible.

Chapter 12 (Reeve)

I throw lines onto the canvas so that I'm not thinking too hard on something that doesn't require my full effort. The focus of the piece will be a massive castle in the background, with an ocean and dark clouds stretching into the horizon behind it. Neither of those needs details at this stage. The foreground will be a grassy plain covered in shadows, with a small rider on horseback. The rider should be a vaguely canine knight.

The client wants the piece to have a foreboding feel to it, but not in a way that'd accidentally evoke horror. I'm not sure if it's at all relevant to the content of the book it'll be cover art for or if the author simply believes it'll be more likely to catch the eyes of potential readers. My job's to bring the client's vision to life, not give them advice.

Sharp lines denote the plains while a rough set of squiggles make up the outline of a rider and horse. The castle receives the bulk of my attention. I give it towering perimeter walls that would cast a perpetual shadow on any realistic fortress. The absurdity should create a strong impact on anyone who sees the cover. The central citadel is even more preposterous, a blocky edifice of stone closer to a mountain than a building that almost makes the walls look sensible in comparison.

The average reader isn't going to analyze a book cover down to the minute detail. I, unfortunately, have too much time to do just that as I check and double-check the sketchy monstrosity I've created. At first I think it's silly, the kind of imposing megastructure you see all the time in fantasy stories, both good and bad. The castle looks to be the size of a city. How would people reasonably travel within it? Who would want to live there? How the hell did they even build it? I'd say magic, but I'm not sure this story will even have any.

Then I start to get intrigued. I don't want to read the story of this knight who's a footnote to the castle. I want to read about the people who have dared to make such a monumental building their home. Maybe they found it abandoned and claimed it for their own. Maybe they've spent decades slowly conquering it level by level, room by room, fending off ancient defenses and unearthing dark secrets.

I put down my pen.

Letting my mind wander is fun, but it doesn't pay bills. I zoom out and look at the sketch, trying to take the piece in as a whole without fretting over details. The far background might be overly simplified. It's lacking in lines and might as well be a void. The foreground is a little better but again, not well defined. The castle gets the right feel across, at least, even if it's a cluster of boxy shapes.

Not good enough to send off yet, but I'm getting close.

I make the clouds more distinct and add a few waves to improve the background. Squiggly trees and tiny farmhouses get added to the plains, along with additional details to the knight so they don't blend in with the horse as much.

Thankfully, I'm satisfied when I look over the piece again. I email the thumbnail sketch to the client along with a note asking about any changes before I move on to the lineart to add details. It's the smoothest start I've had to a piece in a week, and I hope that means I'm getting over the annual slump I endure around the anniversary of Ty's death.

I let my wrists rest for the remainder of the afternoon, sticking to small chores before having an early dinner. Work for me occurs in bursts and is entirely dependent on how many commissions I've taken. Before knocking out the initial sketch for the book cover, I finished a personal piece for someone, so I've done enough to feel productive today. That's one of the toughest parts of freelancing. Setting my own hours means I only have myself to blame if I mismanage my time and don't earn enough. Learning how to handle that required a stressful few months of trial and error as I jumped between taking on too many commissions and not enough. Taking on work for professional clients—like the book cover—required even more experimentation.

Despite what my parents think, I've persevered. I can't exactly say I'm thriving right now, but the bills get paid, and that's what's important in the short term. I'll figure the rest out on my own time.

After dinner, I'm forced to make a decision I've been holding off for a week: am I going to Cascade Games tonight?

The trip has been a Monday tradition for over two years. Construction had been going on nearly non-stop for a month, and the noise had disrupted my work. I couldn't think straight in my apartment. Art that should've taken a couple of days was taking twice that. So many perfect lines were ruined when my claw would jolt from abrupt drilling or hammering or whatever the hell else they were doing outside. I wanted to tell them all to fuck off so I could work in peace, but thankfully I'm not a complete ass so I didn't harass the workers for doing their job.

But the temptation was there, so I knew I needed to find sanctuary from the noise.

One Monday—in the middle of all the ear-splitting construction—I found myself on the verge of missing a deadline for an important repeat client. Rather than hope for a lull in the noise that probably wouldn't come, I packed up my tablet and bolted. I'd planned on settling in the first cafe I came across, but Cascade Games proved to be perfect. There were always open tables, the noise was manageable, and it was a place I was familiar with. No one would ask me to leave because I hadn't ordered anything or was taking up space. I still asked the clerk up front if I was fine working on art there, just to be certain. They only shrugged and said, "Sure".

I returned the following Monday when construction picked up again, and from there it sort of transformed into a weekly tradition. I can pick a table at my leisure, take out my tablet, and draw in relative peace. Sometimes I'll grab a drink from the shop's adjoining cafe, sometimes I'll accept a few Adamant challenges. Whatever I end up doing, it's usually a nice way to unwind on the official start of my work week.

If I go today, though, the fox might be there. The fox whose name I desperately wish I knew. I'm so damn sure he introduced himself at FNA, but I was still wound up after Dad's call and can't for the life of me remember what he said. Maybe it's for the best. The less I know about him, the less I'll think about him. If I'm lucky.

Not showing up will help push him away. He'll see I'm not there, doubt himself, and find someone else to get Adamant advice from. Next week I can go back to enjoying the shop alone. No complications, no horny fantasies about a cute guy who'll only have platonic feelings towards me at best.

I shouldn't have to rearrange my schedule around this stranger, though. Maybe I'm just overthinking shit. After all, I saw him at FNA, and he didn't make any attempt to approach me then. He got some info out of me, and now he's free to throw himself into a wall trying to make Red Aggro work right now. At least he probably won't be making a fool of himself and the deck anymore.

Fuck it, I'm going.

I'm out the door and walking into Cascade Games in less than ten minutes. Hudson's at the counter, as usual, ringing someone up. I give the seahorse a nod, and he nods right back. Three people are trying out a board game, but the rest of the tables are empty. I choose the table furthest from the group and sit where I can keep an eye on the entrance. I don't bother trying to convince myself it has nothing to do with spotting that fox if he shows.

At one point, the wargame players start making noise. It sounds like a spirited argument about unit abilities or dice rolls, shit I know nothing about. I glance over at them to see if any are Adamant players... and to make sure the fox isn't among them. The answer to both is no.

I get my tablet out and start a new canvas. My first few Monday visits were for work, but ever since then I've reserved them for personal drawing. Exclusively doing commissions burns me out, so I make time for myself when possible. It's mostly practice, stuff I'll start and then drop once I've gotten what I need out of it. Overcoming a pose that's given me trouble lately, or perhaps perfecting weapon designs. The only objective I give myself in these moments is to draw. No quotas, no end goal, just drawing.

The first thing that comes to mind as I hold up my pen is automatons, the clanky magical constructs so prominent in Adamant, and I groan as I reluctantly realize why. The fox may not be here, but he's haunting my thoughts. I could pick something else to draw, but then I'd be running away from my own head.

I let myself sketch a few kobold automaton designs. Their art direction has varied wildly in Adamant over the years, ranging from blocky heaps of scrap to clockwork masterpieces. They were some of the first things I drew when I originally got into art. I started by copying the ones I saw on Adamant cards, then moved on to tweaking them with additional bits and pieces, before finally creating entirely new ones from scratch. I even made custom automaton token cards to use instead of dice. I've neglected them in recent years, so sketching a few is fun, even if they keep reminding me of the fox.

I drift towards simpler forms covered in smooth metal plates with few exposed bits as I get back into the hang of things. Some are left as half-finished upper bodies without legs, while others never leave the sketch stage, just glimpses of automatons. No commitment, only practice. I can't underwhelm myself with a piece if I don't have any intentions for it to begin with. Gradually the canvas fills with automatons.

I'm between sketches when the front doors of the shop open, and the fox walks in. Fuck me; he really did come. Not even for a second does my mind entertain the possibility he's someone else. There don't seem to be many platinum foxes in the city—I filled my phone's search history with inquiries like "fox types" and "white gray foxes" to figure that out—and I can't imagine more than one happens to wear glasses and a green stud earring.

He spots me within seconds and stops. I make a piss-poor attempt to not look like I'm staring right at him, but there's no way he's falling for it. He continues in my direction, his gaze only vaguely looking my way.

I save my canvas and turn the tablet off before he arrives.

"Do you want to play Adamant?" the fox asks. I'm sure he's just smiling to be polite, but that's all it takes to fluster me. My tail coils around the base of my chair as I hold back the rash feelings roiling within me towards this dude I know literally nothing about.

"Sure." I think I managed to not sound eager. I could always act like an ass to scare him off, but I don't want to be known as a short-tempered dick, and I can't bring myself to hurt the fox. The only thing he's done wrong is make me horny, and that's all on me.

The fox takes a seat across from me as we get out our decks. Set up and shuffling lets me pretend I'm busy while I figure out what I'm going to do about the fox. Awkward silence could work. It's not like I have to fake being shy, especially around someone I think is cute. The real trick is coming across as bored or uncomfortable, not coy. But I was pretty damn quiet when we met at FNA the first time, and he still approached me later.

Maybe I'm wrong about him wanting to plunder Adamant tips from me. If he's new to Cascade or even just the local Adamant scene, he may be craving friendship, and I'm who he happened to latch onto first. The silent treatment might not work if he's desperate. It's not something I should be encouraging, since I know so damn little about him, but the opportunity to see him more often tempts me.

He finishes shuffling and places his deck before me to cut. I do the same. My starting hand is decent: three locations, a Ritual, a negate, and some cards that'll let me draw more cards. Just a second Ritual away from being a perfect opening, really.

Nothing's preventing me from calling it a night after a couple of games. He doesn't know how long I've been here, and he certainly can't force me to stay. But if I'd thought that'd work, I'd have said that when he asked me if I wanted to play in the first place. It's not that he wouldn't believe me; it's that I don't trust myself to lie to him.

Between choosing my plays and thinking of ways to handle the fox, I end up not saying much during our first two games anyway—victories for me, of course. As I suspected, my silence doesn't dampen his cheery demeanor in the slightest. There's no reason I can't have a polite chat that's definitely not fueled by the fact I want to feel how soft his fur is.

"I see you changed the deck a bit," I say. From what I've seen, he followed my advice to the damn letter. There aren't any stubborn holdouts or bizarre swerves, though clearly he's relying on whatever he happened to have on hand. It's already marginally better than the version I went against last week, for what little good that'll do him. I can think of a dozen better decks off the top of my head, and half of them rarely even get played. He doesn't have an uphill battle; he's looking at a smooth sheer cliff with nothing but a foot of rope and a hell of a desperate prayer.

"Thanks again for your help." God damn it, why does he have to sound so genuine? "I've already noticed a difference online." He lets out a cute, one-note laugh. "I'm still getting pounded by Blue Control, Gold Sacrifice, and Green Ramp, but I've done okay against everything else."

Maybe that cliff isn't as daunting as I think it is. Though players try all kinds of jank online. "That's something." I'm so obsessed with being careful about how I talk to this guy that I'm sounding like an emotionless robot. I guess I won't have to worry about him showing up every Monday if this is the best I've got to offer. I'm suddenly—and embarrassingly—feeling jealousy towards the fox's girlfriend. I mean, he *has* to have one. A flash of that smile and a flick of his tail and surely *any* chick would gladly accept an offer to buy them a drink.

"I've been working on the side deck, too. Since no one's building with Red Aggro in mind, I think I tend to benefit more than my opponents when that's an option."

"Probably."

"And if I'm lucky I'll get a boon or two in the next set. Did any red cards in the spoiler catch your eye?"

I get the most annoying sense of *déjà vu* when he asks that question. I swear someone brought it up in my Saturday stream, too. My attention's been on how the top decks of the meta will change after rotation, so everything not directly related to them just hasn't been on my radar at all. Am I missing some huge shift in favor of red? No fucking way. I'd have heard something about it. The lead-up to new sets always creates wild speculation, and set rotations are even worse. For fuck's sake, last rotation people were convinced Green Control would magically become a thing because of a single rare spell that barely sees use.

The simplest and most honest way I could answer the fox would be to admit that I have no clue, yet I'd feel bad saying something so paltry and blunt. I wish I could give him the same detailed response I could for practically everything else. More than that, I wish I could give him good news. I wouldn't mind seeing Red Aggro do well again, even after its reign of terror two years ago.

"Well, um... not really. I haven't actually put much thought into it." I feel myself frowning and straighten my expression as quickly as possible.

"Ha, no worries! It's a silly thing to ask." We both seem to avoid eye contact for a moment. "Up for another game?"

I agree quickly just to change the subject. Game three starts no different from the others. I keep the fox contained and get out a Ritual. He's running more direct damage spells so I hold back a negate card and keep some locations untapped so I can play it in case he goes after my Ritual. Sure enough, he casts an Unstable Core, a damage spell with enough power to kill my Ritual. The art depicts a grinning, slightly singed wolf wearing goggles. I tap my locations and negate it with an Illusory Distraction, which shows a stern dragon mage blocking a magical strike with a swarm of blue illusions resembling tiny drakes.

I look at the two cards we've dueled with and can't help but scoff.

"What?" the fox asks.

"Nothing. I just think it's funny I used a card with Olarin on it to negate your card with Akelis on it. They're a couple in the game's lore." Regret hits me right in the gut as I realize I pointed out the only prominent gay couple in the game. Most players don't give a shit about the lore, but everyone sure as fuck *acted* like they did when those two were officially revealed as gay. A single line about a kiss in a short story posted on the Adamant website was all it took to get people ranting about how the game was ruined for being "woke." The same thing happened after a concerted effort was made to include more women in card art, so I wasn't surprised by the outbursts. There'd been a lot of support for both decisions as well, but that tends to mean jack shit in Cascade.

I don't know the fox's views on the subject, and for all I know, he's about to start raging about how the game doesn't need "fags" and demanding why I even brought it up. I brace for the worst, prepared to have my dumb crush shattered in an absolutely painful way.

The fox's eyes widen some, but no snarl comes. "They actually added gay characters?" Definitely not anger. Curiosity, maybe? "That's, uh, that's cool." He stiffens and suddenly becomes very interested in the two cards left in his hand, which haven't changed in the last few turns.

That was not the response I expected from him. It's something I'd do. *Oh. Oh fuck. Is he gay?* My tail coils tighter around the chair, the legs digging into it hard, and my heart goes from zero to sixty in a second. He can't be. I want him to be, so my horny brain is making up signs he is, but he can't be. Can he?

Assuming he was straight was the safest bet, but now I'm looking at him and seeing his gay little earring and his gay little glasses and his gay little smile and his gay tight ass and God damn it, he might really be gay.

If he is, he's making an effort to hide it from me. It's a poor effort since he slipped up by showing enthusiasm, but that was only because I stupidly blurted out the bait. For once, we're both on even ground here.

Desperation has me convinced the fox is most likely gay, but I've burned myself that way in the past. I was convinced Mac was the love of my life once, too. I see two options here: I can remain cautious and continue playing as if I didn't notice his reaction, or I can drop another hint that I too have a thing for dick and see how things play out. What I absolutely cannot do is outright say I'm gay, because I need to maintain at least a degree of deniability in case I'm wildly misreading him.

My brain sizzles as I rush to come up with something to say before the moment's passed and I lose my chance at confirming this forever. "Yeah, it was nice getting some representation." Okay, that's a bit more blatant than I intended, but I'm not exactly at my best right now.

The fox's eyes widen, and his face lights up. That fucking smile of his comes back and it warms my currently extraordinarily gay heart. He nods. "I wasn't sure we ever would."

I think I smile. It's hard to tell with my heart trying to punch through my chest and my tail trying to strangle my chair. He *is* gay. I've never known any gay Adamant players personally. My few friends who've played have always been straight. It's not like I don't have gay friends, but this is the first time I've found someone else with me in the tiny sliver of overlap on the Venn diagram of "likes dick" and "likes Adamant".

"They're getting a joint legendary card next set. It's red and blue and makes tokens." Token gays making token creatures. I'd laugh but I'd rather not have to explain that one to the fox. "It's not that great, but the art is..." Adorable. "It's nice." And one of the only times Olarin's depicted smiling, as he's usually aloof and stern.

"That's really cool." I have the strangest, nicest feeling I've somehow made the fox's day by bringing this up. "Good or bad, I'll have to snag one." "Same." What I want is a playmat with the art on it, but I know I'd never feel safe using it in public. And since I don't have any friends left in Cascade who play Adamant, it'd just sit in my apartment collecting dust. "Oh, I think it's your turn now."

The fox looks down at his cards, as if he'd forgotten we were playing. I can't blame him—I did too for a minute there. "Yeah, yeah it is." He untaps his locations, draws a card, and our game continues.

The atmosphere around us changes. I'm not ready to open up quite yet, but my worries about the fox are gone. Before, it was like I was reaching for a pot on a stove without knowing if it was scalding hot or not. If I held back I was safe, and if I kept going my scales could bake and crack from the heat, leaving me curled on the floor, cursing my stupidity. Now I'm glad I didn't avoid him.

Despite our revelations, we don't talk further about the subject. Not out in the open, where we can't be certain a stranger won't decide to take offense even as we keep to ourselves. I didn't think he could look happier, but he does, and I wish I could return a smile even a fraction as inviting as his.

He pulls off a pair of miracle wins before we call it a night. They're the kind of losses that'd usually annoy me at least a little, but I can't bring myself to care about that tonight.

"I should probably call it a night," he says after I swing for lethal with two Rituals. He doesn't throw his deck back in its box like I've seen tilted opponents do, though. Win or lose, he'd gone in knowing this was his last game.

"Same," I say. It would've been nice to play a few more, and not just because I'm wrecking him. He's a pleasure to be around.

When we stand, he holds out his paw. "I'm Zach, by the way."

Why was I so damn convinced his name started with a K? "Reeve," I say, shaking his paw.

His grin widens. "I'll see you at FNA. And maybe next Monday?"

"Yeah." That's about the only coherent thing I can say right now.

I watch Zach leave, aware I'm obviously ogling him but powerless to stop myself. No sooner has he left does my brain turn on me.

I've gone from crushing on a straight stranger to crushing on a gay stranger, and I can't let myself ignore that. Smiling isn't flirting; it's just being nice. There's no way in hell he's single. And even if he was, why would he have any interest in me? Under normal circumstances, I was good at hiding my gayness, so he couldn't have had a clue I was gay when he walked up to me tonight. In all likelihood that was merely a happy little surprise in his busy day of being an excruciatingly hot fox.

I have to be honest with myself. Things have gotten worse. Zach is still unobtainable, but only because I could never be anywhere on his radar. I know the gay scene in Cascade isn't exactly thriving, but he can do better than an artist with a knack for playing Adamant. I'm an underpowered common in a booster pack, not the prize rare.

Fuck, I'm worse off than I thought if that's how my brain's trying to process this mess.

I take a deep breath. Air in, air out. Air in, air out. Over and over again, until my heart's under control. Now I just need to get this crush under control as well. Mom's question about me having a boyfriend is lingering in my head, and I'm starting to worry that's playing a role in all this. It's been a while since I've been in a relationship. I miss... I miss a lot about being with someone. I've leaped into relationships an embarrassing number of times, and they've all ended predictably, sometimes painfully. I keep promising myself I'll learn from my mistakes and then screw up the second I see a dude with a nice smile or remotely charming personality. Maybe for once I'll be responsible enough to avoid making that mistake.

Love at first sight can go fuck itself. I've got too much to worry about as is. What I *should* be hoping for is that I actually get along well with Zach. All we've done so far is play Adamant, and I've known plenty of people I could have a decent game with who I wouldn't want anything to do with otherwise.

I haven't had a single local friend since Yuri moved away, and the isolation is eating away at me now more than it has in a long, long while. It's my own damn fault. Yuri and I only met by chance and I didn't bother befriending anyone else in college. I only gathered a collection of exes I had little in common with. At least I didn't ruin my friendship with the polar bear by lusting after him.

It feels so stupid having to tell myself to think with my head, not with my dick, but here I am. I'm not going to surprise him with a gorgeous portrait that makes him leap into my arms. I'm no humble knight about to win over the handsome prince by dominating a card game tournament. I'm a nobody chasing a cute guy's tail just because I suddenly remembered I'm lonely. It's exhausting.

The miniatures meet-up is beginning to disperse, and the group playing board games are putting things away. I yawn and shake my head as the rest of the day catches up with me. Maybe I just need to sleep on things. I head home hoping my dreams will be about my art or the big set rotation less than a week away. Anything but Zach's fluffy coat and inviting grin.

Chapter 13 (Zach)

It's hard not to bounce on my way home from Cascade Games. Thank God the streets are empty this late at night because I must look ridiculous whipping my tail around with a wide smile on my face. The dark expanse of the CWU campus doesn't distract or dismay me like usual. I barely notice it's there.

He's gay—he *has* to be. Straight people don't casually bring up the fact characters are gay, at least not straight people in Cascade. Then again, gay people here don't either unless they know or at least assume they're talking to someone who'll be supportive. Which means he suspected I was gay too.

My tail droops. Did he notice me staring? I swore I was being good and not blatantly ogling him while we played, and he was still avoiding eye contact until he stealthily opened up. I'd like to think I do a good job of passing for straight, but with how enamored I've been with Reeve, I guess I could've messed up and let something slip through. Or maybe he saw an opportunity to learn more about me and took the risk.

Well, whatever. What's done is done, and I won't let lingering questions sour my mood.

My tail starts swaying again. Tonight doesn't feel real. I worked so hard to temper my expectations about Reeve and convince myself he was straight—because that's what was most likely—and now life has sent me a positive twist for once. I can't hold my thoughts back anymore. He still comes across as rather distant, like he's not sure what to do with me, but not everyone pounces into conversations like I do.

We've also only interacted with each other while playing Adamant, which can be pretty distracting. He seems serious about the game, so he might be focusing the bulk of his attention on that and struggling to juggle anything else at the same time. When we *did* talk for more than a few seconds we stopped playing entirely.

But even playing him is fun! His skill level is way up there, but he isn't a huge jerk about it. He hasn't rubbed in his victories or made excuses for his losses; he just plays quietly and competently. I spent my whole evening playing against him and my only regret is I couldn't play more.

A part of me wants to settle on a second deck to run, maybe a bit higher in the meta than my Red Aggro, so that I can offer him a bit more competition when we play each other. I'm not giving up on my automatons yet, but there's no reason to not have more than one deck around to keep things varied. When I played in high school, I usually had about three decks made at a time. Back then I was mainly tossing together stuff from my collection, though. Keeping up with Reeve and my friends will require a bit of an investment with how expensive Standard has gotten.

At the apartment, Noah is finishing a late dinner while Mr. Wiggles loses another pity staredown.

"Hey, Zach. Long day at work?" he asks, before clearing the last of his carrots. Mr. Wiggles lays down on his chair, defeated.

"No, I dropped by Cascade Games and played some Adamant."

He furrows his brows in thought. "Was there an event there tonight?"

I shake my head. "Just casual games with players who happened to be around."

"Huh, didn't realize Monday nights were that popular."

"The place isn't busy. I just keep getting lucky." I don't know how to explain my crush on Reeve so I decide to keep Noah in the dark about that for now. *Besides,* I remind myself, *I don't have all that much to report yet anyway.*

"Cool," he says, saving me the trouble of coming up with a complex series of lies to cover my embarrassment. "Oh, there's extra spam and rice on the stove if you want some," he adds as he leaves the table and heads into the kitchen.

Seeing his empty plate reminds me I haven't had a bite to eat since lunch at work. "Thanks."

I follow Noah into the kitchen and slide behind him to grab a plate and fork. Two people don't crowd the kitchen, but some careful maneuvering is required since the dishwasher is opened and we're trying to clean up and fill up respectively. I scoop the rest of the spam and rice onto my plate.

"Don't skip your veggies!" Noah elbows me in the side.

"Okay, okay!" I laugh. He's right, I shouldn't be neglecting them. I can't say my body was happy with me when I ate like shit back in college. I add the veggies to my plate as well, even the ones I don't like, lest I incur my roommate's wrath.

When I sit down at the table, Mr. Wiggles pokes his head up, the begging game beginning anew. I look at the home-cooked meal Noah prepared for me, and my eyes start to water.

He didn't have to set this aside for me. He could've saved the leftovers for breakfast or made less. I know it's an easy meal to make—I've helped him with it before—but it means a lot to me, as does everything else he's done since Jay and I broke up. He's fed me, housed me, entertained me, and supported me, all after I spent four years practically treating him like a stranger.

Friday night isn't far from my thoughts. Climbing onto the bed and then him with more confidence than I ever had in high school. Those purrs rumbling through my body, an indisputable sign of unrelenting bliss. I didn't sleep with Noah just because I wanted to get it out of my system. I did it because I wanted to know if any semblance of that old connection we had remained. I'm still not sure.

Look at me. In the last hour, I've jumped between lusting after Reeve and lusting after Noah with equally blind enthusiasm at the drop of a dime. Can I honestly say it's love in either case? I feel like I'm latching onto any hint of attraction that stirs within me. It's obvious I want someone to replace Jay, and while I'll have to move on eventually, I can't be certain these crushes are meaningful. And I may lose so much by rabidly pursuing them. Trying to forcefully rekindle my ancient relationship with Noah would be betraying his kindness and suddenly flirting with Reeve would ruin any potential we have of forming a friendship first.

Having a relationship collapse around me sucked. Being single sucks. Messing with someone else's emotions so I can temporarily solve my problems sucks even more. I've seen rebound relationships fail, and I refuse to willingly do that to anyone, including myself. For my own sake, I need to get a grip.

My food's getting cold while I mope. I take a bite and sigh at the delicious taste. At least food isn't complicated.

Friday marks the official release of the newest Adamant set, Aprivenna. Instead of the usual FNA event, Cascade Games is having a special tournament where players are given a handful of packs of the new set and have to build a deck exclusively from those cards. Release events are always chaotic. It's a miracle if you can put together something with synergy that isn't just held together with a prayer. Luck rules the day, and even the most skilled players can end up swept because they only pulled junk.

The real fun of release events is getting to play brand new cards for the very first time. The whole set has been analyzed and theory-crafted since the first card was spoiled, but today will be the first real test of what the cards are capable of. Players across the country will be discovering overlooked gems and overhyped crap while the volatile new meta waits to be molded into a new monstrosity.

Cascade Games is absolutely packed. The release event has taken over the main back room and swelled out into the Adamant section of the store as well. I've never been to one of these events before, and the sheer number of players here has me hyped up.

"Are release events always this big?" I ask Noah once we've signed up and paid our entry fee. It's more expensive than FNA, but I'm getting a bunch of new cards out of it so I don't care.

"Yeah, for the most part. I think it's a little more crowded because of the rotation, but I've never really kept track." We're hanging out near the board games while we wait for things to begin. I spotted Reeve in the crowd at one point and thought of saying hi, but it'd feel so awkward greeting him and then immediately running off to rejoin my friends, so I restrained myself. I'm sure he's going over the spoiler list one last time, anyway. I don't see him treating the event as casually as we are.

"Yo, Zach!"

The voice is vaguely familiar, but I'm struggling to put it to a face. Then I see the horse it came from waving enthusiastically at us and recognize Cedric. He trots over to us with a long grin on his muzzle.

"Hey, Cedric!" I say. "I didn't think you'd be here."

"These are way more chill than FNA. Wouldn't miss it for the world." He sounds more chipper than usual, and he's rocking his hips to the easy listening music playing overhead. My nose picks up the strong aroma of alcohol with every word he speaks.

"That means he had plans, and they fell through," Noah says.

Cedric shrugs. "Ah fuck, you got me. A friend of a friend was putting something on, but it all fell apart, so now I'm here! The cafe's got some pretty sweet drinks, by the way. The names are all dorky as hell, too; it's great."

Noah's muzzle wrinkles, and his face twists. "I haven't forgotten my birthday party here."

"Didn't think you had, dude." Cedric snickers. "I was giving the heads-up to Zach."

"Did you get wasted at a game store?" I ask.

Noah cringes. "They bought me all these damn drinks, and I didn't want to let them go to waste. That whole night is just a blur to me."

"You should've been there. He was crazy proud of how loud he could chirp." Cedric wraps an arm around Noah and leans against him, causing the cheetah to sway.

"At least I don't claim I can win the Catawba Derby on foot after a couple whiskeys."

"Give me two months to train, and I'm guaranteed to get at *least* top five," Cedric boasts with unwavering confidence. One glance at his middle is enough to convince me it'd take a lot longer than two months for him to tackle any sort of race. He picks up on my skeptical glances and adds, "The other horses will defer to me and slow to a respectful trot."

"They aren't gonna treat you like Wiggles treats Roy," Noah insists. He gives Cedric a pat on the back and slides free of the tipsy horse.

"Have faith in our less-evolved brethren. We still have a deep connection to them unweakened by the eons."

"You've been watching too much reality TV. I'm pretty sure if I came across a feral cheetah it'd eat me, not bond with me."

"Dude, dude. Dude. You'd chirp, and they'd chirp, and then you'd both chirp, and they'd deem you some sort of cheetah king or..." Cedric doesn't finish his line of thought; he just starts giggling. Noah frowns, and I suddenly figure out why.

"Oh. Cause you're a king cheetah."

Noah jabs me in the side. "I *got* it."

I jerk away from my friend's attack, laughing. "Cedric, are you even sober enough to play Adamant tonight?"

"God no. But I'm drunk enough to build a deck that'll keep my opponents on their toes. Ya can't lose with a bad deck if everyone else is building to beat the good decks." He taps a finger to his head as he passes along his sage advice.

"And you can't win if you don't sign up," Noah says.

"Oh yeah. You've always got the best tips, Professor." Cedric slaps Noah on the back so hard the sturdy cheetah almost topples over. He rushes off in the vague direction of the event organizers.

"Ten bucks says he chooses his cards based on how badass he thinks the art looks," Noah says as we watch the horse disappear into the crowd.

I'm not sure if Noah's joking, and I'm not about to lose money finding out. "Maybe he'll get lucky and stumble into something competent?"

Noah snorts, and we both laugh.

We part ways when the tournament starts. I collect my packs and take a seat. All around me I hear the crackling sounds of foil packs being ripped open. The top pack of my pile has the art for the Akelis and Olarin card, which I decide to take as a good omen.

The storyline of the set takes place in Aprivenna, one of many city-states in an area that's basically a fantasy take on Renaissance-era Italy. A lot of previous sets have mentioned Aprivenna, but this is the first time it's taking center stage, and I'm honestly excited. I pay almost as much attention to the art on the cards as I do their abilities, taking in the red-tiled roofs, palazzos, and extravagant nobles. While Adamant doesn't necessarily have the best world-building, I've always found it one of the most interesting aspects of the game.

My card pool proves to be a bit on the weak side. The only real deck options I have are red/white and red/blue. Mono-colored decks are nearly impossible to build in an event as limited as this. Even two-colored decks can be rough depending on what you pull. I settle on red/blue because I can build an alright aggro deck with them. The fact I pull an Akelis and Olarin also plays a not-insignificant role in my choice.

The card creates a weak automaton token with flight whenever you play a spell card, and also gives flight to all tokens that you control. The art depicts Olarin giving one of Akelis' creations spectral wings, showcasing the couple combining their strengths. It's the kind of flavor I adore, but I don't have many good spells to set it off or other token creators for it to boost.

The deck does its best, but I spend most of the event getting trounced by players who got really damn lucky on their pulls. To my delight, Akelis and Olarin earn me a victory tonight, creating enough tokens for me to overwhelm an opponent. At one point, I'm close enough to Cedric to see he's built a deck with at least three colors that probably makes mine look inspired. He's also chatting nearly nonstop with his opponent, who's cracking up at whatever nonsense he's saying.

Reeve is always on the far side of the room or completely outside of it, so I only catch glimpses of him from a distance and never get an excuse to say hello. It's for the best, but I still find myself sneaking glances in his direction when I can.

Despite my underperforming deck and numerous losses, I consider the night a success. It's an interesting break from the usual games of FNA, and I see combinations that likely won't exist outside of this event. There's no trace of the meta here, only risks and surprises.

Once the marches have ended, I meet up with Noah and Cedric so we can share our decks and talk about how good or bad our luck was. It turns out Noah was right, and Cedric went with a deck that looked exciting but apparently played like crap. His combination of suave duelists and visually devastating spells has no direction, but it brought the horse plenty of joy, so I compliment him on it. Noah's especially proud of the white/gold deck he made and is considering looking into the color combination as a secondary deck once the meta stabilizes.

We leave with the rest of the crowd departing Cascade Games as they close for the night. I spy white scales in the far back, but I quickly turn away. Reeve is something I need to figure out later, when I'm not with my friends. He's not easy to forget, though.

Chapter 14 (Zach)

Another Monday, another chance to spend time with Reeve. Unless he skips out on the store tonight to avoid me. I worried the same thing would happen last week though, and that was before he'd seemingly warmed up to me. I mean, I hope that's what happened. He wasn't annoyed with my presence at least, and he clearly felt comfortable enough to reveal he might be gay, albeit in that indirect fashion that queers in conservative places have mastered. We still haven't had much in the way of regular conversation. We've just discussed deck building. I want to know more about him, but this crush is making me doubt my intentions and freeze up. Instead, it's like I've found myself in a completely unnecessary standoff, and I don't know how to end it.

With how complicated I've made things, I try to focus on Adamant, which has somehow become the beacon of stability in my life.

Aprivenna's here, and the meta is on the verge of chaos with the four oldest sets knocked out of rotation. Every major deck has been affected in some way. Control lost its win condition, Gold Sacrifice lost a chunk of its combo, and Green Ramp lost some good early creatures. A few slightly lower-tier decks were hit hard enough they likely won't exist anymore.

I haven't come out of the rotation unscathed, either. A damage spell and two decent creatures went away, but I've still got Ancelot, and one of the new rares looks like a perfect combo for him. It's an automaton that exiles an opponent's creature for as long as it remains in play. It's a powerful ability on its own, and Ancelot ensures that even if my automaton is destroyed, it'll come right back into play and exile the card again. Anything that can deny my opponents a blocker helps my deck.

I'm confident enough in the new card that I ordered four copies of it over the weekend as well as a couple of other cards. Even if Reeve isn't there, I can at least pretend that picking up the cards was a valid reason for showing up.

Reeve is the first person I see when I enter the store, sitting at a back table and facing the door. It could be a coincidence that he's sitting in a way that lets him see everyone who walks in, but I want to believe he was waiting for me. I want too many things right now.

I grab my order from the sea horse at the counter and try not to rush over to where Reeve is. "Hey. Want to play Adamant?" I ask. *No assumptions or desperation, just be polite.*

"Sure." His tone is so casual I don't know exactly how he feels about me being here or about playing or about anything. It's not like talking to a wall. It's like talking to a poker player trying to hide his hand from you. When we're playing it's not as noticeable because a big part of the game *is* hiding the cards you have in your hand, but now I'm starting to wonder if he's this reserved all the time or just around me. There could be a lot of reasons for that, and I'd rather not have my brain jump to every worst possible conclusion.

"Thanks," I say, trying to rein in my smile. I'm afraid of blindly crushing on Reeve like I did on Jay. If a genuine connection forms between the two of us, then that's great, but I can't force it. I can't endure another doomed relationship. I can't walk away from another apartment with junk in a crate and tears in my eyes.

I really wish I'd stop overthinking things right now. Adamant. I have to focus on Adamant.

"I have to switch in some cards real quick. Just bought stuff to replace the ones leaving rotation," I say. I'm already skimming through my deck and removing things to show I don't intend to waste time. "Do you have your deck ready for the new Standard?"

I already sort of know the answer to that from watching his streams this weekend, but I don't want him to know I've been doing that. Not yet. He might start thinking I'm a stalker. Every other game he was switching out cards as he played catchup with the changes to the meta already unfolding online. At this point, the best people can do is report on decks they've seen and make a lot of conjecture about which ones will persist past the first weekend of play.

Blue Control is struggling, though. Forgotten Rituals are only strong if they last long enough to transform, and that's proving to be an enormous, flashing *if.* The old Ascended Rituals had a better chance of getting some damage in before being destroyed. Meanwhile, their replacements have to sit there insisting they'll be a threat one day. Watching Reeve play game after game online, it felt like the wins he managed were mainly against decks that never drew what they needed or were wild experiments that just plain didn't work.

"It's Standard legal."

I don't pry him further.

Forgotten Ritual works well in our first two games, transforming swiftly and avoiding my attempts to zap it before I fall to the onslaught. Reeve's wins weren't entirely the result of outplaying me, though. I drew too many locations our first game and took a risk on my starting hand in the second that left me struggling to cast anything for the first few turns. In situations like those, I'd have trouble against most decks. If I get a more ideal start, Forgotten Ritual might be too slow to handle me. Reeve doesn't react much to victories when we play in person, so I can't tell if he's thinking the same thing.

My suspicion is proven faster than I expect when I blitz right through Reeve the very next game. My starting hand is great, and I manage to drop creatures into play almost every turn. Negates and bounces slow me a little while fueling a lone Forgotten Ritual for transformation, but they tie up Reeve's aether and give me an opening to clear away the Ritual with an unopposed damage spell.

A second Ritual isn't enough to hold me off, and I win the game without taking a single point of damage.

This isn't my first victory against Reeve. He's had bad games in the past where I've gotten lucky, but I've never beaten him so soundly. I can't think of many cards he could've gotten to turn this game around. *Maybe* if he'd been able to draw more cards.

Reeve takes longer than usual to scoop up his cards and shuffle his deck for the next game. Other than that, he's still refusing to hint at any feelings about his deck's performance. Game four is a win for Reeve, but it's incredibly close.

I'm witnessing in real time the dramatic effects of a Standard rotation. Both of us lost and gained only a few cards, so few that on paper, it looked like our decks would be going into this new Standard relatively intact. Reeve had existing replacements for everything, and although they were a bit weaker, his deck seemed to play alright before the introduction of the new cards. Everything I lost was chafe and—unlike Reeve—I actually gained a few good ones from Aprivenna. Six or seven cards were all it took to bring Blue Control's survival in the new meta into doubt, while simultaneously elevating Red Aggro's chances of being viable. As far as Standard is concerned, Adamant is completely different from what it was last week.

This is the kind of change I'd love to talk to Reeve about. I want to hear his early thoughts on other shake-ups likely to happen or how swiftly the players at our local FNA are going to react. Will there be hesitation to adopt new strategies, or will people take risks right away? Do players here actively keep up with online decklists and theories, or will the new meta slowly trickle in as they notice others playing strange, powerful decks?

But as desperately as I want to ask Reeve those questions, I can't see it ending well. Right now, we're not even acquaintances, we're just two guys who tolerate playing with each other. Reeve might be fine answering questions while streaming, but he didn't come here tonight to be interrogated. I also doubt it's a smart idea to bring up something negatively affecting his go-to deck.

Playing in silence won't do either of us any good. If I want to form a connection with Reeve—romantic or otherwise—I need to open up to him more. I've never had trouble rambling on and on to strangers before, so why should being around Reeve hold me back? *Because you still can't break away completely from your crush and fantasies of wooing him,* I tell myself. Being honest about the matter does me more good than pretending my crush doesn't exist.

Start simple and stick to Adamant. That'll sound less odd than abruptly asking him about his job or what music he likes. Obviously I should steer away from the meta and anything related to our decks—I want to chat with the guy, not come across like I'm just using these games to get advice out of him.

"Did you check out the release tournament on Friday?" Of course he did, but again, I'm trying not to give off stalker vibes right now. Or *any* time, really.

Reeve looks startled by my talking and glances rapidly between his hand and me. "Um, yeah."

Not much, but I can make it work. "It was my first time going to one in almost a decade. I forgot how wild it is having to make a deck from scratch that fast with a bunch of random cards. I kept an eye on the Aprivenna spoilers, but even then, I kept getting caught off guard by the stuff people played."

"Drafting online a lot helps," Reeve says. A few words are better than nothing.

"That makes sense. I haven't had a chance to check those out yet." Working to improve my deck means I've ignored pretty much anything on Adamant Online outside of Standard.

I get a nod but nothing else. The conversation's in danger of fading away if I don't keep it going.

"Oh, I actually got an Akelis and Olarin in my packs Friday, so I built my deck around them." That piques his interest. Neither of us seems comfortable being open about our sexuality in public, but this card lets us bring it up in a roundabout way that won't garner unwanted attention. "I didn't get to play it often because I only had one copy, but I think it worked well."

"Did you have anything else to combo it with?" Reeve asks.

"A couple of the commons that create automatons, which helped me fill the field before I got Akelis and Olarin out. After that I sort of snowballed with random spells to create more tokens with flight my opponent couldn't block." I only had one game where everything went smoothly, but it was incredibly satisfying. "It could be a fun deck to build in Standard."

"Maybe." Reeve shrugs, but he's maintaining eye contact with me more now. I'm going to take that as a sign to continue.

"What'd you put together?"

"I pulled a Lord Orseolo and built around him. The set has a lot of solid white and gold cards so going with them is a no-brainer if you pull even one decent rare in the combo." Reeve looks away from me. "I mean, they were hyped up a lot online so if you were, uh, keeping up with all that it'd be an easy choice. And Akelis and Olarin are still good."

I'm pretty sure that's the most Reeve's said to me in one go. "I'll have to look into that next time around. Also I'm glad Orseolo got a good card in his first appearance. He was the best part about the Loreggio novel, even if he only showed up in a few chapters." Loreggio was the last set I played before college. In the lore, Loreggio and Aprivenna are rival city-states, vying for financial and cultural superiority via political intrigue rather than open warfare. In general, it's a whole lot of fancy nobles backstabbing each other in a fantasy version of Italy.

"You read the novel?"

"Uh-huh. My bookshelf used to be full of Adamant novels. They got me into reading." Usually I feel embarrassed admitting a bunch of tie-in novels for a CCG are the reason for that rather than something more popular like *Shadow of the Rings*. Adamant isn't exactly getting turned into blockbuster movies.

"I've never met anyone else who reads the novels. Or really anyone who gives a shit about the lore. Online, yeah, but not, ya know, in person."

Everyone has a passion that'll get them talking, even if only for a few minutes, and I'm certain I just found Reeve's. "I know! It might not be the most spectacular fantasy story out there, but the creators have come up with some fun stuff over the years. Like, there's a reason *Loot & Legends* has used the same setting as Adamant ever since they got bought by the same company. If it weren't for the novelizations of Adamant, I don't think I'd be a writer."

"You're a writer?"

My bubble of enthusiasm bursts. I'd mentioned that without thinking he'd latch onto it. "Sort of."

"Sort of?"

"Well, I have a degree in writing, but I haven't published anything yet." That sounds better than admitting I haven't even written a thing in years. Regaling Reeve with the tale of my astonishing failure to obtain a career is the last thing I want to do. I imagine him going quiet and never showing interest in me again, seeing me as nothing more than another random player at FNA. I don't need depression kicking in, not now. "The first stories I ever wrote took place in Adamant's setting. They were all trash, but you gotta start somewhere." I laugh, but I fear there's some uncertainty coming through.

"So, when you *do* write, is it all fantasy, or do you do other stuff, too?" Reeve plays a card, and I suddenly remember we're still playing a game. I double-check the board and my cards and remind myself to pay attention.

"Almost exclusively fantasy. I read a bit of science-fiction, but I've never had any good ideas for it." When was the last time I had good ideas for *any* story? "I guess it's just easier for me to think about adventurers exploring forgotten ruins and celebrating in taverns."

"Have you read a series called *The Crowns of Sikander*?" Reeve asks.

"I haven't, but I've heard of it. It's been on my to-read list for a long while now." The list is almost long enough to be a book itself. I practically devoured books in high school and college, but after graduation, I could never find the time. My deteriorating relationship with Jay distracted me from touching a single book this last year. Reading never interested him. "Is it good?"

"I think? I've, um, heard good things about it at least." Reeve's tapping a finger on the table, and I'm doing my best to not stare. It's strange seeing him so hesitant in person when I know he has no trouble confidently chatting with an online audience. I guess being able to see how I react might make me more intimidating than words flashing briefly on a screen. "I"—He stops right away and turns his attention back on his hand as if remembering a play he had in mind, but I can tell he's stalling for time as he considers what to say—"I actually drew the cover for it."

"Really? That's awesome!" He's had that tablet with him every Monday I've seen him, but I've never gotten a good look at what he draws. I'd assumed it was simply something he did for fun, not his job. Hints of jealousy taint my awe. He's turned his art into a career in a way I'd hoped to do with my writing but haven't. Why would anyone who's achieved success like that be in any way interested in me and my growing list of failures?

Reeve's stubbornly straight mouth gently curves into a slight smile, the first I've seen grace his face, and I instantly feel shame for my silent bout of envy. "It's the first time a book I've done a cover for has, uh, actually done well. Most of the time I'm doing small jobs for self-published authors or small publishers."

"It's still really cool that you do that for a living." I start to imagine commissioning Reeve for a book cover and seeing it in a store one day, but pessimistic reality is having none of that. I don't know what his art looks like or what a publishable story by my own paw would involve, so the fantasy crumbles while still a vague, merry thought. Holding onto dreams has been close to impossible lately.

"Oh, it's not... it's only part of my income." His smile goes away, and I hate myself for killing it. "I take a lot of commission work and draw for other things, too." He sighs. "But it pays the bills," he blurts out after.

"That's the least we can ask for, right?" I force out a laugh I hope sounds genuine. "Would you be willing to show me some of your work?"

Those red eyes dart between me and his tablet. I may have asked too much, but I'd love to see his art. "Sure."

Reeve places his hand of cards face down on the table and grabs his tablet, clutching it close at an angle so I can't see the screen. He pokes at it, stares at it, and then finally turns it around.

The canvas is packed with automatons in various states of completion, from incomplete sketches to finished lineart and even a few colored pieces. A cluster of kobold automatons radiates from a corner of the canvas, before blossoming into metallic takes on other species. I swear there are a few foxes in the mix, but some features are so simplified they could easily be generic canines. The sheer variety astounds me. Some have a skeletal feel, stripped of their plates with exposed gears making up their bodies. Others are so bulky I can hear the thuds of their footsteps as they lumber around. They're pristine, battle-hardened, trashed, and in progress. Each one tells a different story without needing a single word.

"These are really good." I'm underselling them to a criminal degree, but I'm afraid I'll sound insincere if I react the way I feel. "Have you ever thought about doing art for Adamant?"

Reeve grows silent, pulling into himself. I notice his tail constrict tighter around the legs of his chair, and I feel like I've struck a nerve as he pulls back the tablet. He's an artist, and he plays Adamant. Or *course* he's considered that before. And clearly it didn't go well. I immediately think of the times I've submitted short stories for publication back when I was still writing, only to be met with email rejections. "Did you hear back from the publisher yet?" was the worst question I could be asked, because I would have to admit failure to the few people interested in what I do.

After a pause, Reeve clunkily—but quite fairly—changes the subject. "I think I've still got the original image for *The Crowns of Sikander*'s cover on here if you want to check it out?"

"Definitely." And I don't push the previous topic.

I wait as Reeve searches for the file, my tail wagging unseen behind me. Our game of Adamant is forgotten, but I don't mind. I'm pretty sure I was about to win, but that's far less interesting than Reeve's art.

Chapter 15 (Reeve)

I'm on my second wind as I return to my apartment after hanging out with Zach. I won't pretend my art never gets praise. The pieces I've uploaded to online galleries get loads of likes, and my commissioners gush about my work all the time. But it's felt like forever since I was last able to share my art and witness the genuine adoration in person. Probably not since Yuri moved away.

I set my bag down on my computer chair and put away my tablet and deck. When I'm done, my eyes linger on the painting above my desk. It's a print of the cover I drew for *The Crowns of Sikander*. The focus is a gray-banded kingsnake looking down upon a golden crown held in his claws. Bright, pinkish-purple energy is arcing out from the crown. That'd been added late to emphasize it as a story about magic and not fantasy court intrigue. I thought it was fine without it, but the importance of the commission kept me more tight-lipped than usual.

As beautiful as it is, I remember all the doubts I had while creating it. It was my first big commission. Some work in my online portfolio had caught the author's eye, and they'd approached me about creating a book cover for them.

I came so close to turning them down because of how daunting the project seemed. This wasn't just a personal piece for someone or a competition submission; it was the cover to a book people would be seeing on shelves all over the country. It wasn't going to be a New York Times best seller, but it'd still get more exposure than anything I'd done before it.

I continued being unsure of my work until the moment the client approved of the final design in a long message of ecstatic praise. Holding a physical copy of the book with my art gracing the cover made me feel light-headed. I had to do a double-take when I first saw it in a bookstore. That commission gave me the confidence to take on other big projects and obtain a bit more financial security. I'd be struggling right now if not for it.

The only pieces of mine I like better are the ones I did for Adamant a year ago. The ones I couldn't tell Zach about, though I'm sure he'd love them. He'd ask questions I'm not ready to answer.

Creating card art for Adamant was something I'd dreamed about doing from the moment I decided to draw, but I only looked into it on a whim. When I got a positive response back, I reread every line a dozen times over and quadruple-checked the email address to confirm it was real.

The Adamant art director had been most impressed with the buildings and interior shots in my portfolio pieces, so I was given the opportunity to draw an archive and a workshop for an upcoming set. They also had a single creature card they felt I would be a good fit for. I love the two location pieces I did, but that creature is the single most meaningful piece I've ever created, and it will be a long while before it's matched.

Prints of the three Adamant pieces hang above my couch. The archive and workshop depict the full art that was cropped to fit on the cards, showing off another aisle of floating tomes and a pile of discarded automaton parts respectively. They flank my pride and joy, Ancelot. The full art includes more of his body and additional damaged automatons waiting to be rebuilt.

My direction for the piece was rather simple. They wanted a reptile rebuilding an automaton, and I was given free rein to interpret that. I've since heard they tend to do that to increase the diversity of characters on cards.

I didn't hesitate when I chose Ty to serve as the reference for Ancelot's patterns. Red decks were his favorite, and he included automatons whenever possible. I mimicked him at first, until I discovered how much I loved control decks and switched over to them. He beat me more often than not, but I didn't care. I remember promising him I'd get my art in the game one day so that he could play a whole deck of just my cards. It was a silly dream he never dissuaded me from, and that thought alone makes my eyes water.

Ancelot being mediocre in the meta upon release hit me harder than expected. I'd known it was a possibility—Adamant is teeming with hundreds if not thousands of terrible cards with gorgeous art—but I'd thought the card honoring Ty would be an exception. The first time I ever saw it played at FNA was when Zach got it out against me. Seeing it in a poor imitation of the sort of deck Ty loved was jarring. That encouraged me to help Zach improve the deck nearly as much as my growing attraction to the fox.

Against the odds, the deck is starting to look viable now. It's creeping its way into the lower tiers of the meta, not yet strong enough to see tournament play, but it's starting to show up at FNA events and regular online matches.

The three prints above my couch are some of the strongest examples of the success I'm capable of when I force aside my doubts. I've relied on them to strengthen my resolve after exhausting calls with my parents and to center myself when I hit a snag on a commission. If I can convince Adamant my art is worthy of their game, then maybe I can also convince Zach I'm worthy of him. Or *myself* that I'm worthy of him, at least.

I look up at Ancelot, hoping for a sign, but a painting isn't going to solve my problems for me. If I'm to form any kind of relationship with Zach, I'll have to shake away the anxieties holding me back, and that's so much easier said than done.

The first FNA held after a release event is always chaotic. Players have had a week to theorycraft the shiny new cards, desperate to stumble into the next big thing to conquer the meta. Most of the cards they try out aren't surprising. They're the cards everyone's been ranting about online from the moment they were spoiled. The blatantly overpowered, the gimmicks that only work in niche situations, and the cards that look fantastic in theory but inevitably lose their luster after a few weeks.

I've been guilty of that before. I gave Forgotten Ritual a chance in my deck for three weeks when it originally came out, only giving up when I had definitive proof both online and in person that Ascended Ritual worked better.

Then there's the wild cards, shit you didn't give a second glance to because you knew they wouldn't be useful in Standard. Yet there they are across from you, acting like they've come to prove you wrong. Nine times out of ten they fail miserably and go back in a storage box, hoping for that chance to make a miraculous return from the dead as a combo with a new card two sets later. Thankfully that doesn't happen often, so I've rarely been haunted by the junk of past jank.

I tend to get more wins right after a new set comes out because I'm meticulous about deck building. I tweak decks. I don't rip them apart and hope for the best. Switching out one or two pieces at a time gives me a clearer picture of what's working and what isn't. If I make every change I'm considering at once and the deck plays bad, then I'll have no clue *why* it played bad. All I'll have is guesses, and guesses lead to problems. So while other players radically alter their decks in an attempt to produce an all-star on the first try, I'm ready with my tried-and-true deck that might be fractionally less effective or fractionally more effective. Either way, I've got a better chance at coming out on top.

A set rotation is a very different beast.

I like to think I've got a good feel for the Standard meta at any given time. The few friends I have live far away from Cascade, so I've got nothing to do with my free time other than devote myself to Adamant. Playing a ton of games lets me witness it evolve and stabilize. I read the results of tournaments the average player has no idea occurred, where the best of the best in Adamant are finding new ways to solve the meta. I look at compiled win-loss records, compare them to what I see in the local scene, and adjust my deck accordingly.

But when a thousand cards leave Standard at the same time that a few hundred more get added, I can't even begin to understand the state of the meta. Adamant Online has felt like a damn free-for-all ever since Aprivenna dropped.

Green Ramp survived because it gained more good cards than it lost, and I've seen a half-dozen variants of it as the internet argues over which approach is the best. Common sense pointed towards gold taking a huge hit, but not only are there a plethora of new Gold Sacrifice decks going around, but takes on Gold/White Control are showing up as well. And day after day my once-reliable Blue Control deck is getting worse, despite my best attempts to salvage it.

I have replacements for every single card my deck lost, but they're all a tiny bit weaker than their predecessors. They cost one more aether to play or do one less thing, and now my deck feels like a sluggish shadow of its former glory. Online decklists have given me nothing of value, so I'm not the only one struggling to get Blue Control back into the meta.

The deck in my bag has been with me in some form for the last six years. The original version gave me my first first-place finish at FNA. Before that, the best I'd managed was third on a night most of the best players weren't attending. Control taught me how to play strategically, to think about what my opponent might be able to play and hold back accordingly. I've modified it through a couple dozen sets and multiple rotations, through highs and lows and rare bouts of mediocrity. That's what I'd considered the worst-case scenario of this rotation—a few months of being underpowered before hopefully getting a boost in the next set. I'm already at that point after a single week, before the new meta's even been perfected. I can only go downhill from here.

Whenever strangers have asked me what they should do in this situation, I've always told them the same thing: find a new deck. Nothing stays on top forever, and the meta's better for it. An angry voice in the back of my head has spent days demanding I put Blue

Control away and try something–*anything*–else. But an even angrier voice has been shouting it down with an argument made up of curses and hisses. I won't give up just because of early bad luck. Navigating a new meta takes time.

But that's been my experience with Adamant Online. This is FNA. Things might not be as bad tonight as I fear.

I always linger away from others at FNA because I don't have anyone to talk to. I've got a rough idea of the decks of every regular here, but I don't remember their names or anything else about them. I've never known how to introduce myself to people or what to talk about. The friends I have all approached me first, not the other way around, so thank God for extroverts. Kind of like Zach, now that I think about it. Most of my thoughts lead to him, lately.

I feel my tail starting to wander, and I corral it closer to my body so nobody trips over it. The platinum fox has been in my thoughts too much lately. Hearing him praise my art made me want to pump my fist and jump around, but I'd have died of embarrassment if I had. He radiates joy like no one I've ever met before, in his smile, in his voice, in the way he plays Adamant. I want that joy in my life, but I know I'm setting myself up for disappointment by longing for the fox. At best, I'm just another gay guy he can safely talk to, which isn't necessarily bad, it's just not what I truly want.

There are about ten minutes left until FNA starts. Ten more minutes left alone with my dumb thoughts about card games and a handsome fox. *Hurray.*

Against my better judgment, I scan the room in search of Zach. My search takes all of two seconds before I spot him heading right towards me with three others in tow. I stubbornly convince myself I'm mistaken right up until the moment he stops to greet me.

"Hey, Reeve." Have foxes always had such wonderful smiles?

"Hey."

I look at the three with him. They're a larger cheetah, a snow leopard whose glasses match Zach's, and a deer who's one of the few women who play here regularly. Green Ramp, Gold Sacrifice, and Red/Blue Bombs.

Seeing Zach beside the snow leopard makes my chest feel tight. *That's* Zach's boyfriend; I've got no doubts about that. *God, they look cute together.* That snow leopard has all the luck in the world. He's been blessed both by Zach and the meta. Preparing for the truth has done jack shit, and I'm starting to feel light-headed. I don't know what would be worse right now: falling over or puking.

"Oh, these are friends of mine. I think you've probably played against them before?" Zach says. Played and beaten at various times, yes. He introduces them one by one, and for once I try to hold onto their names and not just their decks. "They're all, um..." He looks around the room. Since I'd kept to the back, we're about as isolated as you can get here, but all that means is a ten-foot gap between us and others. "They're all like us."

My eyes narrow as I try to understand what the hell he's talking about. They're all Adamant players? *Of course that's not what he means, you idiot.* Gamers? Nerds? From the looks of the other three, I'm not the only one confused at least.

Zach twists his muzzle. His voice comes out as a whisper, and I have to lean in to hear him. "Uh, they all think Akelis and Olarin are neat."

"Oh." My abrupt realization is joined in unison by the others.

"That sure is a euphemism," Sienna says.

"Just don't tell my girlfriend," Roy says. The gears in my head turn so fast they're shooting sparks. Sienna elbows him in the side. "Oh come on, Vera would think that's funny."

"She doesn't love you for your jokes," the deer says back.

Noah muffles a laugh that turns into a deep coughing fit. I smile, not for the joke, but for the fact my assumption about Zach and Roy being together was so swiftly proven wrong. And if I was wrong about that, then maybe he's single after all.

"Anyway," Zach says, cutting Roy off from responding to Sienna. "I hope you don't mind the company while we wait for stuff to start.

"It's cool. Honestly, I was getting kind of bored." And angry, and depressed, and a dozen other shitty things if I'd been left to stew alone. I feel like I should be saying more. Not about my mental condition, just more in general. This is already becoming every party I've ever lurked in the back of.

"Well, I'm always free to chat if you see me. You know, if you're feeling it."

"Sounds better than standing around." I'm hyper-aware of every movement I make, from the subtle shifting of my tail to where my gaze is lingering. Am I smiling too much? As if that's ever been a problem. I'm not frowning, am I? How much is my tail twitching? I don't want to look nervous or lovestruck or bored or a million other things I think might ruin my first impression with these people or Zach's opinion of me.

"Trying anything wild tonight because of rotation?" Sienna asks. I take a moment to realize she directed the question at me.

"Not really. Just some tweaks to Blue Control. I'm still trying to work things out." An understatement, but they don't need to know the hardship this deck is giving me.

"Playing it safe like Zach and Noah. I had a Blue/Red Bombs deck but rotation beat the shit out of it." Bombs was a fairly niche deck I never gave much thought to. Sienna sounds a lot less angry than I'd be if rotation ruined my deck. "I'm gonna see how well Gold Aggro works tonight."

"Gold got some of the best cards this set, so it should have potential." Especially against control decks like mine. Experimental aggro decks can still tap and attack to overwhelm opponents, while experimental control decks can easily find themselves unable to play cards or create a win condition.

"I'm just ready for a change of pace. Bombs was fun, but that's all I've been playing for a year, and I've gotten bored of it. Besides, I've got a ton of sweet old-school palaces that deserve to see play."

I can't say I've ever gotten bored of a deck before. Figuring out how to adjust my control deck to the meta every few months is a challenge I usually enjoy. This is the first time it's been a pain, though. If Blue Control was devastated on the same level as Bombs, I'm not sure what I'd switch to.

"Always bet on gold," Roy smirks.

"Didn't your deck get wrecked, too?" Noah asks.

Roy turns his gaze to a particularly barren and uneventful spot on the wall. "It suffered a few setbacks. Which is why I'm going to check out Gold/White Control for a while. There's nothing wrong with a little change now and then."

Switching your deck completely isn't a little change. You have to adopt new tactics, learn new matchups, and gain a whole new feel for what your deck can do in a given situation. It's like saying moving across the country is just a little change. I know what hills to die on, though, and this isn't one of them.

There's no real direction to the conversation. They'll start talking about one thing and then a snarky remark or an abrupt recollection will dramatically shift the topic. I participate as best I can, but all I'm really doing is nodding and responding when asked a direct question. That's still better than I tend to be around strangers, so I don't feel as awkward as usual. Ten minutes fly by, and the night's matches are listed. We disperse, and I say my goodbyes, less tense than I was before they showed up.

I'm not set to go against Zach or any of his friends tonight, which disappoints me more than I expect. It would've been a chance to talk with them more, even if only between plays. Instead, I'm not sure what I'm up against until the moment I take my seat at the table each round.

Round one is against that wasp regular. He's been playing Gold Sacrifice up until now, so he's probably still trying to run it. I realize I'm wrong on turn two when he plays a sanctuary rather than another palace. Gold/White Control it is, then. Matchups like this online have been a crapshoot. I can negate his important pieces while he outright destroys mine. The game stalls out for a while, until he manages to keep a creature out and finishes me off.

Not a great start, but this is what my side deck is for. I switch out bounces for more negates and effects that'll lockdown his creatures. If he's done any research—and his deck seems solid enough for me to believe he has—then he'll either be putting in more cards to let him pull from his discard pile or more ways to destroy creatures.

Discard pile interaction proves the answer to my question, but not the solution to his problem. I neuter his heavy hitters the second they're out, and my creatures survive long enough to swing at him for lethal damage. I stick with my side deck choices. He adjusts his significantly.

Game three starts like game one but gradually gets worse for me. He's come prepared for my lockdown strategy and finds ways around it. I've got no new tricks to surprise him with, and he wins the game to secure victory in round one.

The fact he's a decent player only makes me marginally less irritated at my loss. Deck quality played as much a role in this as skill did. A week ago I had answers to this deck that didn't even exist.

Round two I'm up against a teenager I see here sporadically, and I sweep him in two games. Victory doesn't boost my confidence at all. His deck is a budget take on Green Ramp that's lacking in power. I would've beat him even if my draws had been terrible.

Round three rudely reminds me of how strong a Green Ramp deck in peak condition can be. Normally, I can strategically negate threats while ignoring weaker cards, but *every* creature they play has the chance to be a solid hitter. They're all independently strong and not reliant on fragile combos. The best I can do is slow down the inevitable, not turn the tide of the war. In a complete reversal of the last round, I'm the one who gets swept.

My most humiliating round is saved for last. I go against someone who traditionally plays Blue Control, like me. They've already ditched their old standby in favor of a mess of a Gold/Green Ramp deck that has no right to play well in any scenario, yet fends me off like I'm a joke. I stick with bad starting hands I should've ditched, fumble on side decking against my opponent, and my draws are cursed. My lone win against the deck feels like a damn fluke.

I end the night losing most of my games and winning just a single round, the absolute worst I've done in recent memory. I somehow played worse than I did online.

I'm pissed.

The sheer embarrassment I feel prevents me from making an ass out of myself and snapping at my opponent for no reason, which is about the only win I've gotten this horrible night.

While the wins and losses are tallied up, I hide from Zach inside the crowd so I don't have to reveal how terribly I did. I tell myself he wouldn't care since he hasn't really been playing to win, but "being good at Adamant" is one of the few things he knows about me and may very well be what caught his interest in the first place. Once I've figured out the new meta, I'll admit what happened. By then, this will just be a learning experience on the road to victory rather than the slight on my reputation that it feels like.

"Zach Bridges!"

My head snaps to the front of the room as they announce third place. Zach isn't a rare name—it could easily be someone else they're calling. But no, I see him making his way around the crowd, his adorable smile wider than ever. He looks as surprised as I am.

Confusion, pride, envy, and embarrassment hit me one after another in waves that leave me dazed. I've gotta get out of here.

I scoop up my tail and push through the crowd, trying not to step on any tails or get scraped by antlers on the way out. My breathing's heavy as I push open the door. I'm as ashamed of myself for running away as I am for playing like crap, but I need room to breathe or shout or just mope. Yet even when I'm almost a block away from the store I think about turning around. I want to congratulate Zach on getting third. I want to know if his deck actually did well or if it got lucky and went up against weird jank. I can hear him laughing at accidental wins and stumbling into the top three with a deck no one had eyes on. I'm running from that because I'd ruin the moment. Zach and his friends don't need my dour mood tanking their enthusiasm. I'm doing them a favor by leaving.

That doesn't make the self-loathing go away, though.

Chapter 16 (Zach)

When I hear my name called, I don't believe it. The staff made a mistake, and they'll be calling the correct Zach up any second now. Or maybe the correct Bridges. I probably misheard them say Jack, that's it. Then a slap on my back from Noah jolts me to the reality that I've just gotten third at FNA.

Oh shit.

I've performed decently before but nothing better than, I don't know, fifth? It's not even something I actively aimed for. It just happened. My draws were phenomenal, and I went against decks that didn't have enough answers to aggro. The only round I lost was against Noah, and I made him fight for that win. I knew I did well but, fuck, third?

A nudge from one of my friends gets me moving forward, and I head up front, far giddier than I have any right to be. The staff member running the event is a salmon wearing a Lumberjacks cap. He shakes my paw and hands me a few packs of Aprivenna, along with a foil promo card. After that, the name of second place is called, and I'm left not quite knowing what to do next. I move out of the way and try not to look too awkward as I clutch my prize and grin. I can feel my tail smacking around behind me, but it's out of my control now.

The other two winners are both up here before I even think to look for Reeve. It isn't hard to spot a white and amber python in a crowd, but no matter where I look, I can't seem to find him. My tail slows down, and the whole event loses a bit of its luster.

My time in the limelight is short. The prizes are handed out, and we all get polite applause before the room starts to clear out. My mood recovers when I'm reunited with my friends, but Reeve's absence isn't far from my thoughts.

"Holy shit, dude; you got third!" Noah looks like he's about to swoop in for a hug before he remembers we're in public and settles for another slap on the back. I'm going to be sore in the morning if he keeps this up. Well, that may be inevitable if he's topping me tonight. I think about that a little too much and blush.

"Don't forget us on your meteoric rise to the top," Roy says.

"I got lucky," I insist.

"Lucky my ass," Noah snorts and turns to the others. "I had to pummel this guy's deck into submission. If I hadn't drawn that perfect starting hand in game three, he probably would've gotten second!"

"I'm not so sure about that."

"Have some fun, and be a cocky shit for a moment," Sienna laughs. "Last time Roy got in the top three he had a speech ready and everything."

"I booed him." Noah sounds so proud of himself.

Roy steeples his fingers and shrugs. "I believe in always being prepared. Just like I was prepared for my deck to underperform tonight. Reaching the top requires risks, and sometimes the stars fail to align, and you fall short of your dream."

"How long have you been waiting to say that?" I ask once I'm sure he doesn't have a longer monologue planned.

"Again, it always helps to be prepared." The snow leopard swishes his tail back and forth and smiles.

"He's bullshitting you, Zach" Sienna says. "The dork's just good at coming up with stuff on the fly."

"Is this a new thing, or did I repress a lot of memories of freshman year?" I swear Roy was a lot quieter back then, but I admittedly wasn't as close to him as Noah and Jay were. I wasn't really close to anyone back then.

"I dated a theater major for a brief but exciting year, and a bit of their personality may have rubbed off on me." Roy's smile curves up an inch more, and he momentarily looks elsewhere in thought. "Arctic wolves can be very charismatic."

"Naw, he was already like this before then, he just wasn't open about it," Noah says. If anyone would know, it'd be him.

The crowd has thinned out some, but I still don't see any sign of Reeve. So he really is gone. It's late; maybe he needs to get up early for something so he bailed as soon as his name wasn't called. That's the guess I stick with, even though I can't bring myself to truly believe it.

We can't linger around, but none of us are in a hurry to leave so we take a slow, meandering path to the exit.

"Think Red Aggro decks are gonna start showing up again now that you've run rampant with one?" Sienna asks.

"I didn't exactly run rampant." At least it didn't feel like that when I was playing. Most of the games were close, coming down to small mistakes or good draws. "I got lucky with the decks I went against, and a lot of people are experimenting with stuff. One or two players I beat might add Red Aggro hate to their side decks, that's all."

"Don't be so sure about that," Noah says. "Sometimes all it takes to start a trend is for a deck to do good once, especially around here. I bet a few people are gonna head home and poke around online for Red Aggro decklists to see if they missed something."

"And when they find nothing new, they'll stick to tweaking their old decks."

"Or they'll try to figure it out themselves. Thanks to you, they know it can do well. Congrats on bringing Red Aggro back to life in Cascade." Despite knowing full and well it's coming, I fail to avoid another back slap from the cheetah.

Noah might be speaking from experience, but I can't see my performance tonight as anything but the stars aligning out of pity.

By the next FNA, the local meta will have adjusted itself some more, and I'll be back to rare wins and losing streaks. And you know what? I'm fine with that. If I can still play my aggro deck and not get completely trashed by the competition, I'll have fun. Besides, my deck's fate or where I'll end up in future tournament standings isn't the worry lingering in the back of my head right now. It's whether or not Reeve will be able to weather the storm that is Standard rotation.

I wake with a vivid image of Reeve's tongue flicking over my cock that nearly sets me off. I hold back the pleasure and slide out of bed as quickly and quietly as I can. Noah is still asleep, the top sheet only covering his legs.

A lot of my dreams lately have involved Reeve. They jump between confrontational and sentimental, but inevitably end up sexual in some way, either because we're nude or actively engaging in sex. I've also noticed I always have one the night after I sleep with Noah. It's become sort of a routine. A lot of my life has in the last month.

Every Monday I play Adamant with Reeve at Cascade Games. Every Friday I attend FNA. Every Friday night I sleep with Noah. Every Saturday and Sunday I watch Reeve stream. In between, I have work, which is the only thing in my life that hasn't changed recently.

The routines have helped me feel busy and dwell less on Jay, but now I'm dwelling on Reeve and what my true feelings for him are. I keep hoping for a revelation to answer all my worries so I can move forwards, but all I get is confusion and doubt. I've never been this conflicted over another guy before. With Noah, we just jumped into things and hoped for the best. With Jay, I swooned for him until that miraculous first kiss happened. Determination drove me, and for a long while I swore it rewarded me. Now all I've got in my past is failure.

The weekend drags on as I set my sights on Monday. We're hosting another party next Saturday and I managed the courage to mention inviting Reeve. Noah doesn't have a problem with Reeve coming, but I'm sure he's wondering how I've gotten to know the python lately. I'll work on coming up with excuses for that later. I wish I had a way to contact Reeve so I could ask him right now if he'll come to the party. We've gotten along pretty well lately so that's gotta be a good sign. But he's also shy and has only met the others in the group once.

Watching Reeve's streams only makes me wish I could get ahold of him even more. He spends Saturday's stream working on his Blue Control deck again with no sign of progress. It's never fast enough, never strong enough, never consistent enough—it's just never enough, period. After only two hours he loses his cool and switches from Standard to Aprivenna Draft, which is similar to the release tournament we went to. Free of his old deck, he actually starts to win more than lose. The shift calms him down, at least, and he gets really into explaining how he chooses his colors in draft events.

It's all so obviously a distraction though, something I'm painfully familiar with. His underwhelming Standard deck continues looming over him.

On Sunday, Reeve only gives his Blue Control deck a half-hour of his time before ditching it without success. At the urging of the viewers, he builds a Gold/White Control deck, which has been growing in hype as more pro players sing its praises. His first games are rough, with plenty of missteps that come with running an unfamiliar deck, but he soon proves his ability to adapt. He gets better with each game, his turns speeding up and his losses becoming narrower. Within an hour he's playing like he did before rotation.

The skill is there, but none of the passion. I remember how he used to smile as he countered his opponents' strategies and set up game-winning plays. It was all still a little subdued, but I could feel it in the tone of his voice and how talkative in general he was. While playing the new deck, he talks in a very matter-of-fact manner, informative but dull. It's the difference between someone chatting with friends and someone giving a presentation in front of a class. The soul of the stream is gone.

So when I go into Cascade Games after work the following Monday, it takes every ounce of effort not to immediately ask Reeve if he's doing alright.

Reeve doesn't hide his tablet right away, and I catch a glimpse of a castle. From what little I've seen, his landscapes are as gorgeous as his character work. There's an emphasis on the wondrous features to make them stand out, from towering castles to jagged peaks. It pulls me in at a glance, and I can't be the only one.

The tablet goes dark. "Hey, Zach," he says. He has that very slight, very shy smile he's begun using around me. It's adorable.

"Hey." Okay, first things first. "Oh yeah, Noah and I are gonna host a party on Saturday. Just a small thing—maybe six or seven of us tops—with beer and Adamant. You're free to come if you'd like."

I watch the python's face closely, looking for any early signs of acceptance or rejection. The tiny smile's gone, but nothing bad has replaced it. "Um, sure." His eyes dart away, and his aloof facade cracks sporadically, exposing enthusiasm covered up by his straight-forward response.

I laugh; I can't help it. I don't know if it's because he's shy or what, but it's kind of cute when he holds back like that and doesn't quite succeed. One day he'll be comfortable enough around me to be open. "Awesome! I promise it'll be super chill. Are you okay with sharing Dispatch info so I can pass along directions?"

"Yeah, yeah."

We take out our phones and add each other on Dispatch. My first message to him is the date and time of the party. I have to dou-ble-check the address since my memorization of it relies in muscle memory more than the names and numbers a GPS would use, but I get that squared away quickly and forward that to him too.

The anxiety that's been weighing on me since Friday lifts away. My relief is brief, as I notice Reeve take out the same Blue Control deck that's caused him nothing but anguish lately. I'd hoped that after his streams over the weekend he'd have found something new to try but instead he's sticking to something bound to frustrate him.

We begin the first game, and it's quickly evident Reeve can't keep up with me. I've made time to play Adamant Online every day since Standard rotated, uncovering the weak spots in my deck and doing a fair job of fixing them or at least reinforcing them. The other aggro decks in the meta still outplay it and Gold Sacrifice can be an issue if it goes off right, but control decks aren't the menace they once were. I hit faster and harder now, which puts Reeve at a disadvantage.

I overwhelm him in a matter of minutes. Reeve's already tapping a finger on the table and only stops when he switches cards in from his side deck in between games. Despite putting up a better fight in game two, he doesn't slow me nearly enough, and I still win. Three weeks ago I couldn't even pull off two wins against him in a night, let alone in a row. This should be a moment of celebration where I look back on how far I've come while Reeve begrudgingly accepts my deck has merits. It's marred by the fact I know it only happened because Reeve wasn't playing at his best.

I don't understand why Reeve has reacted so poorly to the changes in the meta. Based on all the games I've seen him dominate and the advice I've seen him give, he should be adapting better than anyone else right now. He values playing well. Sticking with an underperforming deck isn't like him.

Reeve's quiet during and in between our games, as if we're strangers again. My attempts at casual conversation fall flat, getting little more than nods and lifeless *mhmm*'s in return.

Fate shows pity on Reeve, and he pulls off a win in game three after I fail to draw much in the way of locations. Victory only seems to drain the python, who slumps in his chair and shrugs off my comment of, "Good game."

I've been keeping quiet about the matter to be polite, but I can't bear to see Reeve put himself through so much crap for no apparent reason. "The rotation really did a number on Blue Control, didn't it?"

He sighs and seems to deflate a little. "Yeah." He sighs again. "Yeah."

"I've caught some of your streams lately, and it's a bit obvious you're not having fun trying to get the deck to work in the new Standard." I hate being rude, but sometimes you just gotta come out with it.

"Deckbuilding isn't easy." He's shuffling, trying to get me to pull back and play rather than talk. I guess he hasn't realized how stubborn I can be.

"True, but if it reaches a point where it's stressing you out, then maybe you should take a step back and rethink your approach," I say. He's still shuffling. "Have you thought about trying a new deck?"

He stops. "That's what I'm doing right now."

"I mean a *new* new deck, something that isn't Blue Control."

"There's no need to change it."

"I beat you twice in a row. When has that ever happened?"

"Control has *always* been weak against aggro."

"Not *Red* Aggro." At least not for a long time. I cross my arms and keep them far away from my deck so Reeve knows I'm in this for the long haul. "Again, I've been watching you try to fix that deck since before Standard rotated, and this is the best you've come up with. And I mean that in the nicest way possible; you've tried everything. I don't think there's a single Adamant player in the world who's put more effort into making Blue Control fit into the new meta than you, and it's just not viable."

"It hasn't even been a month."

"And it's already losing to untuned decks that are bound to be perfected in the coming weeks." The tapping's returned, and Reeve can't seem to figure out whether he wants to glare at me or avoid me. "Why not try something new and shelve Blue Control for a bit. It could recover in a set or two." Staples of the meta like that don't vanish forever. The recent pseudo-revival of Red Aggro was proof of that.

"You didn't ditch the Red Aggro deck when it was crap, so why should I ditch this?" Reeve snaps.

It's like we've reverted to our first encounters at FNA and the store, when Reeve was merely putting up with me. "That's because winning isn't the reason I play Adamant."

"But you think it's the reason I do?"

"Yes." Those red eyes give up wandering and settle on me. "But that's not a bad thing. You care about winning because you like to outplay people. The happiest I've seen you is when you lure opponents into a trap online. You're good at this game. You know how every deck in the meta works, you know how to adapt under pressure, and you know when someone—or *something*—has you beat. Winning for you is showing off your vast pool of knowledge and the skills you've honed. If you lose and it isn't because of dumb bad luck, then you're doing something wrong that you need to correct. Is sticking with the old deck making you happy?"

I expect silence, but he says, "No." His voice cracks.

"Then why are you still playing it?"

"You wouldn't—" Reeve stops himself and lowers his voice. "I've always been able to make it work."

"Nothing lasts forever." God, do I know that all too well. Now I'm the one avoiding eye contact as I fend off a spike of self-loathing I don't need right now. "There's no shame in realizing you've done all you can and trying something new. At least you tried."

"What if I haven't tried hard enough?"

"You did; trust me." It's so much easier saying that to someone else. We both go silent. Everything else in the store that I've been blocking out seeps back in. I recognize the song playing on the radio and a scene of the music video intrudes on my thoughts. An argument about painting techniques is coming from the miniatures group nearby. Silverware is clattering in the attached cafe. "Why don't we set aside the game for the rest of the night and find you a new deck?"

I look into Reeve's eyes and hope he can't see the fear in my own that I may have ruined our budding friendship by confronting him. But someone has to pull him out of his rut, and if no one else is around to step up then that burden's falling on me.

Chapter 17 (Reeve)

Zach is berating me about my deck like I'm a damn child. I'm feeling overwhelmed by some sort of strong emotion, but I can't for the life of me pinpoint which emotion it is. Maybe I'm just getting hit by all of them at once?

Anger is what I should be feeling, but if that were the case I'd have stormed off or shouted back, and I don't have the urge to do any of those things. He doesn't have the right to tell me what deck to play. He's just some guy who played Adamant in high school and decided to stumble back in. *I'm* the one who's seen the game evolve over the last decade. I've seen every ban, every addition, every damn twist and turn in the meta, not him. He might as well be a newcomer.

But the thing that's pissing me off and keeping me quiet is that I know there's an obnoxious amount of truth in what he's saying. I've run out of ideas for improving the deck. I keep telling myself I haven't, but I can't think of anything else, and neither can anyone else apparently. Adding a second color doesn't work, changing the win condition doesn't work, nothing fucking works.

If I continue playing an underwhelming deck online I'm not just going to lose games, I'm going to lose views. Streaming doesn't earn me much compared to my art, but it bolsters my savings and being a freelancer has taught me that every penny counts. People were fine with me playing the same deck over and over as long as I was showing how to run a meta deck at an advanced level. Running a shit deck into the ground is boring and hurts my credibility.

"What else would I even play?" I don't mean to sound desperate, but I've never been this frustrated with changes to the meta before.

"Have you played anything aside from Blue Control?" Zach's smile is back, after I'd run it off by arguing with him. Maybe he doesn't hate me for being a stubborn ass after all.

I shake my head and almost leave it at that. "A bit of red when I was first learning the game, but other than that I've stuck to blue and control exclusively. I can play other decks well I just..." What, feel bored? Like I'm going through the motions or grinding in an MMO? Or like I'm abandoning the deck that's defined my Adamant experience for years? "I don't know."

"I, uh... I could tell you didn't have much passion when you were trying out Gold/White Control the other day. You did well, yeah, but you didn't interact with the chat as much as usual and looked like you wanted to be doing literally anything else."

I still can't believe he's been watching my streams. I know at least a few of the players at FNA are aware of them, but it's not something I've advertised. It's a side hustle at best. I haven't done anything embarrassing on them lately, have I? Amid everything else I'm dealing with, now my mind's frantically going over my recent streams to make sure I haven't made an ass out of myself or said something that'd alienate the fox, at least no more than I already might have.

I quickly remember to pull out of my inner spirals and respond. "It's a completely different kind of control deck. You trade negates and card draw for creature destruction and discard. It also runs a lot more creatures since some of your cards are fueled by sacrificing things." And in turn those creatures usually do something beneficial when they die. It's been a major aspect of gold since the beginning.

"Alright, but it's not like that difference throws you off when you play. What *specifically* is causing you to dislike Gold/White Control so much you're unwilling to switch to it, even for a single set?"

It's getting harder and harder to avoid his eyes. They're brown, like polished wood, and they aren't leaving me. "It's a dumb reason." Maybe he'll accept that and won't pry any deeper.

"Even if it's dumb, it could help us figure out your new deck."

If I'm going to expose myself as a fool I might as well go all out. "I don't like playing it because even though it's different from my old deck, it's not different *enough*." I catch myself tapping and clench my fist shut to stop. "It's a constant reminder of what I can't play anymore because the dumb devs fucked up blue this set."

"That's kind of harsh."

"It's the truth. Blue Control is dead—that's a fuck up."

"Blue Control just got outpaced by other things. Decks dip in and out of the meta all the time. I don't think they screwed up just because Red Aggro got weak for a while."

If anyone else told me that I'd roll my eyes at them, but Zach's smile makes me feel a hint of guilt. I need to be better at directing my anger. "Fine. That doesn't change the fact I can't play Gold/White Control." Which sucks because I've got nearly all the cards for it, and it's a solid deck. I could make a quick order up front and be FNA ready before I went to bed. Then I'd get my wins but feel like complete shit every Friday night.

"So we've eliminated control. That's a start," Zach says. "Anything else you absolutely refuse to play, dumb reason or otherwise?"

I pour through my memories of decks I've messed around with in drafts or online, trying to think of any that stand out in a bad way. I shrug. "Tribal, maybe? They're too restrictive for me because you have to stick to the one creature type. You always end up with a handful of essential cards and barely any leeway to adjust it when things change." And individual sets don't provide support for every tribe. Aprivenna gave a boost to mercenaries, nobles, and artisans specifically. Other tribes like artificer and automaton got a few good cards, but nothing that interacts with creatures of the same type. Tribal decks frequently have short shelf lives and aren't even guaranteed to last a whole rotation. "I don't want to switch over to something that could end up underpowered by the next set."

"Fair." Zach glances at his deck. "How do you feel about aggro?"

"As a control player, I'm morally obligated to despise them. I took a blood oath and everything." I give him a thumbs down and flick out my tongue.

"Uh-huh. But how do you *really* feel?"

"I don't hate them, but they're not my style." The speedy little shits. How the hell do I explain this without unintentionally insulting the deck he loves and souring the entire evening? "They're too, uh, blunt for me, I guess. I prefer decks that interact in more ways than just attacking. I mean, they do other shit, too, but that's their focus, and that's not what I'm interested in."

Zach laughs, which I'm going to hope is a good sign. "You don't have to love aggro decks to"—His face twitches and he stumbles for a second—"to appease me. Though we're starting to run out of decks. What about Gold Sacrifice?"

"I'm not convinced they're gonna hold out much longer. The ones I've seen online are real iffy. They'll likely end up being a third-tier or low second-tier deck at best." Good enough to win the occasional game or round at FNA but that's it. Barely a step up from my current deck.

"Zap?"

Zap decks are a variant on Red Aggro that uses direct damage spells to defeat opponents rather than creatures. "Still aggro."

"A few ramp variants are showing promise."

"Ramping into big creatures doesn't impress me." And it's annoying getting stuck with hands full of large creatures and none of the ramp to get them out.

"If complicated is what you like, then what about a combo deck?"

"So we've narrowed it down to the vaguest archetype in all of Adamant." I don't want to sound like an ass, but I'm telling the truth. "All or nothing style decks aren't my favorite, either. They always look great in theory but fall apart when you remember your opponent can destroy one piece and crush your entire strategy in an instant." Though it is hilarious watching people concede in Adamant Online just because you negated a single card.

Zach should give up on me. I already have. If I cared about any other archetype I'd have found out by now, and we wouldn't need to go through them one at a time to find the magical answer to my stupid issues. This is all a waste of his time.

Zach's eyes suddenly widen and so does his grin, showing off his fangs. "Akelis and Olarin."

"Yeah?" It's a cute card, but I don't see what that has to do with my problem.

"Build a deck around them!" He leans in, and I pull back a little. "Aprivenna added some good cards that produce and boost tokens. Combine them with solid control spells, and I bet you can make a midrange deck that overwhelms opponents with flying automaton tokens."

My gut instinct is to dismiss the idea outright. Zach's as desperate to find a solution to my deck problem as I am to fix Blue Control, and it won't end any better for him. He's just latching onto an okay card with a lot of personal meaning to the two of us. I've seen a couple of decks using Akelis and Olarin online, and midrange is about the best way to describe them. They both came across as a half-assed hybrid between a zap deck and a control deck, without any win condition other than the legendary creature. But they weren't horrible, just unfocused.

"It might work."

"So you'll try it?"

"I'll try to put together a decklist. If it looks crap on paper then I won't even bother playing it though." I've already embarrassed myself enough lately. "Hold on, I've got Adamant Online on my phone. Let's see if your dream deck is viable." I shouldn't get my hopes up, but I find myself wanting it to work more and more with each passing second. Midrange decks fall in between aggro and control when it comes to complexity, and I've put up with them in the past.

"Awesome! Wait, let me come around so I can see the screen." Zach is out of his chair before I can say a word. He rushes around to my side of the table, not even a foot away from me. I look down and see my tail coiled in a death grip around the chair. Hopefully he'll assume that's a thing that snakes do all the time, and not just me when I'm nervous.

I take a deep breath and return my attention to my phone. I rarely use the mobile version of Adamant Online. The UI is awkward and the cards are so tiny I have to squint to figure out what's on the field half the time. Building a deck in it is even worse, but I've already resolved to do this so I'll just have to suffer.

One of the nicest features of the deck builder is that you can design a deck without actually having the cards in your collection. You have to have the cards to play anyone online, but you can at least go against a bot and get a feel for sample hands and turns before you obtain new cards.

I start with four copies of Akelis and Olarin, since they're the star of the deck. The program automatically adds in twenty-four locations split evenly between workshops and archives, which covers the legendary creature's two colors. It's a nice feature for new players who don't quite know what percentage of locations a deck needs, but I almost always end up tweaking it myself.

From here, I'm in uncharted waters. I haven't exactly been tracking any midrange token decks. I do a search to narrow down the Standard-legal cards in blue and red that create tokens. There's another creature with a similar ability to Akelis and Olarin called Academy Instructor, so I add four of them to bolster my token-creation strategy. I also add a few spell cards that create creature tokens outright. They're alright on their own but will provide great value if Akelis or the Instructor happens to be in play.

"Add Veteran Mechanic. It boosts the strength and defense of automatons," Zach's voice comes over my shoulder. I'd forgotten how close he was. It's not like we're ever that far when we're across the table from each other playing Adamant, but now we're side-by-side and working on something together, and my face feels warm as I grow flustered.

"Sounds good to me." The Mechanics will enhance all the tokens the deck creates and turn an attack from a weak pinch to a finishing blow. It can also produce automaton tokens for four aether, which will be a nice added bonus on turns I have nothing else to use my aether on.

I shift my focus to spells and add a few that were core to my control deck, giving me negates and card draw. Having access to red means direct damage as well, which will protect me from early aggro.

The deck comes together faster than I expect. I adjust the number of copies of a few cards so that I've got a better balance of early and midgame options, tweak the number of locations, and that's it. The deck is done. It looks good in theory, but so has every other failed deck idea in Adamant history.

"Time to see if it can handle the bot," I say. The bot player is incredibly basic. It randomly selects a simple starter deck and honestly just plays cards and attacks until it's inevitably defeated. Playing it won't improve your skills or test your deck in any meaningful way, but at the very least it'll give you a hint as to whether or not your deck works like you intend it to. You'll see what kinds of opening hands you'll get, how often you're able to play certain cards, and how long it takes for the deck to do something. If it's too slow and weak to beat the bot, then something is terribly wrong.

The deck Zach has coerced me into building is straightforward to an extent—get out creatures, cast spells, make tokens—but I start to notice the amount of thought that goes into every play. Do I use a spell right away to disrupt my opponent, or do I hold onto it for later when it can fuel Akelis and create creature tokens? Do I sacrifice a token now to hold off an attacker, or do I save it until I get cards out that can turn it into a threat?

My first game is acceptable. I get out Akelis and Olarin and beat the bot with a modest army of tokens in only a few turns. Two more test runs prove the first wasn't a fluke, and that I can win without getting Akelis and Olarin into play. One of the greatest weaknesses of my control deck was losing my Rituals and thus the game. This midrange deck seems to have more flexibility.

"That's a promising start," Zach says.

"It takes more effort to lose to the bot than to beat it."

"But you still beat it." I wish I knew how he manages to stay so enthusiastic about the dumbest little things. "Are you willing to give it a shot against a real player?"

I have almost every card needed to build the deck. Playing draft events boosts my collection and I buy quite a few packs for every new set. Even if the deck doesn't work out, I won't lose anything of value. Well, my pride, maybe, but my shitty performance with the control deck has wrecked that enough already.

"I guess." I don't want him to know how worried I'm getting about this. If it doesn't work out, I'll be stuck either humiliating myself with Blue Control or mindlessly running Gold/White Control while brooding over how it usurped my old favorite. I can't tell which would be worse. I finalize the new deck and make it official, naming it simply "Akelis Token Midrange".

"If you want, you can play me a few times first."

"How, the deck only exists in here right now?" I wave my phone at him.

Zach pulls out his own and waves it right back at me. "You're not the only one who bothered downloading the Adamant Online app. Work gets boring."

"Okay." A flood of tension I didn't even know I had bottled up is released. Zach's the only one as invested as I am in this deck being viable so I won't get laughed at if it fails miserably. His deck isn't part of the meta—not yet at least—but it's leagues better than anything the bot would use and will give me a feel for how I fare against aggro in general.

We add each other as friends on Adamant Online and Zach returns to his chair. Our abandoned game is still on the table, my inevitable loss frozen in time as we shield our phones from each other.

My starting hand is solid. I've got three locations, Akelis, a creature, and two spells. Everything is playable as-is aside from Akelis and Olarin, which will need one more location that I'll hopefully draw by turn four. Zach gets a creature out right away, and I get one out on turn two. I let his first attack go through because I want to keep my lone creature alive for now. He's able to cast a creature a turn, but has only dealt four damage to me by the time I get my first

Academy Instructor, followed by Akelis and Olarin. My token-making engine is out.

Zach zaps Akelis and Olarin on his next turn and swings at me again. This time I block with a creature and take out one of his. On my turn, I zap him right back with a spell and play the Veteran Mechanic. The two tokens I've got out are now strong enough to menace the creatures Zach has left and instantly slow his momentum.

He plays a creature and passes the turn. I play a spell that creates two automaton tokens, which becomes three once Instructor's ability kicks in. I've now got him outnumbered. Zach attempts to zap Instructor on his turn, but I negate it, saving my creature and creating another token in the process. I draw and play a second Mechanic, zap another of Zach's creatures, and I officially take control of the game. Zach holds out for a few more turns before my boosted creature tokens finish him off.

"Good game."

I look up to see Zach smiling at me, and I'm happier for that than the win. "Yeah, good game."

"So?" he asks while I stare at him. "How do you like the deck?"

"It's got potential. I need to shuffle around some spells and see what complements the deck best. Maybe adjust some creature numbers." It's too early to tell if it's better than my bad control deck, but I've got a good feeling it is.

"But do you like playing it?"

I think I do? Again, it's too early, but the card interaction is more interesting than the average aggro deck and keeps me engaged. "Sure." I'm not going to bore him with my self-reflection, but I'm worried I keep coming off as a robot by not saying much. "I can't make any promises until I've had a chance to play it more, though. I felt happy with the control deck, too, up until it started getting thrashed by everything else."

"So you're up for a rematch, then?" Even if I hadn't been hoping he'd say that, I don't think I could've said no to that smile.

"Yeah, I'll beat you again." I try to give him a small smile in thanks, though it doesn't last long as I start to feel self-conscious about it.

I back up my boast and defeat him a second time in a much closer match that leaves our boards devastated from zaps, negates, and sacrificial blocks. Zach's deck has gotten significantly faster since Standard rotated, or maybe he's just gotten better at playing it. It doesn't pack the same punch as previous Red Aggro decks I've seen in Standard, but a set or two of new cards could change that.

Seeing the effort he put into improving the deck and making it viable makes me feel pride. I remember my frustration when I first played him. I was dealing with a lot that night—Dad's call, memories of Ty, the sudden crush on Zach—and I'd funneled all of it into pure disdain for the platinum fox fucking around with a deck that deserved better. After thinking it was doomed to obscurity, seeing Ancelot in play, the figure I'd modeled off of my brother, really fucked with me. In hindsight, I was being unfair, but maybe that annoyance spurred him to seek me out and improve the deck. And if that hadn't happened, I wouldn't be sitting across from him right now, trying not to ogle him too much as we play Adamant and I figure out a new deck. I guess there can be good things in screw-ups after all.

Between each game, Zach asks me if I'm sold on the deck yet, and each time I feel a little more confident that I actually am. It isn't a perfect replacement for control—nothing can match the years and connection I have with that deck—but it's satisfying to play. Blue Control was always my thing, and Red Aggro was Ty's. A part of me felt like borrowing his strategies, his preferences in Adamant, would be like robbing the grave, but maybe with this combination of colors—in a very little and only symbolic way—there's a little bit of Ty still supporting me like he always had.

We play six games and end up tied for wins and losses. Zach doesn't even say anything after the last game. He just looks at me expectantly. "Okay, it's fun." I want to be more enthusiastic about it, but in the back of my mind, I'm going over all the ways things could go wrong. The meta might crush it. It might be exceptionally easy to side deck against. Everything else might surpass it when the next set comes out. Zach might be holding back against me.

No no no, that's unfair to him; he wouldn't do that. He slipped up a couple of times but that happens, especially when going against unfamiliar decks.

"I'm ready to take it online," I say.

"I knew you'd like it!" He shoves his phone back into his pocket and rushes back around the table, his fluffy tail swaying with every step. It looks so soft.

"You didn't even think of the idea until the second before you suggested it!"

"I still knew you'd like it."

I still get flustered when he arrives beside me, but I'm less stiff than last time. Well, most of me is. "Let me side deck in some gold hate real quick. I know they're gonna be a pain in the ass to go up against."

"You've got way more threats for them to choose now, you'll be fine."

"Right until they casually drop a board wipe and drop something heavy the next turn." No color annihilates creatures quite like gold.

"Then just beat them before they do."

I laugh once and then a couple of times more before stopping myself so I don't draw any unwanted attention from the rest of the store. I want this moment to stay between Zach and me. I want it to be something more. But this is nice for now, and I'll cherish what I can get.

Chapter 18 (Zach)

"What chips should we get?" I look back to Noah, who's pushing our empty cart and idly glancing at the aisle of options.

"Chips."

"Ah, of course, my favorite brand: Chips. Seriously, Noah, what should we get?"

"Anything, Zach, seriously," he says right back with a smirk.

"You've gotta have a favorite. Or know something the others like."

"It's chips. Once they're drunk, they'll eat any brand."

I guess he has a point, but some direction would be nice. I grab a small variety I think will go well with dip, which reminds me we have to pick up some of that as well. "What about dip? Actually, never mind." I already know the answer is going to be the same as it was for chips. I add a variety to the cart and we move on.

"You learn the art of partying quickly."

I roll my eyes and refuse to legitimize his act.

We're planning on ordering pizza again to feed the party, so all we need to grab besides chips and dip is booze. Safemart's got all the basics we could hope for. Noah hefts a case of Cascade and a case of

The Gold Standard into the cart. I add a couple six-packs of hard cider on top of them.

"Getting the fancy stuff, are we? What's the occasion?"

"It's not fancy; it's just cider." And cheap cider at that. It's not like it costs much more than a six-pack of beer.

"If it's in a bottle and not a can it's automatically fancier than everything else we're getting." Noah waves a paw at the beer in the cart.

"I want to make sure we've got some variety. And also to contribute more. Last time I felt more like a guest than a host."

"Dude, you'd just moved in. You were dealing with stuff and sleeping on an air mattress."

"I'm *still* sleeping on that air mattress." Much to my back's dismay.

"Why don't we go mattress shopping before the party on Saturday?"

God, a real bed would be so nice. Even a mattress on the floor would be better than what I've got now. "But mattresses are such a pain to carry," I groan.

"I'll help you grab it, you dope." Noah starts prodding me in the back and doesn't stop until I've scooted away from him.

"Alright, alright, I'll get a mattress." I feel a buzz in my pocket and pull out my phone. A Dispatch message from Reeve is waiting for me. I swiftly unlock the phone and open the message. There's no text, only a picture of sleeved cards spread out on a table. I spot copies of Akelis and Olarin, along with Veteran Mechanist, and that's enough for me to realize it's a physical copy of the deck we put together last night.

Hell yeah! I type. *Can't wait to see how it does at FNA!*

Reeve responds with a simple smug snake emoji.

"Sharing lewd deck photos?"

I have to clutch my phone tight so I don't drop it. Noah snuck up on me while I was distracted. "It's just a deck we were theorycrafting."

"Oh yeah, Blue Control got wailed on by the rotation. He's switching to Gold/White Control, isn't he?"

I put my phone away. "No, he... he decided to change things up for a bit. I convinced him to try out a midrange deck based around Akelis and Olarin."

"Huh, didn't even know that was a thing. Guess I'll have to watch out for it."

"We're still trying to figure out if it *is* a thing." Reeve managed a decent record last night in the games I saw him play. He did well against aggro decks but going against control decks of other colors was tough. Helping him out was nice.

"Hmm. I was really surprised when you introduced us to Reeve last Friday and you were all buddy-buddy with him. Zach, when *did* you start hanging out with Reeve, anyway?" Noah asks. He's got me boxed in between the cart and the beer coolers. "Uh, a while ago."

"He warmed up to you pretty quickly after that one FNA, then, didn't he?" His smug smile reminds me so much of Roy I half expect the snow leopard to reveal himself from behind the Seattle Lumberjacks cardboard cutout at the end of the aisle.

I knew he'd start asking about us eventually, and despite all the time I've had to prepare, I still can't think of a good answer. I'm not sure I'm ready to open up about my crush on Reeve yet. What am I going to do, admit I've been so desperate to fill the void left behind by my failed relationship that I started lusting after the first cute reptile I met? And it'd be awkward as hell admitting that to Noah, who I've been fucking for the last few weeks. It's bad enough I keep worrying about whether or not I'm a terrible person for crushing on one person while sleeping with another.

No. No, that's not how that works. We're not in a relationship together, we're just providing each other with an outlet for our desires. If Noah invited Cedric over for a quick fuck, I wouldn't feel envious; I'd give them a thumbs up and pray the walls are thick.

I can't dodge Noah's questions forever. We're roommates for Christ's sake. He can casually ask me about Reeve whenever he wants. I don't have to tell him the whole story, though, just bits and pieces that'll leave him content.

"Look, I ran into him by pure coincidence the Monday after that first FNA. I was buying cards for my deck after work, and he happened to be dueling people at Cascade Games. I thought maybe I could figure out what his deal was so I challenged him, and we played a few games." Also I think he's hot.

"And then?"

"And then nothing. We hang out at Cascade Games on Mondays and play Adamant, that's all. I guess he liked having someone to chat about decks with."

Noah leans in closer, still smiling. "No ulterior motives for wanting to hang out with a snake who happens to share our super-secret very special interest." There's no one else in the aisle but he keeps his voice lowered to a playful whisper.

Oh fuck me and my preferences. He's probably been suspecting something was up from the moment I introduced him to everyone. "He's just fun to play with."

"I bet." Noah snickers and punches me in the shoulder. "Did you really think I'd forget your type?"

"A guy can dream." I sigh.

"Don't worry; I've been on to you for a while now."

"You have not." I'm not falling for his silly master detective act. He's smart but not *that* smart.

"Let's just say you've been getting rowdier on Friday nights, and I haven't exactly been laying on the charm to deserve it." Noah winks at me.

If I could hide in the coolers I would. My ears are bent back, and I'm biting my lip in a vain attempt to keep my face straight. I didn't think I'd easy to read in bed of all places.

"Were you thinking about me with a big chunky tail or smooth scales whenever you had me from behind?" He's grinning so I know he's teasing me, but I feel like I need to curl up in a ball and hide. He hasn't forgotten a single one of my turn-ons.

"I'd never do that to you; I swear. I don't *only* find reptiles attractive." I almost ramble on about how handsome Noah is, but that is not a conversation for the beer aisle at Safemart.

"I could always buy one of those lizard *kigus* with the big fake tails, and we can *roleplay*."

My mind betrays me and immediately crams a vision of Noah in the *kigu* in my head. He's wearing one that resembles a leopard gecko to match his colors and spots. The Noah in my head is swinging his large felt tail around and cackling, enjoying my torment as much as his real-life counterpart would. I hate how cute he looks.

"I'm not hearing a no."

No way in hell am I calling his bluff, because I will lose, and he *will* strut out of his bedroom one day in a lizard *kigu* and give me confused horny thoughts. "No."

"Well shucks. Guess I'll have to settle for watching the forbidden romance between aggro and control."

"I hate to ruin the soap opera love story you're putting together, but this thing is entirely one-sided." If only it wasn't. "Reeve's really quiet for the most part so I'm not always sure what he's thinking."

"He likes you enough to play you one-on-one and accepted the invite to the party, so that's something, right?"

"That means he's shy and wants to make friends." Not that I can blame him for wanting more friends. I've spent the last month nurturing new and old friendships myself.

"Yeah, so?" Noah's taken a step back so I'm no longer backed against the cooler door. "Get to know him better, and maybe it'll turn out he's interested in more than just playing Adamant with you."

"Maybe it's better that he's not."

"Huh? But you're crushing on him, right?" Noah checks our surroundings again. We're still in the clear.

"Yeah, but I'm worried I'm only interested in him because I want a replacement for Jay." The idealized version of Jay I fell in love with, not the incompatible one.

Noah looks me right in the eyes. "I can understand why that'd worry you, Zach, but try not to overthink your feelings for someone. You might deny yourself something nice because you're convinced you aren't supposed to be happy yet. You know how Roy said he met

Vera at a bar?" I nod. "Well, he didn't say he was at that bar getting wasted with me because his boyfriend had just dumped him."

"The theater major?"

"No, some other hospitality major. They were together for over two years and things abruptly went south. I, uh, never really asked him about the details; I just know he was pissed. But he hadn't even been single a week before he started dating Vera, and they both seem happy together. So be careful, but don't forget that sometimes life will spontaneously decide to treat you well."

Or maybe Roy and Vera got lucky. "I'll consider it."

"Good! Now let's finish shopping so we can go home and browse mattresses online like a married couple." Noah takes control of the cart and starts pushing it down the aisle.

"Don't phrase it like that," I say, both because of how silly it sounds and the fact another customer has wandered nearby. Fortunately they seem more interested in the beer than our conversation.

"Alright, then we're gonna find you a fuck pad."

The other customer's ears flick at that. "You made it worse, how did you make it worse?" I hiss under my breath.

"Easily."

"I can't believe you're going to be a professor." I wish I could say that was only because of his silly attitude, but the fact we've railed each other before is playing a not insignificant role.

"That's because you've never seen me in action." Noah's beaming.

"I'll have to ask Cedric about it on Saturday." Now *that* makes the cheetah's ears flatten.

"Cedric likes to say a lot of things, and not all of them are true," Noah insists.

"I'm sure the only ones you'll say are false are the ones related to you and him." If there weren't people around I'd be more vulgar just to see *his* face scrunch up for once.

He scoffs. "There's plenty of other stuff I'd call out. You've barely had a chance to hear any of his frat stories yet. Those are the ones you gotta question."

I feel like I could benefit from a tall tale or two about frat house antics right now. "You know that's the first thing I'm gonna ask him on Saturday, right?"

"Good! He'll be too busy talking your ears off to say anything embarrassing about me."

"Well damn, I've fallen for your nefarious plan yet again," I say in the most monotone voice I can manage without cracking up.

"And that's why I'm the one getting a doctorate." He tilts his head up haughtily and almost veers the cart into the aisle for his efforts.

We both burst into brief laughter, my worries about Reeve, Jay, and everything else temporarily forgotten.

Chapter 19 (Reeve)

To make it to Zach's party on time, I would've had to leave fifteen minutes ago. Sixteen now. I push my phone away so I can't see the time.

I want to go, but my legs won't take me anywhere, and my brain isn't offering any direction. No suggestions to find my wallet and keys or to double-check my deck before I leave. There's no urgency, even though I'm going to be late. I wish I didn't know why I was being plagued by last-minute second thoughts. At least then I'd have the excuse of not being able to get over them.

Anxiety has its grip on me. Zach was kind to invite me to his party, and I'm terrified of making an ass out of myself in some way. What if I drink too much or break something or insult someone or can't get along with his friends? What if drunk Zach is completely different from the Zach I've come to know in Monday games of Adamant? I've only seen a fraction of the fox, and the rest of him could surprise me in the worst possible way.

I throw those thoughts aside as quickly as I can, refusing to sour my feelings towards Zach by dwelling on hypotheticals.

This party is my best chance to make a positive impression on him and figure out what our budding friendship actually means to either of us. But when have I ever done well at parties? When I went to them in high school I clung to friends who were there and barely said a word to others. I was there, but I wasn't. That doesn't matter when you're at a huge party with classmates you'll never interact with otherwise, but it'll be awkward at a small get-together with nowhere to hide.

Bailing on the party isn't a solution. I don't want to imagine Zach having to explain why I never showed. I can't even lie and message him that I'm feeling sick because I sure as hell looked fine when I was streaming Adamant Online earlier today, and I know he was watching.

At least that went well. My new deck has been consistent enough that I can say with confidence it's a solid second-tier deck. Even with the meta still evolving, I think it'll hold. It plays better on average than my last attempt at fixing the Blue Control deck, and I've gotten the hang of how to handle specific matchups. I'm also seeing more variations of the deck online, which is a good sign. Having a totally unique deck in Standard tends to mean you've either just stumbled upon the next big thing or you're running something everyone else already knows is crap, and the latter is far more common than the former. Imitation in this game is confirmation you're on the right track.

The other deck I've been seeing more of is Red Aggro. Not quite as much as everything else, but they're there. I fought and won against one last night at FNA, which thankfully wasn't as much of a disaster as last week. I didn't place in the top three, but at least I had fun and played well this time around. When Zach caught up with me, I knew his friends by name and not just deck, and we had a nice conversation until the store closed. I also reaffirmed that I was going to go to the party I'll now be late for. The one I'm still thinking about ditching for no good reason. God damn; Zach deserves a better friend than me.

What if I told him I had to stay home to finish a commission? It'd be more believable than me suddenly becoming sick, but it'd also make me seem irresponsible for putting off something that important. And why would I have streamed Adamant Online if I had important work to do?

All the excuses I'm coming up with are shit. They either make me look bad, or they'll make Zach feel bad, and I'm unwilling to choose between the two. I guess that's the thing about excuses. They're always shit. Looking back at all the times I've ditched my family the last few months has made it clear. It's always shit. I'm better than this. I let out a loud sigh. I *should* be better than this. The difference is, my family only ever makes things harder. Zach, in his own little ways, has made so many parts of my life easier, more bearable, fun even. I'm not protecting myself by trying to find a way to get out of this. I'm just letting my parents win, letting them hook their shitty ideas into my head and make me believe what they keep saying, that I can't make it out here on my own.

Going to this party will be good for me, despite all the reservations my dumb brain is pulling out of thin air. It's a chance to make some new friends and give myself a better excuse to stay in Cascade aside from avoiding my parents and their plans for me. It's not the only reason I should go, but the extra motivation it provides gets me up and moving. I grab my wallet, my keys, and my deck. It's been hot all day so I stick with shorts, a t-shirt, and a light tail sleeve that'll protect it without getting too warm.

The walk to Zach's apartment takes a little longer than I thought it would, even with me going at a brisk pace to make up for lost time. Thank God it's a pretty direct route. All I have to do is make my way to the other side of the university and take a right. When I get there, I still check the apartment number saved in my messages with Zach just to be sure.

I can hear music and laughter coming from inside as I knock on the door. Seconds later it opens, and Zach is on the other side, all smiles.

"Yo! I hope the walk wasn't too bad," he says, welcoming me into the apartment. I slide off my shoes and my tail sleeve, which I hang carefully from a hook on the wall I assume is usually meant for coats.

"Uh, sorry for being late. I was doing a last-minute chore, and it took longer than I thought it would, and I lost track of the time." Not one of my best lies, but it's better than any excuse I was trying to come up with earlier.

"No worries, we've still got plenty of party left. Let me give you a quick tour of the place," he says.

"Sure." Honestly, he could ask me to walk with him all the way to Hillmart, and I'd say yes.

"We've got the kitchen over here," he says, bringing me into the cramped space. I let my tail stick straight back so it doesn't block the path. "Do you want anything to drink? We've got Cascade, TGS, and some ciders."

"I'll take a Cascade." Nothing breaks me out of my shell quite like liquor. Though really, it's less breaking and more like poking a few peepholes. I'm not planning on getting wasted—I did that once in college and almost gave up booze entirely after—just buzzed enough to talk. I take a sip while Zach is watching, but the moment he's got his back to me I gulp as much as I can to speed along the process and dull some of my growing anxiety.

"There's the living room, and the table we'll be playing Adamant on later." He points it out. "The spotty cat hiding out on the chair at the far end there is Mr. Wiggles. Sometimes he's shy, but he's a good cat. Do you like cats?"

The question catches me off guard, and I rush out an answer without thinking it through. "I dated a cat once." Briefly. He was a caracal friend of a friend of a friend, and we didn't last four months together. "I mean, a real one. Bipedal." Well, I sure as fuck sound drunk already.

Zach lets out a short laugh. "I assumed so. The bathroom's over there." He points across the room as we head towards the back. "And my room's in there, but it's not much at the moment. I've only been here a month. I guess that's all, really."

"It was a fantastic tour," I say, hoping I sound more amused than snarky. He's still smiling, so I must have gotten my point across right. I'm going to be worrying about shit like that all night, aren't I?

"Oh yeah, I think you've met everyone here but Cedric."

A horse tilts his ears at the name and then waves at me with his beer before taking a drink. It takes me a second, but I recognize him as one of my opponents from the Aprivenna release event. The drunk one with the odd deck who played like shit but looked like he was having a blast.

"Yo!" Cedric stumbles over and holds out a hoof, and I take it. He gives me a rigorous shake that probably would've spilled my beer if I hadn't drained most of it already. "Who are you again?"

"This is Reeve," Zach says. "He's another Adamant player from FNA."

"Nice to meet ya, dude." Cedric takes a quick drink and then looks at the can in confusion. He holds it up to his ear and gives it a shake. "Gotta do a beer run; talk to ya later!" He's trotting off to the kitchen before I can say a word in return.

"I swear he's usually a lot more talkative than that," Zach says.

I nod. "I played him at the release tournament so yeah, I've got an idea." I've already learned he's as boisterous sober as he is drunk. Though maybe he's already drunk.

"I hope he behaved himself." Zach laughs, but it sounds forced.

"He was fine. He played a very bad deck very well which is, uh, impressive I guess." It was like he'd built the deck drunk and then played it sober.

"He's a horse of many contrasts." Zach laughs again. "Oh yeah, we'll be playing once pizza's arrived and we've all had a bite to eat. You like pizza, right?"

Maybe it's because I'm nervous, but I swear that's the funniest question anyone has ever asked me before, and I have to stifle a laugh. "Yeah, probably a bit too much." Though my size is about average for my species. Pythons have to work their asses off to get lean.

"You look fine. I mean, I'm pretty sure I've heard pythons are thicker than other snakes, and no one gives bears or elephants a bad time for being bulkier than cheetahs, so..." Zach quickly trails off as he starts stumbling over words.

I'm surprised he even knows what general species I am. Most people can't even make an educated guess due to my coloration. The fact he took the time to figure it out unexpectedly flusters me, and I have to avert my eyes from him.

"What's this about bulky cheetahs?" Noah has pulled away from the other group to join us.

Zach's ears flatten, and he frowns. "That's not what I was saying, I was comparing elephants and cheetahs." Noah raises a brow as he stares in silence at the fox. "Wait, no, I was contrasting them, *contrasting*!"

Noah taps him on the shoulder. "Relax, my hearing's not *that* bad." He wiggles an ear with his finger before turning to me. "Enjoying yourself, I hope?"

"Yeah." I've only been here a few minutes, but I guess it's not a disaster so what else can I say?

"Good. So, what do you do when you're not wrecking people in Adamant?" he asks.

Something I haven't been doing in a few weeks. "Uh, I draw a lot." It's the first thing that enters my head.

"Cool! Do you draw comics or something?"

"Oh God no, I don't have the patience for projects that big." I've tried creating a few short, one-page comics in the past, but each time I've felt all creativity leave my body. I have no grasp of panel layout and don't know how to write engaging dialogue. "I just do commissions and the occasional book cover."

"Shit, that's just as cool. You could draw the cover to Zach's first book whenever he writes it."

The suggestion makes my face feel warm, and my imagination runs wild. I don't even know what sort of stuff he writes, but I love the idea of being a part of it.

"I don't think I'll have anything done any time soon," Zach says. I'm all too familiar with his tone and the look in his eyes. It's the same thing I go through when I'm doubting my art. I feel like I should be offering at least a few token words of support, but I can't think of anything to say that wouldn't sound either hollow or overly sentimental, so instead I'm shamefully silent.

"You'll get there," Noah says before turning to me. "What's the coolest thing you've drawn for?"

Adamant is the first thing that comes to mind, but I stop myself from blurting it out. I've actively tried to keep my Adamant and artist lives separate as much as possible. For my work with Adamant, I went by R.A. Lucas, and since I don't tell people my last name no one ever makes the connection. I also don't mention I'm an artist when I stream. The focus then is on the game, not my personal life, which I'm happy to stay quiet about.

Fortunately, I *can* think of something almost as impressive. "My art's in a *Loot & Legends* manual."

Zach and Noah's eyes both go wide at that, and my heart flutters. "Seriously?" Zach asks.

"Yep." Any amount of approval from the fox boosts my spirits.

Noah leans in close to Zach and slaps the fox on the back. "We played that game all the time as kids. You've gotta be talented to get your stuff in there."

"Well, it's just a few small pieces." Fuck, I hope I didn't accidentally build myself up too much there. Now they probably think I did a cover or a bunch of monsters or something. "They were in a supplemental campaign guide, nothing major." Dad would be so proud of how easily I diminish my own accomplishments. "It was a ranger firing their bow, some equipment, and a scene of adventurers in a temple."

"That's still something," Zach says, while Noah nods in agreement. His moment of listlessness is gone now that we've shifted away from talking about his writing.

"Yeah, I guess." The praise is nice, but I'm reluctant to be the center of attention. I want to impress Zach, not come off as conceited. I've never been great at starting conversations, though. "So Noah, what do you do for a living?" Wow, I sound like a confused interviewer. Smooth.

"Nothing yet," he says in a surprisingly chipper tone. "I'm actually still working on my degree."

"He's gonna be a teacher," Zach says.

I didn't get teacher vibes from the guy. Then again, I'm not sure I'd get those vibes from anyone outside of a classroom. "What grade?"

"College! I want to teach people about Roman History so they know more than just Caesar got stabbed a bunch or that Nero fiddled while Rome burned—which is a myth, by the way. The history of the loser is usually written by the winner, which can lead to a kindhearted person becoming mundane, a mundane person becoming a monster, and a monstrous person becoming nothing short of the Antichrist. Uh, Nero's situation is probably closer to the latter but, like a lot of ancient history, it's a complex mess of contradictory sources and questionable motivations." The cheetah scratches the back of his neck as his speech is met with silence from Zach and me. "Sorry, it doesn't take much to send me into lecture mode."

I snort, and I'm pretty sure Zach is covering up a giggle. "You obviously picked something you're passionate about." I go so out of my way to not accidentally sound like I'm mocking him that I end up sounding uncertain instead. I have to move forward before either of them notices.

"Did you go to CWU, too, Reeve?" Zach asks.

"Yeah."

"When did you graduate?"

"2019."

"We're both class of 2017," Zach says, pointing to himself and Noah. "What dorm were you in?"

"Hunter Hall." It was one of five nearly identical dorm buildings all next to each other, and I'm not sure any were distinct enough to be memorable. Giving people directions to it was always a pain in the ass.

"I think I remember that one." I've got my doubts, since he looks like he's still thinking about it. "We were in Moore Hall."

"Oh yeah, the big one." It was right across from my dorm, too large to forget. It looked a lot nicer than mine on the outside, but I never had a chance to see if that was true on the inside, too.

"We were only there for freshman year. Spent the last three up north at the student apartments," Noah says.

"Same." It suddenly hits me that there was a whole year where Zach and I lived in the same complex. There are a lot of buildings in that complex, but there's still a decent chance we crossed paths without realizing it. What if we'd bumped into each other then rather than four years later? What if we'd spent the last four years as friends rather than strangers? What if we'd become something more in that time?

What if, what if, what if, what if! Creating an unfeasible fantasy to hook myself up with Zach doesn't do me any good. I still need to build a *real* friendship with the *real* Zach right in front of me. I also still need to convince myself I deserve to be a part of this guy's life.

"What was your favorite dining hall, and why was it obviously Village Market?" Noah asks energetically.

The silly question sparks a genuine debate that even I get caught up in. Zach and I both favored the Central Market, which had way more variety even if it felt like a mall food court. I'm happy to latch onto any connection the two of us have, no matter how insignificant in the grand scheme of things.

I take a drink of my beer and finish it off. I'm not buzzed yet, but I'm feeling less stiff and more willing to talk, and even if it's only psychological, I'm glad for it. I crack open a second as soon as I get it, and we continue talking about college.

Despite going to the same school at around the same time, our experiences have little in common. We all took different majors, so we can't reminisce about specific shared classes or professors. Even our electives didn't overlap. Zach chose astronomy to fill out a science credit while I chose biology. I was dipping into accounting courses while they were taking basic math I had tested right out of.

It's fun hearing how different college was for all of us. Or maybe I just like hearing about Zach. Really he could talk about anything, and it'd at least *sound* pleasant.

Sienna makes her way over to our group and taps Zach on the shoulder. "Hey, I need you to tell Roy he's wrong."

Zach looks over his shoulder. "You're wrong."

"That doesn't count," the snow leopard calls from the other side of the room. Cedric isn't in sight, so I guess he's either grabbing another beer or taking a piss.

"You heard the jerk, come settle this in person."

"Can't this wait for later—whoa!" Sienna pulls Zach away, a few drops of cider spilling from his bottle.

I want to follow, but I'd feel bad abandoning Noah, and Zach might only be away for a second.

Cedric comes out of the bathroom as Zach is dragged along and laughs at him, before taking a meandering route around the couch over to us. The horse has Zach's positivity dialed up to eleven, grinning and bouncing along to the music. "You're another one of Noah's conquests, right?"

I'm the only one that question could possibly be directed towards, but I've got no clue why he's asking it or if he's making a joke I'm too stunned to laugh at. Noah looks like Cedric just sawed his Adamant deck in half so at least I'm not alone in my confusion.

"No?" My voice comes out as a strained squeak. What else could I say?

"He's Zach's guest, dude," Noah says.

"Oh, my bad. So you're one of Zach's conquests, then?"

I suddenly feel very dizzy. I've fantasized plenty of feeling Zach's warm body beneath mine, my claws running through his fur as my tail slithers around him. Hearing someone else so casually state that fantasy as if it were fact rattles my brain.

Noah's horror hasn't gone away, but he's looking at me, waiting for an answer. Waiting for a denial. I shake my head, unable to respond with anything coherent that wouldn't blatantly give away my feelings for Zach. Shit, I hope he didn't hear the question. My eyes dart past Cedric to where the fox is, but he seems entrenched in his role as peacekeeper, thankfully unaware of what's happening in our corner of the apartment.

"Cedric, dude, I love ya but"—Noah reaches over and clamps a paw around the horse's muzzle as he opens it to talk, probably doing us all a favor. Wait, are they like, a thing?—"but please don't terrorize our guest. I'm sure he's happily taken."

"I wish." The words tumble out, and I feel like I can see them crash to the floor as permanent monuments to how desperate I must have sounded.

I expect a look of pity or to simply be ignored, but, instead, Noah raises a brow. "I'm sure you'll find someone," he says.

Cedric is trying to talk, but Noah hasn't taken his paw away so it's a muffled mess. Noah finally releases him. "Yeah, with an ass like that someone's bound to come calling." He points his beer at my butt. Noah immediately takes aim for his muzzle again, but Cedric leans back and avoids the swipe. "Fastest land animal my ass!" He breaks into a laughing fit.

I can't help but join him. Laughing gives my brain a chance to recover.

"I swear he's usually better than this. Sometimes he doesn't know how to behave when he gets drunk." Noah gives up on his quest to silence the brazen horse.

"It takes more than two cans of Cascade to get me drunk," Cedric snorts derisively. "I'm only buzzed."

"He's fine." And I know he's capable of some degree of restraint since he definitely didn't go off about my love life or my ass when we were playing Adamant in public. Unless he somehow gets less vulgar as he gets drunk.

"See, Professor Spots, nothing to worry about." Cedric flicks his tail and wiggles his hips in what I can only assume is a victory dance.

"Sometimes I wonder." Noah rolls his eyes. He promptly directs the conversation away from our sex lives while I drain more of my beer to regain my composure. There are a hell of a lot of beers I enjoy more than Cascade, but I appreciate the confidence it's giving me to talk. Or tricking me into thinking I've got that confidence. If it works, it works; I'm not complaining.

I talk about what led me to stream Adamant Online, and we share how we started playing Adamant in general. Cedric dominates the conversation with long-winded stories that keep me smiling in between drinks. I'm fine with his rambling. Even being a passive participant is refreshing. It's been forever since I just talked with others like this.

I'm feeling positively loose by the time the pizza arrives. I'm allowing myself to smile more often, and I'm wiggling the tip of my tail to the beat of the music. There won't be any singing or dancing out of me—those require shots, and I'm aiming for chill drunk vibes not puking in the morning vibes. And if I get too drunk I might not remember my time with Zach, which would piss me off more than any hangover.

We gather around the table to grab greasy slices of pizza we slap on paper plates. There are enough chairs for all of us, but no one sits. It's easier to get more beer or napkins or slices this way, and conversations continue between bites. Noah's cat is the only one who claims a seat, watching us all feast intently and never getting so much as a single pepperoni slice for his effort. I've had enough beer that I'm starting to notice the similarities between the cat and Roy, which Cedric has helpfully pointed out about five times since we began eating.

I drift over to Zach because I want to be near him again, and I hope everyone simply sees it as the new guy sticking to the one person he knows.

"Who won the argument?" I ask before chomping into a slice of supreme pizza.

There's a stretch of silence as Zach quickly finishes chewing and swallows. "No one, which I'm beginning to think is usual. It was just about that really gory horror franchise, *Slice*, and since I've only seen one of the movies, I was deemed not knowledgeable enough to tell Roy he was wrong about what a mess the timeline is or something. Instead they tried convincing me to marathon it with them even though that'd take like a whole day, and I don't have the stomach to watch beaks and tails torn off in rusty traps." He looks down at the rest of his pizza and frowns. It's a while before he takes another bite.

"I'm sure you did the best you could," I say, now more amused than disappointed he got snatched from me.

The pizza's wiped out, and the boxes are tossed out to clear the table. Empty beer cans get shoved aside and small spills wiped up, while paws, claws, and hooves are cleaned off.

I haven't played casual Adamant with a group in years. The matches I play online are against faceless strangers who I have no way to chat with. Even the infrequent duels I'm challenged to at the store always have an impersonal feel. I've never bothered with small talk or getting to know my opponents. I've spent years focusing entirely on the decks I'm up against, not the people playing them.

Now I have the chance again to play without any stakes on the line. My rank doesn't matter here, my reputation doesn't matter here, my viewer numbers don't matter here. We're just going to have a good time playing Adamant, and maybe gain some bragging rights in the process.

I do my best to shake my usual competitive mindset before we start. The beer helps.

I'm up against Cedric first. He seems to like talking in general, which is fine with me since all I have to do is nod and react to sudden questions. The dude's friendly, if a little overwhelming, and I know it'll take me time to get used to him. He's running an underpowered Green/White Tokens deck that he plays surprisingly well considering he's drunk.

My first impression of Sienna is that she's Cedric if he showed restraint. She's chatty but she gives me room to breathe. She's been playing Adamant even longer than I have and sounds overjoyed to have someone else to relive the old days with. We talk about how Standard looked years ago and the things we're grateful changed. Her deck philosophy is almost the exact opposite of mine. She jumps between archetypes all the time, with only a slight preference towards aggro and zap. It's the kind of flexibility I wish I had. The Gold Aggro deck she brought tonight has potential, but I'm able to stall it and win.

Roy offers my first challenge of the night with his Gold/White Control deck. I don't care much when I lose, since it's a matchup my deck is weak against. The snow leopard is less talkative than Cedric or Sienna, but we still manage to chat about the set rotation. I guess he's a cat person, because Noah's cat spends the entire match sitting on his lap and purring loudly. It is rather funny how much they resemble each other.

I figure my game against Noah will be quieter since we've already talked so much, but he finds plenty to chat about. College keeps getting brought up and so does Zach. The two have apparently been friends forever. I'm envious of the time they've had together, of that connection forged from years of growing up in the same city and attending the same schools. None of my friendships have endured that long. Booze and stories about Zach fend off the gloom. I lose to Noah, but it's a close loss.

Zach is the last to slide into a chair across the table from me. This feels familiar and different all at once. I block out the others around us, my attention solely on the smiling fox who's unwittingly had a hold on me for weeks now. I don't hold back my smile this time.

The game itself isn't any different from the many we've been playing Monday nights. He tries to rush me while I try to stall long enough to fly over him with tokens. He has the advantage in the early stages of the game, while I start gaining steam in the midgame. No one gets aether-screwed or flooded with locations and we both always have something to play. It's an absolute definition of a stalemate between our decks. Which makes holding a conversation far easier.

Even an entirely mundane chat with Zach feels refreshing. I like the way his voice sounds and how he inevitably starts gesturing with his paws when he talks. I like answering him and seeing flashes of curiosity shift back into that wide grin of his. It's been a while since I last felt this incredible simply being in someone's presence. Pulling off the win against him is a nice bonus.

There are more games to play, and I have to bid farewell to Zach as he switches seats. Two more full rounds of games pass before liquor and wariness force us to put away our decks and return to talking. I can feel the party starting to wind down. This is the most fun I've had playing Adamant in months, maybe even years. It was like being at a mini FNA event, one I felt comfortable talking to people at. If I had the energy to play more I would, and the others clearly share that sentiment.

I stick with Zach as he gathers his deck. "Hey, Reeve, did you want to check out my Adamant collection? It's not huge, but I've got a lot of the older stuff from when I first played."

"Sure, sounds fun." I'll seize any chance to be with Zach. This is the longest we've been around each other, and my desire for him hasn't faded at all. He's still smiling, so hopefully I haven't been a bore.

We leave the others and stop at the shut door to Zach's bedroom. He grabs the doorknob and hesitates. "It's, um, it's kind of a work in progress."

His warning doesn't prepare me for how utterly sparse the room is. He has a desk with a tilted office chair, a small bookcase crammed with books, a mattress on the floor, and a storage bin serving as a nightstand. Everything is mismatched and old, like it came from a thrift store. I'd expected something more vibrant. Movie posters covering the walls, a shelf full of figurines from fantasy games, or maybe even a rainbow flag. I suddenly feel like I'm intruding.

"I haven't really found the time to decorate," Zach says as he watches me take in the nothingness. "I swear I don't normally sleep on the floor."

I laugh. "My old roommate, Yuri, slept like that. Always said it was easier for him to just roll in and out of bed. He was a polar bear." Seeing the mattress makes me nostalgic.

"Well, he's got a better excuse than me. I've just been obsessed with Adamant and keep putting off buying a bed frame." His shame has mostly vanished, and his smile is returning.

I glance back over at the bookshelf, the one thing in the room that didn't surprise me. It holds row after row of books I'm unfamiliar with. I only recognize a couple prominent fantasy series, along with the Adamant tie-in novels. The spines on most of the small paperbacks are cracked from heavy reading, leaving their titles nearly illegible. A copy of *The Crowns of Sikander* sits atop the bookshelf.

"Oh, you have *The Crowns of Sikander*."

"Yeah! I've been meaning to look into it forever, and when you brought it up a while back, I remembered and finally nabbed a copy." He speaks so fast I struggle to keep up with him.

I'm embarrassed to admit how gratifying it is to see my art in Zach's room, even if it's only the cover of a book. "Are you liking it?"

"I'm only halfway through, but yeah, I am. The story has me hooked and the protagonist is really fun. And handsome. I mean, the author describes him as being very handsome and your cover helps fill in the blanks." His words speed up again, and he looks away from the bookshelf and me. "My collection's over here. Feel free to take a seat on the, uh, mattress."

Zach plops down on the mattress next to the storage bin. I walk over and slowly lower myself down on the mattress beside him, fearing I'll flip it if I'm careless. The door to the room is half-closed. I can hear the others but can't make out anything they're saying over the sound of the music. It all blends into ambient noise.

This is the first time I've ever truly been alone with Zach. Our Monday night get-togethers have all been in public. For once, I don't have to dance around the fact that I'm gay. I clutch my beer bottle tight.

"Are you feeling alright?"

I jolt at the question. "I'm feeling great. I just haven't hung out with people in ages." I'm juggling the high of socializing with the fear of alienating everyone. The alcohol hasn't quite drowned out my anxiety yet. "The last party I went to was in college."

"I can only imagine the sort of parties art majors host."

I snort. I can't help it. "I was a business major." I see the surprise on his face and know the questions he'll ask next. He'll wonder why I'm not using my degree, why I didn't dedicate myself to art if I'm a freelancer now, and what I plan on using the degree for anyway now that I have it. Answering those questions one by one just feels like an interrogation, so I've learned to head them off and answer at my own pace.

"My dad was keen on me getting a practical degree." I've got a whole slew of excuses and redirects if he tries to press me for details on that. Most people are sympathetic about the situation, but it's not something I like discussing, especially when I'm trying to have fun. None of that will come up if I keep talking, though. "I'm decent at math so business school wasn't that bad." Just an enormous bore. "I managed to take a few art courses here and there when I could. Really the only bad thing was that I didn't make any friends in my major because I was just going through the motions with it."

"Yeah, I know that feeling," Zach says. "Sort of. I met a ton of people in my major, but I never found the time to click with any of them, I guess." His smile shrinks and loses its luster. He's a lot better than me at maintaining a positive mask, but I'm starting to notice when it wavers. I'm used to the broad smile he has most Monday nights, the one I see when I lay in bed thinking about him.

Maybe that's why I feel like shit when I'm comforted by the fact we both shared a lackluster college experience. I don't want to see him sad, but I don't want to be alone in my regrets.

Zach rebuilds his smile. "Let me get out my collection."

He clears off the storage bin and drags it around front. Based on the state of his room, I expect the collection to be a mess. Instead, it's organized in binders and smaller boxes. It's a time capsule of cards I've read about but never included in my own decks. Zach eagerly points out the cards that were the bane of his existence years ago. I share my knowledge of more recent cards that have made them seem tame in comparison.

The meta and our current decks aren't brought up. We laugh at cards with silly art or convoluted text. We rave about the plotlines we enjoyed and the ones we wish they'd return to. I don't think I've talked about Adamant this casually with anyone since Yuri left.

By the time Zach puts away his cards, I'm as drunk on the moment as I am the beer. "Thank you so much for inviting me." God, that's such a bland response. Booze might make me more talkative, but it's never made me better with words.

"I'm glad you came." Zach's smile warms me more than the beer.

I *have* to say more, while we still have privacy and the beer's making me bold. "I haven't told you how good our Monday games have been. No, they've been great, like, *really* great." Words are so hard when you don't have the time to think them through, but I can't stop now. "Hanging out with you in general has been a blast, and I'd probably be having a shit time playing Adamant if you hadn't put up with me being so stubborn and gave me advice. Thank you." It's hitting me like a truck how much I've missed being with other people. How the hell did I not snap before meeting him?

His brown eyes wander for a moment before returning to me and freezing in place. "It was the least I could do after you agreed to play against me, and you helped me out with *my* deck first. Honestly, you've helped me out more than you know."

Zach tilts his head down, and I follow his gaze to my tail. The tip is resting on his lap, and I realize I've absentmindedly embraced him in a sort of side hug with my tail, like I used to do with past boyfriends. I frantically retrieve my tail and coil it up on the other side of me so it can't embarrass me further. "Sorry! The stupid thing wanders when I get distracted." I smack my tail and try to laugh the incident off, but my voice cracks.

"It's fine. I think it's... I think it's charming."

I feel a broad smile growing on my face and look over at my tail to hide it. The fox sounds so pleasant when he speaks. "My tail's always been more mischievous than charming. It gets tripped over, it bumps into everything, and it's always getting in the way." My thoughts drift to Zach's tail. "I'm sure yours doesn't cause as much havoc. People probably call it cute all the time, too." I wish I had the courage to say it myself. The indirect approach will have to do for now.

Zach lets out an adorable little laugh. "Some have. But yours is cute, too. And... and so are you."

It takes a second for that last part to really hit me, and I refuse to believe I heard him right. But what else could he have been trying to say? No, it was just a compliment, like Cedric mentioning my ass or thinking I was Noah's booty call. It's not like he said I was hot. There's nothing wrong with friends telling friends they're cute. Are we friends now? But if it was just a compliment then why did he hesitate, why is he silent, as if waiting for a response?

I need to tell him I feel the same way. My tail's coiling tight beside me, and my heart's pounding so hard it's shaking my body. Three words. It's three fucking words; why can't I say them? Since I can't speak, I do the next best thing. I dart forwards and kiss Zach on the cheek so quickly I'm not even sure I get past his fur.

Why did I do that? That was way out of line! I'm roaring in my head at my stupidity. Everything will be awkward between us from now on because I couldn't say a few dumb words literally anyone else could've managed. I won't see Zach on Mondays anymore, he won't be approaching me with his friends at FNA, and I'll never get invited to another party again. I've turned a perfect night into a disaster, just like I feared.

Neither of us is speaking. Zach is staring at me, his mouth slightly ajar and his glasses crooked. Shit, I must have bumped them while making an ass out of myself. "It's getting late, I should... I should leave. Thanks again." I bolt up and flee the room before I can make things worse, my tail dragging behind me.

I narrowly avoid plowing into Noah in the living room. Everyone else is putting their shoes on by the door and getting ready to leave. Good. Now I won't have to risk screwing up an excuse for leaving early. I hear the others telling me goodbye and saying it was great to hang out, but my head's spinning as it replays my mistake over and over again. I stumble trying to put my tail sleeve back on.

"Are you okay to walk home?" Noah asks. I realize I'm still holding my empty beer bottle in a death grip. Great, he probably thinks I'm shitfaced now. I guess that's better than knowing I'm ashamed of myself for kissing his roommate out of the blue. "I'm sure someone can walk with you if you want."

Before I can say no, Zach hurries over. "I will."

I look up at the fox. He's not scowling or lost in thought. He's smiling, and my heart freezes. Maybe I didn't fuck up. Maybe he also thinks I'm drunker than I really am and is blaming the kiss on the beer. If that's the case, then I can't give myself another chance to make an ass of myself tonight. "I'll be good." My voice is quiet.

"I don't want to worry all night about you falling into the irrigation canal. I need to work off the beer and pizza anyway." He laughs.

I want to tell him he's fine just the way he is, but thankfully my words are still failing me. I'm too selfish to turn down the offer a second time. "O-okay."

There's another round of goodbyes and promises to host another party again soon. My panic attack is starting to subside, so at least I think I'll be invited again now. I force a smile and walk out of the apartment with Zach right behind me. I worry this is going to be a long walk home.

Chapter 20 (Zach)

The fresh air was supposed to clear my head and help me process the last few minutes, but in truth it's only given me new scenery to stare at in confusion. The exterior walkway of the building gives a sweeping view of the parking lot. If you lean over the rail, you can almost see the CWU football field through a row of pine trees. Even on a Saturday this neighborhood gets pretty quiet after sundown, so the silence is only broken by occasional passing cars. My gaze is stuck on the metal railing and the parking lot below, with Reeve on the edge of my peripheral vision.

He kissed me.

I don't know why I chose to open up to him right before he was about to leave. Maybe I was thinking about the Halloween party with Jay and the last-minute confession and kiss that began our doomed relationship. If liquor was to blame, I'd have called him a lot more than just "cute." I swore I'd ruined the night by saying that.

Then he kissed me. He struck fast, like he was afraid I'd get away from him, but it was definitely a kiss.

Whenever I replay the kiss in my head, I tell myself he's drunk and teasing me. He didn't seem drunk when we were playing Adamant, though. Tipsy, sure, but not wasted. And he's not teasing me right now as we stand alone outside the apartment. Stressed. He's stressed and nervous. But is that because the kiss was genuine and he thinks I've rejected him, or because he didn't mean it and now he's worried I'll take it seriously? My heart's begging for the former while my brain is convinced it could never be anything but the latter.

He *kissed* me. It wasn't followed by a laugh or a loud declaration he'd won a bet. Reeve feels something towards me. He just might be uncertain of what it is. That's something we have in common.

Reeve doesn't really need an escort home. It was the kiss that made him stumble around at the door, not the beer. I couldn't let us depart on that awkward note, though. We need privacy so we can talk about what happened and maybe figure things out between us. My failure to do that with Jay is probably a reason our relationship became unsalvageable, and that's a mistake I refuse to repeat.

The others have already vanished, walking home or getting into their arriving rides, leaving Reeve and me alone out here. I glance over my shoulder at the window to the apartment and catch Noah peeking through the blinds. His eyes widen, and the open slat falls down as he retreats, leaving us alone completely.

I'm the reason we're both out here together, so it's up to me to get things started. "You live around Old Downtown, right?" I'm pretty sure that's what he said when I was giving him directions.

Reeve twitches, as if I just startled him awake. "Yeah."

"That's not too bad a walk then. It's quiet at night, too." I shatter the silence with my first two steps down the stairs. They groan like the floorboards in a haunted house, the loudest I've heard them yet. I half-expect them to snap beneath my feet and send me plummeting to the ground.

"Are you sure it's safe, Zach?" Reeve asks.

I look over my shoulder, and the sight of his slight grin makes me blush. "Trust me, they just *sound* like they're on the verge of collapsing. I hear kids storming up them all the time, and they haven't been reduced to splinters yet."

"I'm fatter than most kids."

"I'll try to break your fall if the stairs can't handle you."

His eyes dart to the side, and the tip of his tail starts wrapping around his shoe. He nudges it away and then lifts his whole tail, holding it close to his chest. Jay did that when he didn't want his tail to drag behind him. I let the lizard's memory brush past me and focus on the python who's actually here.

Reeve joins me. The stairs creak less for him.

I continue down one step at a time. Slowly, so that I don't outpace Reeve. "Noah told me the noise gives the stairs 'character'."

Yeah, they sound like an ancient witch cackling as she plots the protagonist's doom."

"I was thinking more along the lines of a gnarled mentor still capable of providing a lesson or two."

"Optimistic."

"Sometimes I remember to be." Though my confidence about the path ahead still wavers.

We make plenty of noise on our leisurely descent, but the stairs hold, as they have for everyone else who used them today, yesterday, and all throughout the years. They don't need to be perfect to do their job.

We walk through the parking lot and down the street in silence. The way to Old Downtown has become second nature to me thanks to all my walks to and from work. That gives me time to think about Reeve's kiss and what my next move should be.

I could always profess my love for Reeve right here and now, tell him that "cute" is an understatement and that he's held my attention since the moment I saw him at the game store. It'd be a fantastic way to make him shut down again or bolt from the dude admitting to having a crazy crush on him. This needs to be handled delicately, for both our sakes.

Time doesn't have the courtesy to slow down for me, and we're passing the CWU track before I know it. So far all I've decided on is to not be an absolute freak, which doesn't bode well for me. For all the praise I get about being sociable I'm sure doing a terrible job at it when it matters most.

Seeing the track reminds me of Cedric. "Reeve, did you know Cedric used to be a pole vaulter?" I've gotta break the silence between us somehow.

"How?"

His response makes me laugh. "I had the same reaction when he first told me, and I didn't quite believe him until I saw pictures. He used to be in better shape."

"Oh. Duh."

"It's kind of wild how dramatically people can change in such a short period of time, right?" Or how dramatically they *seem* to change when they've been holding their feelings back. Jay and I went from loving to broken in a matter of weeks, while Reeve and I have gone from acquaintances to something a lot more complicated in a matter of minutes.

"Yeah."

"So, what do you think about Cedric?" I'm hoping that talking about anything other than us will make it easier to transition to the subject of the kiss.

"He's a lot." I don't think I've ever heard a more concise and accurate description of the horse. "But he's fun to be around. I think."

"Yeah, he sort of grows on you."

"Then he's always like that?"

"That's the impression I've gotten. I've only known him a month though, so maybe he's just being extra rowdy because he graduated." He can't be bad if Noah likes him. "I'll have to ask Noah, since he's known him the longest. He was his tutor for a while, too." I almost tell him what else they've gotten up to, but that's for Cedric to blurt out at an inappropriate time, not for me to reveal. I also want to be there when he inevitably does tell Reeve, just to see the reaction on the python's face. He *did* chat with Cedric and Noah for a while tonight. Maybe he already knows?

"I can't even imagine what it'd be like to tutor Cedric. Or teach him."

I haven't figured out how to bring up the kiss, but at least we're talking and not stewing silently in our own thoughts. I'll have to keep finding things to talk about until a solution comes to me. Otherwise, I'm bound to be dumb and spontaneous, like I was when I told Reeve he's cute and started this whole mess. I shouldn't consider it a mess. It's confusion, that's all.

"I guess spending eight years learning how to teach came in handy."

"That's a long time to spend in college."

I've been graduated for as many years as I attended, and the fact Noah is still going blows my mind, too. "Yeah, he's definitely getting the most out of college." Which reminds me of a question that might be too serious for our anxious walk home. "Do you feel like you really got the full college experience?"

"I'm not sure." Reeve answers faster than I expect. "I haven't thought about it."

He's luckier than me, then. "I thought I did for the longest time, but over the last month I've been wondering if that's the truth." How do I say this without mentioning him? I exhale. "I sort of fell into a holding pattern after freshman year and focused on one... thing at the expense of all others. I'm noticing more and more opportunities I let slip through my fingers, and now I'm starting to feel like I squandered my time at college." I can't make that mistake again. But would a relationship with Reeve be repeating the past or learning from it? Convincing myself every new relationship I enter will be Jay all over again is dangerous, and will leave me forsaking love for the rest of my life.

"Honestly, I probably didn't have the full experience either. I didn't make many friends, I wasn't part of any clubs, and I didn't go out much in general. College just feels like a thing I did, not a whole chapter of my life that, I don't know, defines who I am or shit." He lets out a one-note laugh that comes across like a scoff. He looks at me, his red eyes shining in the glow of the street lights. "If you had a chance to do it all over again, would you?"

I think of how I could've changed things, but Jay is such an imposing presence in my college years I don't even know where to begin. "I don't know."

"Same. Some days I feel going to college was a waste, but if I hadn't, I wouldn't have met Yuri. It seems shitty saying I'd erase those friendships out of some blind hope things would be better."

I glance across the street, at the campus hidden behind a line of trees that must have been planted so long ago and have only recently begun to provide on the investment of landscaping, watering, and most of all, patience. Somewhere, just on the other side of that pseudo-natural barrier, exist the rooms and halls and staircases that lead people through an equally pseudo-natural stage of life, thousands at a time. Some will later reflect on those as the best years of their lives. Some will see it as only a stepping stone to the next thing. If I consider my drawn-out relationship with Jay to be my biggest failure in college, did any successes come from it? I met Roy but quickly forgot about him, and I got a bounty of writing advice I've yet to use. I made very few personal connections and absolutely zero professional ones. I can shamefully say I've made more friends in the last month than I did in the entirety of college. My time there just seems like a series of failures.

But the only reason I'm walking with Reeve right now is one of those failures. If I hadn't met Jay, I wouldn't have broken up with him and ended up getting back into Adamant at the right time to connect with Reeve. I may have met someone else—for better or worse—and Reeve would simply be a potential friend I thought looked cute. Thinking up a mountain of alternate scenarios is pointless when the real one is all that matters.

We've reached the corner of Cowboy and University Way, the border between campus and Old Downtown. I'm running out of time, and the best I've managed is getting us both to admit we had a less-than-stellar college experience, which has nothing to do with the kiss. The pedestrian light to our left has started counting down, and in ten seconds we'll be crossing the street, and who knows how long we'll have left to talk?

I'm all out of ideas so it's time for desperation. I turn to Reeve. Even at night his scales look beautiful. There's a shine to him, like porcelain with golden accents. The blurry, glowing countdown timer of the crossing light is behind him, reminding me I need to make my move now. I lean over and kiss Reeve on the cheek.

I don't linger, pulling back a half-second after touching cold scales, but the simple act makes me feel so lightheaded the rest of the world ceases to exist. He freezes in place, staring at me, waiting for an explanation.

"I meant it when I said you were cute." I give up on trying to think through what I'm saying because it's all just jumbling together in my head. "You're handsome and smart and just being in your presence has been enough to boost my mood." I stop myself to give him a chance to react, *and* so I don't embarrass myself further if it turns out I've completely misread him tonight.

Those red eyes look into mine. "Really?"

I'm so nervous I laugh. "Really."

Reeve looks all around us at the empty sidewalks and barren streets. "You... look good, too."

It's such a little thing, but I want to grab him and lift him off the ground in a back-breaking hug. I'm not sure I'd even be able to lift him that much considering his weight. Regardless of his physique, I know that python tails are a whole lot heavier than the fluffy ones us foxes have, and the full length of muscle is often the equivalent of a whole other person.

But I have no reason to hold back the compliments anymore. Just once, I need to use that stupid degree of mine and let the words tumble out, even if they're the equivalent of a sloppy first draft. "I think your patterns are some of the most beautiful I've ever seen, and your scales are so shiny and well cared for."

"I don't know many people who notice that sort of thing," Reeve says, rubbing his arm.

The vast and wonderful diversity of our world means the average person is oblivious to the particulars of other species. I know how to properly treat a fur coat, but I have no clue what goes into the care of an avian's plumage. "I dated a lizard once." For a very, very long time.

"Your fur looks really pretty, and I love your smile. Uh... I mean 'like'. I *like* your smile."

For him, my grin widens further. This moment doesn't feel real. My harsh mind tries to tell me this is because we're both drunk and still riding the high of a good party, but the words shared between us are too genuine for that. Clunky but genuine. I don't know how I managed to be this lucky, and convincing myself I deserve it is hard. Chunks have been taken out of the barriers we'd put up around us, and it's like we're probing the unexplored territory or our mutual affection.

"Thanks. I try my best." At least I have recently.

"Um, would it be okay if I feel your tail?" The hesitance in his voice as he asks such an innocuous question is adorable.

"Go for it. Just don't tug." I make an effort to freeze my tail in place so it isn't rapidly wagging back and forth.

Reeve inches closer to me and scopes the area out again. Aside from the occasional car zipping past, we're alone out here. He reaches out with his claws and brushes his fingers through the fur of my tail with such caution you'd think he was handling glass. People at the antique store aren't this delicate with handling things. Jay would sometimes flick or tousle my tail to tease me, but he never caressed it in the way Reeve is now. Only Noah's ever given it that kind of attention before. I'm going to have a lot to tell him when I get home.

"I'm not dreaming, am I?" Reeve asks in a murmur as he stops stroking my tail.

"If you are, I don't want the dream to end." The lights have changed back and forth as we've been standing here confessing to each other. Down the street, I see someone heading in our direction. Our moment of privacy is gone. "I guess we should probably get going."

"Yeah," Reeve sighs.

We cross the street but instead of heading South into the cluster of apartments squeezed between Old Downtown and the suburbs, we make the same turn I've made on the way to work for the last month and go along the edge of Old Downtown itself.

"Wait, do you *literally* live in Old Downtown?" I ask. I'd assumed he meant he lived nearby it, since Old Downtown is primarily businesses.

"Yeah. After I graduated I needed a place with one bedroom that was cheap, and I guess everyone else was too because I found jack shit for like a month. Then I dug up a listing downtown that was an okay price and a good enough size, and I jumped on it." He's looking at me when he talks now, his slight grin a constant reminder that the kiss was the right decision. "I've been there about two years, and it's still working out."

"It's gotta be nice living within walking distance of so much stuff. Groceries, restaurants, Cascade Games." We're actually only a couple of blocks away from it.

When Reeve guides us down another street, it's the same one work is on. Have I seen apartments this way before? When I used to walk the other direction home, I never paid much attention to my surroundings. I could've been passing his complex every day without realizing it. He stops abruptly in front of a door between two storefronts. I look up, and for the first time I notice the apartments sitting above all the stores on this side of the street. I can't hold back the laughter.

Reeve looks at me like I've gone mad. "Sorry. See that building over there." I point across the street at Tabitha's Treasures. "I work there."

"No way."

I nod. "For four years now." I'm amazed we've never stumbled into each other before. How many times have I left the store to head home right as he was looking out his window or arriving back at the apartment? It's like when we lived a few buildings away in the student apartments for a year. We've been so close for so long, all while being completely oblivious to each other's existence.

"Is that where you've been coming from every Monday night?"

"Right after work."

We laugh together, keeping our voices down so they don't echo down the streets of Old Downtown. There are still people out, heading home from bars and restaurants. We raise our barriers again, acting like friends and not two lovestruck fools.

"It was lovely having you over tonight; it really was," I say. "It's always lovely hanging out with you."

"Same. Monday's are the highlight of my week." Reeve looks away for a second. "I, uh, I almost didn't come tonight. I'm glad I changed my mind, because that would've been the biggest mistake of my life."

I guess luck was on both our sides tonight. "I'll see you Monday, then?"

"Hell yeah."

"Goodnight."

"Night."

We reach out at the same time and grasp our hands together, paws in claws. The connection lasts only a moment to protect us from prying eyes. I want to kiss him again, but even at night I worry about being seen.

I wave at Reeve as he passes through the door and disappears, leaving me alone beneath a mountain of euphoric thoughts.

I'm overwhelmed and for once it's in a good way. I want to shout and dance and laugh and jog home with a smile so wide everyone I pass thinks I won the lottery. And really, I did. When you're gay, the odds of having a crush on a stranger being mutual are astronomical. I may have used up a lifetime of luck finding Reeve, but it's worth it. I hope it's worth it.

A few shared compliments won't necessarily lead to true love. I still need to make sure this crush isn't merely a passing whimsy to help me get over Jay, who has six years of roots deeply entangled in my head. Messing this up wouldn't only hurt me, it'd hurt Reeve as well, and I'd never be able to forgive myself for that.

When I cross the corner of Cowboy and University Way, I set sights on CWU and the tangle of memories it's become. I cross the street again and pass the wall of trees, entering campus.

Red brick buildings rise above me, their windows dark. The campus on a summer night is so eerily different than it is during the school year. Paths normally filled with students of every species are empty and silent. No one is stumbling home from a frat party or last-minute study session in the library. It isn't completely devoid of life during the summer, but tonight I seem to have been left alone.

I have to make my way through a maze of tightly packed buildings to reach the main pathway that crosses the campus. Memories of Jay confront me on the route—all the times we met after classes to get lunch, the school events I followed him to, the lazy talks of how our days had been.

Campus opens up to give space for the wide-open East Mall. I used to dream about basking in the grass on sunny days with Jay like all the straight couples could without worry.

I stop on one of the many bridges that cross the Irrigation Canal and listen to the water flowing gently beneath me. Moore Hall is a bit downstream, and I see lights in the windows. I only lived there a year, and yet it played a decisive role in how the next seven would go.

I reach up to my ear and feel the smooth surface of the stud earring. When Jay showed up with his brand new nose ring I acted like it was the coolest thing I'd ever seen. Thinking back, I'd have likely felt the same if he'd showed up with a tattoo of a rubber duck on his head. Everything he did was amazing to me then.

Right away I'd considered getting a nose ring myself to impress Jay, but thankfully I'd chickened out before it ever became more than an impulsive fantasy. It was too big a change. I still wanted to stand out to Jay, though, which was why I settled on the ear piercing.

I was terrified that wearing anything too fancy or showy would out me as being gay—I still am, shamefully, despite the fact it'd probably go unnoticed. A simple disc stud seemed like the perfect compromise, but then I fretted over the color for the same reason. *Too much of my life revolves around paranoia.* In the end, I chose the shade of green that came closest to matching Jay's scales. He never noticed it, even after we started dating. If he did, he never cared enough to mention it. All these years this earring has been a symbol of our shallow relationship. The fact I looked at it every morning in the mirror without realizing that is just another sign of how firmly I convinced myself everything was fine.

I carefully take off the earring and hold it between two fingers. Its color is dull at night. I remember the steel starter earring I had to wear for a few weeks while the piercing healed. I'd hurried back to the dorms to show it to Jay. Noah and Roy teased and congratulated me, while Jay only complimented it once in passing.

The relationship with Jay was a mountain of mistakes we both allowed to build up until it collapsed in on itself. I need to accept that I can learn from it and not repeat it with someone else. Whatever sort of relationship is forming between me and Reeve right now can't end up like that one. Even if this doesn't actually go anywhere, I'll make sure no one comes out of it hurt.

I resist the urge to throw the earring into the canal. Part of me still cares for Jay, though I have no idea when I'll see him again, if ever. Instead, I place the earring down on the broad stone handrail of the bridge. It'll probably end up in the canal anyway, but at least now it has a chance to be found and given new life. "Bye, Jay. I hope you find the right person for you someday."

I turn away and head towards my new home and my new life, and I wonder how long it'll truly take me to move beyond the old one that's barely begun to leave my mind.